ENDGAME AT PORT BANNATYNE

An Alison Cameron Mystery

MYRA DUFFY

www.myraduffy.co.uk

http://myraduffy-awriterslot.blogspot.com

Cover design by Mandy Sinclair

www.mandysinclair.com

While the story of James Hamilton is true, some historical incidents may have been adapted within the framework of the Pelias Productions 'script.'

A number of real locations have been used in the novel, but details may have been changed or added for purposes of the plot.

Also by Myra Duffy

The Isle of Bute series

The House at Ettrick Bay

Last Ferry to Bute

Last Dance at the Rothesay Pavilion

* * * * *

When Old Ghosts Meet

The Isle of Bute

The Isle of Bute lies in Scotland's Firth of Clyde, off the west coast of Scotland, a short journey from the city of Glasgow.

It has been occupied for over five thousand years but rose to prominence in Victorian days when its proximity to a major city made it a favoured spot for the wealthy to build summer houses and the not-so-wealthy to enjoy the delights of the seaside in the many rooms available for rent during the holiday season.

Bute is the ancestral home of the Stuart kings of Scotland and the 800 year old Rothesay castle (now ruined) was built by a hereditary High Steward of Scotland, from which the name is derived.

Today the island is a haven from the hustle and bustle of city life with quiet beaches, woodland walks and an abundance of wildlife, including seals.

For Paul and Judith

PROLOGUE

Gertie hummed quietly as she moved quickly from room to room, deftly pushing the trolley along the silent corridor. She didn't mind the hard work. It was a regular job and it was exciting to have the Coronet Hotel on the seafront at Port Bannatyne refurbished, restored to its former glory and once again busy with guests, thanks to the arrival of Pelias Productions on the Isle of Bute.

To be truthful the film they were making, *A Man Alone,* set in the early nineteenth century, didn't sound the kind of movie she enjoyed. She much preferred a bit of modern romance, rather than actors in fancy costumes. Still, mustn't complain, it was good for tourism on the island and if the film was successful it would attract lots more visitors to Bute. Look what had happened with other films set in Scotland. More visitors, more employment.

She lifted a bundle of sweet smelling clean towels from her trolley and knocked on the door of number 251, not expecting a response. The crew and the actors would have left for the film set long since.

She hesitated, the entry card poised above the slot. What if the occupant of this room was still here? Hopefully it wouldn't be like that time when she'd surprised one of the guests in the shower.

She chuckled at the memory of the startled look on his face as he'd reached for a towel to cover his embarrassment.

She opened the door and edged her way in.

'Room service,' she called in a very loud voice, just to be sure.

For a moment Gertie thought the man sprawled on his side across the bed was still asleep and prepared to back out quietly, to return later, though it would interrupt her routine for the day. In a way she wasn't surprised to find him in bed. She'd heard the bar at the Coronet Hotel was doing a roaring trade every night.

'Sorry,' she said very loudly, 'I'll come back later,' hoping this would startle him into wakefulness and she could get on with her work.

There was no movement. The man lay perfectly still. She moved closer, clutching the bundle of towels tightly. It was then she saw the shining handle of the knife embedded in his chest.

1

If my husband Simon hadn't taken a contract in America, if I hadn't sold my book on James Hamilton of Kames to Pelias Productions and if I hadn't met Robert Broughton by chance in a café in Glasgow, everything would have turned out differently.

As I boarded the ferry from Wemyss Bay to make the short crossing to Bute that morning in early summer, I'd no idea what lay ahead. I was off to the island to work on an exciting new project and every time I thought about it, a little shiver of excitement ran through me.

'Want to come outside?' said Robert, nodding in the direction of the seats out on deck, at present the preserve of a few smokers. 'It looks as if it'll be a really pleasant sail across the Firth of Clyde today.'

I shook my head. Having paid a large sum of money for a new honey blonde hairstyle, I didn't want to subject myself to the sea breezes just yet.

'I'm happy here in the passenger lounge,' I said, 'but I'd be grateful for a cup of coffee before you go.'

'Not a problem,' he said and headed off to join the queue while I settled myself at a window seat.

Robert was an old friend from my first post as a newly qualified teacher, before he'd gone off to Canada and we'd lost touch. I'd bumped into him in a café in Argyle Street a few months previously and we'd delighted in the opportunity to catch up on the intervening years.

It was a lucky coincidence to discover we'd both be in Bute at the same time and when he offered to help me with the move saying, 'I've sent my luggage on ahead,' I accepted gratefully.

Left on my own with a welcome cup of coffee, I remembered with pleasure the phone call from the Pelias Productions film company saying they'd like to option the short book I'd written about James Hamilton of Kames Castle.

The story of James and his wife, Harriet, had long intrigued me. I'd written the book without a contract, but fortunately this episode of the history of island life interested many readers and it sold well.

A few weeks later I'd been approached by the director, Sol Makepeace, to help with the script and it was difficult to disguise my delight at this new opportunity.

Little by little, over the succeeding months, I learned more about the proposed film, wrestled with the terms of the contract and tried to work out exactly what was expected.

When Maura, the eldest of my three children, said, 'Shouldn't you ask a legal expert, someone who specialises in this kind of thing, to look over the contract you're being offered,' I brushed her concerns aside, putting it down to her usual cautious approach to life.

Maura has always assumed a special responsibility for family matters. Alastair's a typical academic - vague and absorbed - and Deborah as the youngest is, I fear, somewhat spoiled, though at present she's working in Edinburgh and long may it continue, given her previous record in finding and keeping jobs.

'This is a reputable film company,' I said. 'I've checked them out on the internet. They've decided to make this film about James Hamilton and his tempestuous marriage to Harriet Wynne in the place where the events actually took place. It's bound to be a success, given the current appetite for historical drama.'

Her silence should have been a warning.

I ferreted in my bag for the envelope with the information I'd been sent by Tracy Holmdale, the PR for the company, anxious to be fully briefed and flicked through till I found the draft (very draft, as she'd had been at pains to tell me) flyer. It would be unforgiveable if I got the names of the stars wrong.

At the various production meetings in Glasgow, I'd also met Matt Trickle, the chief scriptwriter, but the other members of the cast and the crew were unknowns for now.

Problem was, I'd packed my handbag with all the odds and ends I thought I'd need for the journey and it took me several minutes to rifle through everything before I found the envelope with the flyer.

Pelias Productions

present

A Man Alone

The tempestuous love story of
James Hamilton of Kames and Harriet Wynne

Starring

⁕**Franklin Todd** of *Heart and Home* as
James Hamilton

⁕**Juliet Rae** of radio's *Country Found* as
Harriet Wynne

And Introducing

⁕**Quentin Quizling** as Daniel Hamilton

As the ferry swung into the calm waters of Rothesay Bay, I stuffed the information back in my bag and stood up to watch the graceful movements of the crew as they threw the heavy ropes with a deceptive ease on to the pier to berth the huge ship safely. Outside on the decks a number of people craned over the rails, anticipating a relaxing holiday on the island, while the regular commuters lined up patiently.

The sight of Robert loping towards me jolted me out of my daydream. He was nothing like my husband, Simon - he was tall, very tall, at a guess somewhere around six feet six and his slightly long hair was now a peppery brown, with flecks of the original red, but his eyes were still the piercing blue I remembered from our younger days.

'Ready, Alison? We'll be there soon.'

He stood over me, his pale face flushed from the sea air and I drained the last of my coffee, tossing the cup in the recycling bin as I passed.

'Had I realised there was so much luggage, I would have hired a car,' said Robert as we wrestled with my baggage stowed beside the exit, but it was said with a smile.

The house in Glasgow had been let fully furnished and the place I was renting in Port Bannatyne was also furnished, so apart from a few precious items and my personal belongings, the move entailed little effort. Or so it had seemed when I'd first planned it, so how had I acquired all these small cases, holdalls and plastic bags?

As we waited for the ferry to berth, I said, 'How are you planning to spend your time on Bute?'

'I have a notion to write a book about my time as an academic,' he replied. 'Something in the nature of a memoir and I thought the peace and quiet of Bute would provide me with the impetus.' He grinned. 'Where I live now may be exciting, but you could not call it peaceful.'

Robert lives in a very smart, modern flat in the centre of Glasgow: ideally located for access to the many theatres, restaurants and art galleries, but not ideal for any work requiring concentration.

'You mean an autobiography?'

'No, more a recollection of the days when being an academic was exactly that, before the bean counters took over and we all had to worry more about finding grants than undertaking research.'

The ferry doors swung open and we followed the other passengers down on to the pier. The little town of Rothesay, nestled snugly in the curve of the bay, lay bathed in sunshine, a higgledy-piggledy collection of houses, tenements and shops.

Up on the hill the large Victorian villas, built for summer living, were carefully screened by thick woods. In spite of giving the impression of a prosperous destination, Bute was suffering as much as the rest of Scotland from the economic decline. Many people hoped this film would be exactly what was needed to give the island a boost.

We headed for my car, conveniently parked at the Albert Pier near the ferry exit and spent a few minutes loading it up, cramming everything in.

'Are you taking me to my cottage right away?' he said as I headed left out along the Shore Road. 'I thought I might come and help you unpack, make sure everything was satisfactory.'

'No need,' I replied. 'There's not much to do and it would mean a double journey.' Aware how ungrateful this made me sound I added, 'I am rather tired at the moment. We can catch up later.'

He turned away to look out of the window as we sped towards Ascog and when we reached his holiday cottage a few minutes later he opened the car door without a word.

Feeling badly about my abrupt dismissal of his offer, I leaned across the passenger seat to say, 'I am most grateful for your help, Robert, I couldn't have managed without you.'

He visibly softened, though his reply was somewhat formal even for him.

'I was glad to be of assistance, Alison. Phone me when you are settled and we can arrange to meet up for dinner or a drink.'

I smiled, but made no reply and waved and revved up the car to drive off. Glancing in the mirror, I saw him standing at the door of the cottage looking after me as I rounded the corner and headed back towards Rothesay.

Oh dear. This wasn't meant to happen. Trouble was, there was no denying he was a most attractive man.

2

The house I'd rented in 'the Port' as it's affectionately called, wasn't really a house at all, but a two bedroomed upper flat at the top of the hill in Castle Street. It was reached by an ancient, steep, winding stair, the handrail pitted and worn, though it had the advantage of a small terrace outside the living room, giving a clear view over the hotchpotch of houses and old grey stone tenements down to the boats bobbing at anchor in the waters of Kames Bay far below.

Already I could picture myself sitting out with a glass of wine after a day of being on set with the film crew, chatting to the actors, suggesting improvements and tweaks to the script.

Port Bannatyne was looking at its best: the stone containers on the slipway bright with busy lizzies and begonias, the window boxes and tubs on the houses along the front newly planted. Many of the shops had had a fresh coat of paint and the acrid smell of gloss mingled with the tang of the seaweed strewn along the pebbly beach. The three storey Coronet Hotel, temporary home to Pelias Productions, stood on the corner of Marine Road, its gently curved frontage also newly painted in cream and maroon, gleaming in the sunlight.

When I reflected on it later, much later, I realised how silly my expectations had been. Even the title of assistant scriptwriter was a misnomer, no more than a cover for what turned out to be a very lowly role indeed, somewhere below the lady who dispensed tea and gossip in large quantities.

But for the moment I was filled with anticipation and excitement and, after stowing my belongings in the limited accommodation, I checked my phone. There were no messages. There'd been no word from Simon for the past couple of days and I'd have to contact him soon, find out how he was getting on with his contract - a *Career Readiness Initiative* sponsored by the Education department in California - an ideal opportunity for him given his experience of further education.

Things hadn't been going too well between us lately. It might be no more than the difficulty of adapting to a new way of living together - me with my writing career, Simon with his as a consultant - which meant both of us worked from home, something which isn't as delightful as it sounds. Perhaps this breathing space would help us resolve our differences.

In the meantime I had to make contact with Pelias Productions and I pressed the number on my mobile for Tracy, the PR and liaison person on the production crew.

'Hiya, Tracy isn't here at the mo. Leave a message, why don't you?'

Drat - her voicemail. Referring to herself in the third person wasn't a good start and I abandoned a message half way through. I'd try again in an hour or so, speak to her directly. Meanwhile there was plenty to sort out here at Castle Street.

From the vantage point of the little terrace, furnished with a tiny glass bistro table and two fold up chairs, squeezed in beneath a riot of pale pink clematis covering the side wall, I could look down over the Port to spy out any signs of activity where the film crew had set up.

To my surprise, instead of numerous lorries and vans occupying the road along the seafront between the Coronet Hotel and the boatyard at the end of the village, which is what I'd expected from my (admittedly limited) experience of film productions, there were only a couple of rather dilapidated caravans parked outside the hotel.

Of course! The film company had taken most of the rooms in the hotel, newly refurbished after years of neglect. At a guess, the owners were glad of this block booking to give their business a good start and such extensive accommodation meant the film company wouldn't require a fleet of dedicated trailers.

Figures scurried about, some evidently in costume, but at this distance it was difficult to make out who they were, if they had anything to do with the film. No point in waiting here for a call from Tracy, it would be better to go down and introduce myself, find out what was happening.

Decision made, and with a tingling sense of anticipation, I put my mobile in my bag, grabbed a cardigan from the hallway and closed the front door with a bang to hurry down the hill to join the rest of the company.

A knot of villagers had gathered outside the little Post Office cum general store, enjoying the sunshine and chattering loudly as they waited, no doubt hoping to spot some well known personalities. I wasn't the only person excited by all this commotion in the Port.

Waving to one or two people I recognised, I crossed the road and joined a couple of men from the production crew, judging by their T-shirts emblazoned 'Pelias Productions'. They were leaning on the bright blue iron railings, gazing out over the water, watching as a sailor rowed his dinghy towards one of the smartly varnished wooden boats at anchor in the bay.

'Excuse me, I'm Alison Cameron,' I announced in a loud voice.

Quite what sort of response I'd expected, I'm not sure, but their cursory, 'Hi, Alison,' before going back to their diversion of watching the sailor, was disappointing.

'Can you help me? I'm looking for Tracy,' I said.

The taller of the two men turned round again and waved vaguely in the direction of the old stone quay.

'She was here a minute or two ago,' he said, but made no further effort to help and went back to watching the sailor.

Disappointed by this reception I moved away, but a few minutes later, as I approached the far side of the gaily painted bus shelter, I spied Tracy deep in conversation with one of the actors, judging by his old-fashioned costume of knee breeches, embroidered floral waistcoat and green velvet topcoat. He was standing beside a woman in a very modern outfit of jeans and a t-shirt.

Tracy's first reaction, in reply to my, 'Hello, there,' was less than enthusiastic. She said nothing, merely stood and stared at me.

She was someone you wouldn't easily forget. For one thing, she was about six feet tall and apart from her bright pink hair, she was dressed to call attention to her size, wearing a stretchy top almost matching her hair colour and emphasising her ample bust. This garish outfit was completed by a flared floral skirt below the hem of which peeped a froth of silver net and her over-large sunglasses were exactly the same shade of pink as her top. This was a woman who liked to be noticed.

'I wondered if you needed me for anything?' I tried again, sounding less sure this time, realising she'd completely forgotten me in spite of having met me at one of the production conferences.

She drew back, frowning as she appeared to recognise me. She looked pointedly at her watch saying, 'All the extras were supposed to be here two hours ago. I'm not sure there'll be time to costume you up before we start shooting. This really won't do, you know. This is how everything gets behind.'

The smile on my face faded.

'I'm not one of the extras, I'm Alison Cameron, the assistant scriptwriter. I'm part of the production team.'

14

She frowned at me again, obviously baffled and as she looked me up and down I became conscious of the dowdiness of my pale blue summer skirt and t-shirt in contrast to the dazzling outfit she was wearing.

'Did someone ask you to come along today for any special reason?'

'No, but I thought I'd be needed, that there would be a number of changes required as the filming went on.' I stood on tiptoe the better to meet her gaze adding, 'I was also told my knowledge of the island and of the story of James Hamilton would be critical, would make me, as assistant scriptwriter, someone useful to refer to.' I said the words "assistant scriptwriter" in a loud voice, hoping to jog her memory.

'Can't imagine who'd have told you that. I certainly don't remember being informed you'd be coming.' She shrugged. 'Besides, why would we want to keep changing the script? The actors are confused enough already, believe you me.'

Determined she wouldn't dismiss me so easily, I said, 'It was Matt, Matt Trickle, the chief scriptwriter,' aware of the rising note of desperation in my voice, seeing all my plans, not to mention the money I'd invested in renting the flat in the Port, suddenly disappearing. 'He told me to report to the set as soon as I arrived on Bute; said there would be opportunities to help with the script.'

Tracy laughed, an ear piercing screech, causing the young man standing beside her to jump back, a startled look on his face.

'Oh, Matt. What does he know? He's always making mistakes. Or you must have misheard him. Yes, you must have misunderstood what he said.' Problem resolved, she turned away.

Something in her attitude put steel in me. There was no way I'd misunderstood. I might only be the assistant scriptwriter, but hadn't I been assured my contribution was essential to the success of this venture? Wasn't the original story mine?

'That's as may be,' I said frostily, 'but I'd be grateful if you'd check it out with someone more senior,' placing great emphasis on the word "senior".

She rolled her eyes and pouted.

'Oh, I suppose so. I'll ask Derek. He's the casting director and the only person around at the moment who might know what's going on.'

The middle-aged, silent woman standing beside her stepped forward, seemingly embarrassed by Tracy's rudeness. 'Hello,' she said, 'I'm Linda Fortune.' Her smile lit up an otherwise unremarkable face, framed by a cascade of light brown curls. 'We're still a bit at sixes and sevens. It's early days yet.' She moved closer, placing herself between me and Tracy. 'I'm responsible for the props...and the make-up...and the hair. You'll find on this production most of us have more than one job.'

Tracy ignored this attempt to pacify me and turned to flounce off along the seafront, wobbling dangerously on her high heeled sandals.

Linda shrugged. 'I'd better go along with her, check out what's going on. Won't be long. I'll come back and let you know.' She smiled, her calmness comforting as she patted my arm. 'Don't worry, it'll all sort itself out.'

As she disappeared after Tracy, I was left alone with the young man and there was an awkward pause before we both spoke at once.

'Are you an extra in this film?'

'What parts of the script did you write?'

We laughed, the ice broken and he said with a hint of pride in his voice, 'I'm Franklin Todd.'

'I'm Alison Cameron,' I stuttered. 'I'm so sorry, I didn't realise…'

How could I have failed to recognise Franklin Todd, one of the best known actors of the day through his role in the long running soap *Heart and Home*. Probably because of the costume and the wig, not to mention the thick make-up he was wearing. He didn't look the least bit like the character of a young 'man about town' he played on television.

He laughed, showing a set of pearl-white teeth and then, as though he'd read my mind said, 'We don't look quite the same as we do on screen, especially when it's a costume drama.' Pointing to his elaborate breeches and waistcoat, 'And this outfit isn't what I'd usually wear.' He shuffled his feet. 'It's so uncomfortable and hot in all this gear I'll be glad to get out of it. Sometimes we actors have to suffer for our art.'

'It does look very dashing,' I replied, unsure if this last remark was a joke, but he smirked as though this compliment was no more than his due.

We chatted amiably for a few moments about the film and his starring role as James Hamilton before Tracy came thundering along, still teetering on her impossibly high heels, with a swarthy and very dark-haired man behind her, panting and trying hard to keep up. In spite of her promises to help sort the situation, there was no sign of Linda.

'Hi,' he said, extending his hand and nodding to Franklin. 'I'm Derek, the casting director. Matt is along at the castle set at the moment with Sol discussing some changes to the script, so I'll try to help. I guess you haven't been briefed on what to do?' He wheezed as he said this, his chest visibly rising and falling under his over-tight shirt.

'That's an understatement,' I muttered, but aloud said, 'I'm happy to help in any way I can. I believe there may still be some work needed on the script.'

As he put his arm round my shoulder, I instinctively drew back.

'You see, Alison, it's like this. At the moment we're trying to organise the scene, so it may be some time before you're called for any questions we have. You can hang around if you like, take in the action, but there won't be much happening for a while. The sound boys are still working on the noise levels, especially with these pesky seagulls everywhere.'

As if on cue, a number of seagulls swooped and dived overhead in a loud cacophony, wrongly convinced there would be some titbits for them soon.

'I'd like to shoot them down,' said Derek grimly, waving his fist in the air, 'but apparently that's not allowed. They're a bloody nuisance and a nightmare for the sound crew.'

Encouraged by the sight of a raised fist, mistaking it for someone about to throw food, the gulls swooped in closer. I could understand Derek's problem. The seagulls were everywhere: perched on the railings, bobbing along the shore, swooping and diving above us, riding the waves close to the water's edge, their noise making it impossible to work.

'I'd like to wait around, if that's okay?' I said. 'I know little about making a film and I'm sure it'll be very interesting, that I'll learn a lot.'

Franklin gave a loud 'Hrrumpp' at this and Tracy glared at him.

'This is what it's all about, if you want to hit the big time, Franklin. This isn't your two-bit soap opera now. This is a real production.' There was almost a look of triumph on Derek's face as he spoke, realising he'd touched on a sensitive area.

For a moment it appeared Franklin was about to snap back, but instead he turned away quickly and pulled out a cigarette from the packet hidden in his costume.

Derek looked round. 'I'm afraid there's nowhere to sit, unless you want to wait inside the hotel or here in the bus shelter.' He tugged at his shirt, trying unsuccessfully to pull it down to cover his ample stomach.

It appeared the usual bus service from this stop had been suspended and the film crew seemed to have taken over the Port, careless of the disruption. With a sinking feeling the thought struck me that this had all the appearance of a low budget production. Even Franklin, though known for his part in *Heart and Home*, wasn't the main star of that particular television series. Well, I'd have to make the best of it and the experience of working as a scriptwriter, even on a film such as this, would be a good addition to my list of skills.

Shrugging on my cardigan against the chill wind that had sprung up over the bay, I wiped the slightly damp seat and settled myself down in the bus shelter. Better to make the most of the afternoon, rather than stay indoors. As I looked back, Tracy was walking off towards the Coronet Hotel with Derek, their heads bent together in animated chat, but Franklin was left gazing after them and the expression on his face showed he was far from happy.

3

The rest of the afternoon was no better. If anything it was worse: Franklin fretted backwards and forwards along the seafront, smoking cigarette after cigarette before finally announcing he was fed up waiting.

'I'm off to the bar,' he said. 'It's ridiculous to have spent all this time in costume and make-up without a call.'

Tracy had returned, still without Linda, and became increasingly strident as it became obvious there'd be little action any time soon.

'Sol will be furious if there's no filming today,' she kept muttering, scrolling through her phone as though seeking an answer there. 'And if the director's unhappy, we're all unhappy.'

After half an hour in the bus shelter, I headed for the café in the Post Office for a large cappuccino…and then a refill. The crowd of curious locals who'd gathered early, only to be kept well away from the central area by a couple of heavies - not the kind of people you'd mess with - had also grown tired of waiting and straggled off. I heard one of them mutter, 'They'll never get a film made if they go on like this,' and I could only agree as his companion added, 'Anyway, there are no big stars here. Nothing worth hanging about for.'

As for me, I'd no idea what to do. It was clear my lowly status as an assistant scriptwriter merited no attention and my dreams of being deferred to as the film was shot - 'Could you suggest a re-write for this scene, Alison?' or 'If you could put in some extra dialogue in this part, that would be great?' - were so much pie in the sky. A belief confirmed when eventually Matt arrived from his meeting with Sol and the look on his face made it clear he hadn't expected to see me at the shoot.

'I'll leave you to it,' said Tracy and off she went again.

'Why, h...h...hello, Andrea, h...h...how are you doing?' A wide grin lit up his boyish face as he attempted to disguise his nervousness. Matt had either inherited excellent genes that gave him his fair and smooth complexion, or else he was a fan of Botox. Either way, his face belied his fifty-odd years, though the comb over he'd adopted couldn't disguise his thinning hair, a style he was having difficulty keeping in place in the wind blowing in from the bay. He was slim to the point of emaciation, probably because he seemed unable to stay still.

'It's Alison, actually,' I replied, trying to sound upbeat. Surely we'd met often enough in the pre-production stage for him to recognise me?

'Of course, of course, h...h...how could I make that mistake? Welcome to Bute, Ali,' he said, adjusting the dark rimmed glasses that seemed rather too large for his face.

If there's one thing that sets my teeth on edge it's being called Ali by people who don't know me well, but I was in no mood to argue and even more annoyed by his "Welcome to Bute" considering one of the reasons for engaging me was for my knowledge of the island, probably a good deal better than his.

'So you're going to h...h...have a little break here and you've come along to find out h...h...how the film process works? I'm sure you'll learn a lot from watching real professionals.' He accompanied this statement by a wink as he once more smoothed his hair down.

He was making a lot of assumptions.

'No, actually I was under the impression I might be needed here on set, as the assistant scriptwriter.' How often was I going to have to repeat the same story?

He drew back, seemingly confused by this and scratched his head, completely destroying what was left of his carefully arranged hair style.

'Did we tell you that? I guess there's been a bit of a breakdown in communication. Once the script is finalised, it's over to Sol for the duration, though he h...h...has to consult me about any changes. Not,' he added hastily, 'that we don't value your input, but it makes more sense to h...h...have one person in overall charge of the final script, so that any changes can be minimal. Cuts down on costs, apart from anything.' He giggled, but it was a further sign of nervousness and he scanned my face to gauge my reaction to the news I was very much surplus to requirements.

By now, anger had replaced frustration.

'You will remember I was the person who wrote the short biography of James Hamilton, the reason you engaged me in the first place. You wanted me here to make sure the facts were correct and as I'd already done all the research…' I let my voice trail away; let him fill in the blanks.

This seemed to confuse him even more.

'Mmm, of course, of course, Ali. We were very impressed, but really and truly I'm the person who knows h…h…how it all works. Your stuff was quite good, but I've h…h…had to take the material and give it that oomph we need for film. A film is different from a book, you know.'

This speech was accompanied by much hand waving and a wealth of facial expressions I'd have found fascinating had I not been so cross. A suspicion was beginning, one I didn't dare acknowledge. My biography of James Hamilton of Kames Castle had been very well received, was very popular and the reason Pelias Productions had contacted me in the first place.

Now it was becoming clear Sol had sweet-talked me into the role of assistant scriptwriter in order to use my book for his own ends. That way, there'd be no problem about using my copyright material. Too late, Maura's words of caution came back to haunt me.

'So what happens now?' I said, determined not to slink away and leave them to it when I'd gone to all the trouble and expense of letting out the house in Glasgow and renting a place on Bute.

This stopped him in his tracks and I could almost see his brain ticking over as he tried to come up with a plausible reason to get rid of me. Perhaps he hadn't anticipated I'd be so determined, had thought I'd meekly back off? Or wouldn't have been interested enough to take up his offer of coming over to Bute, something he now appeared to regret.

As he was about, I'm sure, to give me some tin-pot excuse, Tracy came tearing along the seafront as fast as her considerable bulk and her very high heels would allow.

'Where's Derek? He's needed at once, along at the set. They're going to shoot one of the crowd scenes, try to get something in the can today.'

She gazed around wildly, as though we were deliberately hiding him somewhere. 'Sol will go mad if he's not there in a couple of minutes.'

As though he'd heard her, Derek came strolling out of the Coronet Hotel to join us. He edged closer to Tracy, who recoiled as the alcohol fumes from his breath hit her. 'Get along to Kames, now, Derek. Sol's freaking out. He's some questions about the extras you hired.'

Derek coughed to disguise a hiccup, none too successfully. 'Is everything in place, Tracy? All the extras for the scene costumed up?' He spoke in that slow, deliberate manner of someone trying to control his every word.

Tracy nodded, seemingly calmer now Derek had arrived.

'Well, I suppose so. I've put out a cattle call, though there are fewer than we thought, even including the children we've recruited from North Bute Primary school, and we might have to resort to a bit more in the way of computer graphics to make it look as if there's a large crowd.'

'Oh, for goodness sake - why are there so few extras? I thought we'd decided to go with my suggestion of engaging lots of the local people for the crowd scenes. It's hardly rocket science.' His face was suffused with rage - or alcohol - and the buttons on his shirt looked ready to pop at any minute.

Tracy glared at him, put her hands on her hips.

'You're the casting director, Derek. It's not my job. I'm doubling up as it is.'

'You can't expect me to do everything, Tracy.' Now Derek was shouting, the purple veins standing out on his forehead. 'I told Sol I needed help, but would he listen? ...oh, no. Now there aren't enough people from the island for the crowd scenes.' He leaned in towards her and she shrank back, all bravado gone.

Derek refused to let the subject drop.

'But you have plenty of extras for the scene at the castle? What's happening about that?'

Matt stood tapping his fingers on the railings, all attempts to keep his hair under control forgotten and a long strand flapped about like a bird on top of his head. Fascinated, I could only watch as it blew to and fro.

Tracy fiddled with her phone. 'Well, there is one teensy weensy problem. The woman who was playing the lady's maid to Harriet has had to go off the island to help her daughter with a sick grandchild.' She paused. 'We've no idea when she'll be back.'

For a moment it appeared Derek was about to explode.

'How inconsiderate,' he shouted, waving his arms and stamping his feet. 'You can't trust anyone. You give people a contract, try to help them with employment and this is what happens.'

He glared at Tracy, who was cowering under this onslaught.

'It's hardly my fault,' she whimpered.

Matt swung round to face me.

'Wait a minute, Derek. We might h...h...have a solution. You'd be ideal for the part, Annabel. There's not much to it, Tracy will fill you in.'

Too astonished at this suggestion to pick up on yet another wrong use of my name, I squeaked, 'Me? I've no acting experience at all, unless you count a part as an angel in the school Nativity play when I was five.'

Derek brushed my concerns aside.

'Nonsense. It's a great idea, Matt. Of course you can do it. You've very few lines to say - you'll know them, won't you, as you helped write the script? It won't be a problem.'

This was unlikely: it had been some time since I'd looked at the script and how could I explain most of the actors' lines had been written by Matt, without losing face?

My input was checking the facts, filling in the details, adding lines here and there when historical accuracy was needed. And I suspected those lines I had contributed had been severely chopped.

Yet, there was this feeling no matter how much I protested, Derek would refuse to listen and besides, if I wasn't wanted here for my input to the script, what was I going to do? It might be fun to be involved, to be doing something, rather than waiting on the sidelines for the slight possibility I'd be called to give advice. Even so, I wasn't going to agree too readily.

'I expect I'll be paid for this,' I said. If money for the production was as tight as it appeared he might decide to do without my services and save me having to make a decision.

'Of course, of course.' Derek dismissed my concerns with yet another wave of his hand. He appeared to have recovered from his earlier outburst, now a solution had been found.

'But it's a speaking part,' whispered Tracy. '*Equity* won't be pleased. There are rules about…'

Derek was having none of it.

'This is an emergency,' he said grandly, cutting her off in mid sentence. 'I'll deal with that side of it.' He leaned back against the railings, consciously trying to keep his balance.

What more could I say, in spite of my many doubts? I'd come to the island expecting to be on the set helping with any changes to the script, providing information about the Hamiltons, correcting any historical inaccuracies and here I was with a role in the production, though mine might well be among the scenes to end up on the cutting room floor.

4

Thinking it would be Robert trying to contact me, I'd deliberately ignored the latest messages on my mobile. I didn't feel in the mood to meet up with him at the moment, with all that was happening, or rather not happening. Truth was, I felt guilty after all the help he'd given me moving to Bute and I made a decision to contact him soon but, exhausted after the first day of waiting around for some filming to take place, all I wanted to do was go back up to the house in Castle Street and sleep through till morning.

'It won't take long to get you sorted,' Derek had assured me as he hustled me towards the props caravan to leave me in Linda's care.

All my concerns about my role as Harriet's maid were quickly swept aside, but it wasn't as easy as Derek suggested. The first problem was my costume. In spite of Matt's grand assurances, based on no more than an idle judgement born of desperation, it immediately became obvious that the defaulting granny and I weren't anything like the same size - or height.

Linda Fortune shook her head, setting her brown curls bouncing as she brought out the costume for the lady's maid.

'Surely Derek realised how difficult this would be? You can't go changing actors like this - it never works well.' She pushed and pulled me into a tight-laced, dark grey costume, heavy with decoration, 'Take care how you move. Try to walk as slowly as you can. Fortunately it's not a big part today and by tomorrow, with a bit of luck, I should be able to do the alterations.' Even her calm manner was being tested by the difficulties of this film production.

What was the point in protesting? It was too late to refuse and all I could hope was that by some piece of luck the recalcitrant granny would appear on the next ferry, the crisis would be over and I'd be released.

But it was not to be and eventually, suitably garbed and very uncomfortable, I emerged from the props caravan to board the minibus waiting to ferry the actors and the crew along to the set where the day's filming was to take place. The area round Port Bannatyne was used for the outdoor locations, but replica rooms had been constructed in the old barn at the far end of Kames for all the indoor shots.

Next came the problem of actually shooting the scene. The long and wearying afternoon seemed to consist of take after take, none of which pleased the director, Sol. This was the first time I'd actually met him, a large, burly man, with a shock of unruly white hair that looked more like one of the costume wigs than real hair.

When I'd first talked to him on the phone, I guessed he was American and sometimes he sounded as if he was, but his accent kept slipping in a disconcerting way. Perhaps he'd been born in America and spent a lot of time in Britain. Whatever the reason, no one else appeared to notice, or if they did, failed to comment.

He leaned heavily on an ornately carved wooden walking stick, but whether he needed it for support or whether it was merely for show was hard to say. He certainly made use of it to keep the cast in order, waving it around in the air at the slightest opportunity.

'Hi,' said a voice next to me as I hovered nervously at the side of the set, waiting for instructions on how I'd be cued in.

I turned to see a man similar in build to Sol, but younger and with dark hair instead of Sol's thick, white thatch.

'I'm Perry O'Brien, the cameraman,' he said. 'Don't look so worried. There won't be any problems. Just make sure you follow directions, keep to your mark and you'll be fine.'

'You make it sound so easy.'

'I've worked on a lot of films with Sol - don't fret.' His grin re-assured me as he acknowledged a shout from the director and hurried over to the camera stand, giving me a thumbs-up as he left.

I tried hard to remember Perry's words of encouragement, but by the end of the day if I was to hear that clapperboard going one more time and Sol shouting 'Action,' I'd scream. Not that I'd much to do in this short scene except speak a few words and curtsey several times, always remembering to keep my back to the camera so that the last minute stitching Linda had resorted to wouldn't be noticed. Nothing pleased Sol, who kept making remarks about 'wooden acting' and people 'having a poker up their back.' At least that's what it sounded like from a distance.

My scene should have been straightforward. Arriving back on Bute after a spell in Edinburgh with Harriet and her friends, I'd been sent ahead to make sure all was prepared for her return to Kames Castle, only to be met by a crowd of furious locals who despised her and everything she stood for.

My lines were hardly difficult, consisting of 'Let me pass,' and, 'How dare you treat us like this.' It sounded simple when Derek briefed me, but it's amazing how easily you can muddle words up, especially when your nerves are in pieces after umpteen takes.

So I went through, 'Let me pass you/Let me treat you/Let me dare you,' until finally I managed to get it right and Sol shouted, 'Cut' though I did hear him as an aside say, 'Where did you find her?' and he wasn't being complimentary.

Relief flooded through me as I left the set, where Quentin Quisling, in the role of James Hamilton's brother Daniel, was waiting to be cued in.

For all these reasons, the last thing on my mind when I reached the house was returning any phone calls, though before going to bed I decided to check the names on the 'missed calls' list, even if I lacked the energy to reply.

There were a couple of messages, not from Robert, but from Simon. Neither sounded urgent and as a calculation of the different time zones ruled out calling him back straight away, I resolved to call him in the morning. But once in bed I tossed and turned, all kinds of scenarios coming and going, drifting into nightmares. Worse still, I'd been told in no uncertain terms to be on set for six the next morning, dressed in costume and fully made up and ready for the next scene when Harriet arrived home.

The more I tried to sleep, the more difficult it became and eventually about four o'clock, as dawn was breaking, I gave up the struggle and slipped out of bed to make a large mug of coffee to take out on to the terrace. The gauzy early morning mist over Kames Bay was slowly lifting with the promise of a day of sunshine. At this hour even the most energetic of dog walkers hadn't yet made an appearance, but there were signs of activity down by the Coronet Hotel, just about in my line of sight if I stood on tiptoe and craned round the far edge of the terrace.

I'd been warned yesterday's rushes might not be good enough and the whole scene might have to be shot again. Somehow, even at this early stage, I didn't think the film business was for me and my admiration for those who chose to make it a career was increasing with every take.

Why didn't I cut my losses, pack up and go home? Then I remembered this course of action wasn't open to me: even if prepared to forgo the money I'd paid to rent this house, I'd have nowhere to stay in Glasgow for at least three months. It seemed I was destined to be stuck here on the island, involved in this mad film, becoming more and more depressed about the likelihood of its success.

There was a lack of crew members, as Tracy had reminded everyone on several occasions: most seemed to have to double up, take more than one role. So I discovered Linda Fortune wasn't exaggerating when she said she was not only the wardrobe mistress and the props supervisor, but she also did the make-up for most of the cast, a difficult task she managed with a commendable calmness and cheerfulness.

And though Perry O'Brien went by the grand name of director of photography, he operated the camera, assisted only by a young lad who appeared to be on a forced work placement, so little interest did he show in what was happening. Perry was constantly explaining the details to him, trying to encourage him, but met with little response.

'You're very patient with him,' I'd said to Perry the day before as we stood waiting for the call to re-shoot a scene, while Matt and Sol huddled together at the far end of the set, discussing the latest changes.

He laughed.

'It would be good if he showed any interest, but I'm afraid he's a lost cause. Stop worrying so much about everything, Alison. It'll all work out in the end. It's been better planned than it looks.'

There was a pause and as there was still no sign of action, I said, 'You've been in films for some time?'

'Mmm. That's right. It's all I ever wanted to do, though times are tough at the moment. Let's hope this one brings in the money.' He winked. 'We really need to make a profit, else Pelias Productions is in trouble.'

This sounded ominous, but before I could quiz him further, Sol called over and we were off into shooting the next scene.

There was no point in idling out here on the terrace any longer, thinking about that conversation with Perry: best to go down to the sea front and find out what lay in store. Several times I'd tried to eat breakfast, but the butterflies in my stomach had other ideas and I made do with another coffee, though perhaps it would have been better to stick to decaffeinated.

By the time I was ready to walk down to the Port the mist had all but disappeared and there was the promise of a perfect day, surely a good omen. As if to confirm it, when I reached the seafront the café at the Post Office was opening up, the little zinc tables and chairs set out on the pavement under the striped awning, ready for the first customers.

In spite of the Coronet providing meals - and drinks - for the film crew, the café was doing a brisk business in snacks throughout the day. At least one part of the island economy was benefitting from this invasion by Pelias Productions.

Down by the Port Bannatyne quay, everything was quiet. There was no one around in the bus shelter, though it was strange not to find Franklin hanging about on the seafront for his pre-filming dose of nicotine. The palm trees next to the beach nodded in the breeze from the water and in the large plant pots beside the shelter the burgeoning fuchsias were a riot of colour, lending the village a continental air in the bright sunshine.

I checked my watch, but as it was well after six o'clock there should surely have been more signs of activity? Unless, of course the start time was more flexible than I'd been led to believe, in spite of all the warnings the night before about "being ready early".

At the Coronet Hotel I greeted several people huddled in the doorway, but my 'Good Morning,' elicited no more than a few muttered responses as they stared at me, then turned away again.

Tracy was standing on the pavement outside the door of the caravan that served as the props and costume department, snuffling and crying, her eyes red-rimmed, her mascara running and making little streaks on her face.

'What on earth's wrong?' I said. In spite of our differences, I didn't like to see her upset like this.

'Oh, it's Derek,' she wailed. She pulled another tissue out of the capacious yellow bag which today echoed the colour of her low-cut top and dabbed her eyes, smearing the mascara further over her face. 'It's so awful. No one can believe it.'

'Why, is he ill?' Sadly I have to admit this idea didn't concern me greatly: it might be better for me if he was off the scene for a while. He'd turned out to be a perfect nuisance and if he was ill, there was only one thing that could have been the cause, judging by the last time we'd met.

She shook her head.

'Ill? No, of course he's not ill. He's dead.' She went back to wiping her eyes, crying softly.

This was said so starkly, with so little emotion, it was a moment or two before I could take in what she'd said.

'Dead? Was it a heart attack?'

That was the first thing that came into my head and though it was more likely an over indulgence in alcohol had led to his sudden demise, I refrained from saying so.

'No, no,' said Tracy beginning to sob loudly again, blowing into the soggy tissue, 'It looks as if he was murdered. We're waiting for the police to arrive.'

'Murdered? How do you know that?' Derek hadn't been the most popular member of the crew, but it was hard to believe he'd been murdered. She must be making a mistake.

'Because there was a bloody great dagger sticking out of his chest,' said a voice and I turned to see Franklin who'd come up behind me so quietly I hadn't noticed him.

If Tracy was upset, Franklin gave no indication he was in the least disturbed by the news.

'He won't be missed,' he growled and then as both Tracy and I looked shocked, added hastily, 'Though who'll take on his work I've no idea.'

'Who found him?'

'The woman who went in to clean his room in the Coronet Hotel. She thought at first that he was sound asleep. We did wonder why he hadn't appeared this morning.'

Linda came running out of the hotel and stood beside me.

'I should have known nothing would go right with this production. It's been nothing but trouble from the beginning. I'm going to find out if there's any way to get out of this contract, because...'

The sound of a siren approaching stopped her in mid-sentence and a few moments later a car screeched to a halt beside us and a smartly-dressed young man carrying a case opened the door and jumped out. This could only be the local doctor come to certify the death and we watched in silence as one of the police officers accompanying him began to move the curious crowd away from the front door before disappearing inside with a roll of blue and white tape.

'What happens now?' I said, thinking about Derek's death. But Franklin either misunderstood, or chose to misunderstand.

'It buggers up the whole schedule,' he said, pulling out another cigarette.

I waved the smoke away as he lit up. 'I mean about poor Derek. I expect the police will want to interview us all?'

'Sure they will. In the meantime I'm off for some breakfast,' he said. 'I'll have to find Sol, see what he wants me to do. Today was to be my big scene, the showdown with Harriet. I was rather looking forward to it. Are you coming, Linda?'

'I could do with some coffee,' she replied, trotting behind him towards the Post Office café.

So far I hadn't met Juliet Rae, who was playing Franklin's wife, Harriet, but I pitied her, having to deal with this huge ego, given how little Derek's death seemed to have affected him.

Then again, perhaps Franklin was being a realist. In spite of any sympathy we might have for Derek, there was no doubt this unexplained death would bring the production to a halt, at least temporarily.

Much as I regretted what had happened to the casting director, I hadn't really known him. With Derek dead, there might have to be some changes. Perhaps my skills would yet be called upon.

5

In spite of the commotion following Derek's death, it was impossible to ignore Robert any longer. He'd put a note through the door of the flat in Castle Street, claiming he was "just passing" - not that I believed that for a moment. You don't "just pass" a house at the top of a hill on a bike.

He seemed delighted to hear from me. 'I wondered if you would like to have dinner,' he said.

For a moment I hesitated, about to plead a busy schedule, but how ridiculous did that sound? Even with this bit part in the production, I wasn't exactly in the inner circle of the cast, which seemed tight knit, unwelcoming to outsiders. Besides, there was a real possibility that with Derek's death and the ensuing police investigation, the production might be in jeopardy and the film might be cancelled, if one of the many rumours going round was to be believed.

The police had been very business-like, especially the C.I.D who had come over from the mainland, but this was a murder and had to take precedence over everything else, in spite of the number of occasions Sol tried to remonstrate with them about "lost production time". In the politest of terms they made it clear that, while we'd all been subject to a preliminary questioning, there would be further calls on us.

My decision was made. There was no point in hanging around with the rest of the cast where there was only one topic of conversation - how soon filming would start again.

I said to Robert, 'You'll have heard about Derek?'

'Yes, word travels quickly. I thought meeting up for dinner might take your mind off all of this.'

Pleased at this suggestion I said, 'Good idea, I look forward to that. Where do you suggest?'

'How about the restaurant up at Mount Stuart House? It has an excellent reputation.'

The venue agreed, we settled on seven as our meeting time, and he refused my offer of a lift saying, 'I can travel round the island easily on the bicycle I've hired and Ascog is not far from Mount Stuart.'

With a brief, 'See you then,' I shut down the phone and wandered off along the seafront. There was a police car parked outside the Coronet Hotel, but otherwise there was no sign of activity. Perhaps I could sneak in, find out what was happening from some of the cast. They were almost certain to be sitting in the lounge bar, passing the time with a drink or two.

Since the first police interviews, there had been little activity and sure enough, that's where I found them, most of them very unconcerned about poor Derek and very concerned about their parts in this production and how his death was going to affect them.

Franklin, as was to be expected, was holding court or attempting to, though the bored look on the faces of some of the other members of the cast crowded in to the far corner of the lounge told its own story.' ....about Derek,' he was saying, 'but there's no way filming can be held up. After all, none of us can possibly be responsible for what happened. The show, as they say, has to go on. And as casting director, his work was more or less finished.' He waved his hand in the air to emphasise his point. 'We can manage fine without him.'

He gazed round, but no one rose to the bait, no one replied. One or two shuffled their feet as he spoke, others avoided his direct gaze, making me suspect he'd been waxing on in this vein for some time. There were a lot of egos in this group, each concerned only with how Derek's death would affect them.

A tall, slim woman, squashed in to the high backed bench in the corner, wriggled her way out past the others and stood up.

'If there's nothing happening, I'm off to look at my script, darlings. When we do start again, Sol's sure to want to move very quickly.'

'Yes, milady,' said Franklin standing up to let her out, his tone of voice mocking. Or it might have been no more than he couldn't get out of character and James Hamilton had taken him over completely, though I heard him mutter, 'La-di-da,' as she passed.

Of course! This must be the actress who was playing Harriet, the wife of James Hamilton. Her elegant appearance was striking, not only because of her height and her slim build, but because of her raven black hair piled up on top of her head. It was impossible to tell if it was natural or dyed, but in spite of Franklin's comment her open face made me think she was someone I could get on with.

She smiled as she reached me and, encouraged by her friendly manner, I said, 'Are you the actress with the lead role in this production?'

'I suppose you could say that, I'm Juliet Rae, darling,' she smiled again, holding out her hand as I introduced myself. 'Ah, you're the scriptwriter who's been persuaded to take the part of Harriet's maid?' She chuckled. 'Everyone seems to have to double up on this production.'

'Yes,' I said. 'When I signed up as assistant scriptwriter I'd no idea I'd end up in the film.'

A frown crossed her face. 'That's if production ever resumes.'

'I've heard a rumour the film might have to be cancelled. The police want to interview everyone again.'

'Mmm, there's no gossip about any suspects so far: we'll have to reconcile ourselves to a lot more questioning,' she waved her hand to encompass the others, 'which is the reason we're all huddled together in the hotel like this.'

'You surely don't think it's someone from Pelias Productions who's responsible for Derek's death?' I shuddered at the thought.

She shook her head. 'Let's hope not. I don't see what possible motive anyone here could have. For all of us it's incredibly important to make sure this film is made, finished on schedule.'

'And get out of here as quickly as possible,' muttered Franklin behind her, but she ignored him.

'I guess everyone's upset,' I said, 'and only too anxious for filming to start again,' omitting to add there'd been little evidence of any great sorrow.

'I know, I know,' she sighed, 'and I am sorry about poor Derek. He wasn't the most popular person on the crew, but it was a dreadful way to go. I have some idea…'

Perry came wandering over from the bar, clutching a beer and broke in before she could finish.

'The police will sort it out, I'm sure. Let's hope it's nothing to do with any of us.' He gazed slowly round the room, as though daring someone to confess.

Franklin stood up and glared at everyone, shaking his fist, making his feelings clear.

'Good riddance to that bloody man. He was a nuisance to all of us, kept messing the extras about, those he could persuade to join us that is. Mind you, what could you expect with the pittance they were being paid. Why are we worried about what happened? Whoever killed him did us a favour.'

There was a shocked silence. Many of those sitting around in the bar would no doubt echo these sentiments, but expressing them in public was quite another thing.

Matt, who'd been sitting beside him, stood up and put his hand on Franklin's shoulder in an attempt to calm him down, quieten him, but he shook off Matt's arm angrily and said, 'Don't tell me you're not all thinking the same. I'm the only one with the courage to say it and of course...'

Perry shook his head and went over to join some of the crew at the bar.

As Franklin continued to rage on, Linda came rushing in.

'What's going on here? The police are going to want to know.' She looked frightened, upset, so unlike her usual self the room fell silent and everyone turned to look at her.

'Know what?' Matt said.

'Calm down, darling, what's the problem?' said Juliet.

Linda looked over and pointed at Franklin. 'I've been going through the props while there's a break in the production, checking everything, making sure there's nothing that urgently needs mending.'

'So?' Matt waved impatiently.

Linda bit her lip. 'It's just that ... with Franklin's costume as James Hamilton... there's a difficulty.'

'For goodness sake,' shouted Franklin. 'It was fine when I took it off - you won't find any rips or tears there.'

'Yes, yes,' said Linda, appearing close to tears. 'But the dagger is missing.'

6

Franklin said nothing for a moment, then in an angry voice, 'I've no idea where it went. I did report it missing, you know.' He pulled out the cigarette packet, then impatiently crushed it in his hand as the barman said, 'You can't smoke in here, sir.'

Sol came over from the far corner of the bar where he'd been perched on one of the high stools unnoticed, sipping his drink, refusing to engage in conversation. 'Oh, yeah,' he said, his tone of voice making it clear he didn't believe a word. 'So why haven't we been told about this before. Surely you must've been suspicious?'

'Of course I wasn't,' said Franklin scornfully. 'I thought I'd dropped it somewhere and someone had found it and put it back in the prop box. Anyway it was, as has been pointed out on many occasions, only for display. Given the budget for this production, I wouldn't have been surprised if it had been bought in the nearest toy store.'

'Excuse me,' said Linda. 'It was an authentic dagger. That's why it had to be kept under lock and key.' Her eyes glittered as the mild-mannered Linda relished Franklin's discomfort.

Sol wasn't going to let this go quite so easily.

'Oh, yeah? Who did you report it to? Not to me, you didn't.'

'No, of course it bloody well wasn't to you. Although you seem to think nothing can function without you, that none of us is able to get on with what we're supposed to do without your input.'

For a moment Sol appeared to be taken aback by the vehemence of Franklin's statement, but he quickly recovered.

'Of course it's all to do with me. I'm the director. You're only the actor. A monkey could give as good a performance as you're giving right now.'

It looked as if blows were about to be exchanged, but Tracy stepped forward and positioned herself between them, her action and her bulk causing them to halt. Her brief adoring look at Franklin confirmed my suspicions she was more than a little smitten by him.

'Franklin reported to me,' she said loudly. 'He told me on Tuesday he couldn't find his dagger, asked if I'd seen it anywhere.'

'On Tuesday? Why was he reporting it to you? Why didn't he tell Linda? She's the one in charge of the props.' Sol waved his stick as he spoke.

Tracy hesitated and looked over at Franklin, but he refused to meet her gaze. She shrugged, saying, 'I was in the props caravan at the time. Linda had asked me to double-check the order for more make-up and I...'

Sol was momentarily distracted.

'More make-up? What do you mean? We ordered enough make-up at the beginning of this production for the entire island.'

Tracy took a step back. 'Yes, in theory we did, but there've been a lot of hold-ups, people being costumed and made up and then nothing happening...' Her voice trailed off as she saw the look on Sol's face. It was clear he couldn't abide criticism of any kind, but suddenly he seemed to make the decision to ignore this last comment.

'Whatever,' he said dismissively, 'but we'll have to let the police know. They'll be wanting to interview you again, Franklin, buddy. Another hold up in production.'

As they stood there, the anger between them simmering in the air, a thought struck me. Surely Tracy wouldn't have been in such distress if all he'd done was report his missing dagger? Franklin wasn't being entirely truthful - anyone could see that.

Linda, who'd stood looking from one to another during this exchange, said, 'How could Franklin lose his dagger and not notice? Why wasn't I told?'

Tracy shrugged, springing to Franklin's defence.

'It's only part of his costume, surely, concealed by that long frock coat he wears. He didn't actually have to use it at any time.' She gave a nervous titter, as though suddenly realising how inappropriate this comment was.

'That's not the point. He knew he had to be careful with the props in the interests of health and

48

safety. Anything remotely dangerous has to be kept in the locked box. It couldn't have been made clearer.'

'Well, perhaps it was a mistake, h...h...he didn't realise,' Matt intervened timidly. Like most of the members of this production, his main interest was himself. What happened to the others came very far down his list.

Franklin shouted, 'Excuse me, I'm still here you know,' but there was no expression of sympathy: it appeared everyone was well used to his outbursts and chose to ignore him, while I decided now was a good time to let Sol know I wouldn't be around in the evening, in case he arranged an impromptu rehearsal.

Dinner with Robert was increasingly appealing. Not that anyone had the slightest bit interest in what I was doing. And though it was really none of my business how the props department worked, I couldn't resist saying the obvious, 'What makes you so sure the dagger wasn't stolen from Franklin?'

Matt and Tracy turned to look at me, the expression on their faces making clear they thought this suggestion nonsense.

'W...w...who on earth would want to do that?' said Matt while Linda added, 'Even Franklin, bored as he appears to be with everything to do with this production, should have noticed his dagger was missing.'

'I've no idea what might have happened,' I said, wishing I hadn't joined in this conversation. 'But someone wanted Derek dead.'

Matt looked thoughtful and said, 'That's true.'

'Anyway,' said Perry briskly, 'it's up to the police to find out. In the meantime we've a film to get on with.'

'Exactly,' said Sol. 'Let's do it.'

As though on cue, Linda's mobile rang and she went wandering out and off along the seafront, talking earnestly.

We stood in an awkward silence for a few moments and finally I said to no one in particular, 'I'd better move.'

Sol made no effort to detain me and Matt and Perry headed back to the bar, leaving me with the impression the fewer conversations we had the better as far as Matt was concerned. He must surely feel guilty about the way I'd been treated.

Saying, 'See you all tomorrow,' I left the hotel to head to Castle Street. No one replied, but looking back I saw Perry had come out of the hotel and was standing gazing out over the bay, leaning on the railings, lost in thought. Perhaps what I'd said had disturbed him, made him re-consider what had happened. In the meantime I was going to meet Robert at Mount Stuart. The concerns of the film crew would have to wait.

7

The meal with Robert later that evening was more enjoyable than anticipated. He was good company and although we spent some time talking about our early years of teaching, exchanging up-to-date news about old friends and acquaintances as we made our way through a substantial first course of a fish platter, we soon progressed to other topics of mutual interest.

As an academic who'd decided to retire early from his post in the department of Accountancy at the University of Maple Ridge in British Columbia, Robert was unexpectedly very interested in what I was doing, in my new career as a writer, especially as a scriptwriter, and such attention is always very gratifying.

The questions he asked about the film, the cast and the crew sounded genuine, rather than merely polite, especially as his area of expertise was the Media.

'So tell me more about this project, this film, Alison. I gather that it's the story of one of the famous sons of Bute?'

There was a moment's interruption as the waiter arrived with the next course before I said, 'Yes, James Hamilton of Kames - you know the castle at the far end of Port Bannatyne? He bought the property from Lord Bannatyne of Bute who originally inherited it from his mother.'

'Of course – I have noticed that huge statue of Lord Bannatyne on the promenade, the one the seagulls seem to favour.' He laughed. 'So why did he sell it?'

'They were both Edinburgh lawyers and according to the story Bannatyne got into debt – gambling debt - as happened to so many in those days - and had to realise some of his assets. He was described as being of a "gay and easy disposition" so you can guess that's code for saying he went through the family money pretty quickly.'

'And this James Hamilton has an interesting story? Tell me more about him: is it intriguing enough to make a film of his life? This is what…the early eighteen hundreds?'

'Mmm. Of late there's been a revival of interest in anything historical.'

I went on to tell Robert as briefly as possible the story of James and Harriet, how Harriet was a member of a very famous family of the time, but when her father got into financial difficulties in 1796 they left England to travel extensively on the continent till worries about Napoleon made them decide to return.

'They were well connected, knew Lord Nelson and her father was very friendly with Casanova.'

This was the short version and Robert nodded from time to time as I continued with their story: how she had married James Hamilton and they came to live in Kames castle.

'Unfortunately the estate wasn't the source of money, nor the Isle of Bute the social whirl Harriet anticipated and James was forced to sell some of the belongings of the estate to keep up appearances,' I said. 'While she was in Edinburgh having her portrait painted by Raeburn, James had to sell the bedroom furniture.'

Robert chuckled.

'Good gracious. But why is the film called *A Man Alone*?'

'The marriage deteriorated and the couple spent more and more time apart. James is buried not far from Kames Castle at Croc-an-Rath, opposite the ruined church. The locals call it Lone Man's Grave.'

Robert was trying his best to maintain a look of interest but it was clear he didn't think there was enough in this tale to make a full length film.

'And that's it? Where would Sol find a producer for a film like this? I thought the box office demanded lots of action in any historical movie? Whoever is funding it must have deep pockets.'

'No idea who that might be,' I laughed. 'The main part of the story is about his marriage to Harriet Wynne. She was accustomed to a life of luxury. It's not exactly a romance as it was a tempestuous marriage by all accounts and some say he's buried alone because he couldn't bear to be in the same grave as her.'

I put down my coffee cup. 'How did you know about Sol being the director?'

He dismissed my question with a wave of his hand saying, 'Someone mentioned it. Or I came across an article somewhere.' He leaned forward, with no intention of explaining. 'Tell me about the filming - how is it working out? They are using your script, I hope?'

A little worm of reluctance to admit to my lowly part in this project made me say very cautiously, 'Not exactly. They've used my story, but I suspect they only engaged me as an assistant scriptwriter to have access to the information without any copyright issues.'

'But it is commercial enough to have attracted sponsorship?'

'Yes. I haven't really thought about that. I guess there must be enough people interested in providing the money, though from what Sol keeps saying, we're on a tight budget.'

My disappointment must have been evident, because Robert leaned over and said, 'Everything will be fine, Alison. Historical films do well,' though he did add as an afterthought, 'Usually.'

Robert seemed to believe I was a lot more clued up about the world of filming than I really was. Of course I should have come straight out and said how limited my knowledge and experience were, but sadly pride reared its ugly head and it was too late to retreat.

I was grateful when we changed the subject, even if that subject was the death of poor Derek.

'Did you know him well?' he said, toying with his coffee spoon.

'Not at all. I only met him once – as casting director he was the one who persuaded me to take on the part of Harriet's maid. Apart from that I know absolutely nothing about him. He wasn't at any of the meetings I attended in Glasgow.'

'Any idea what happened?'

'Apart from the fact he was murdered, you mean?'

'Someone must have disliked him a lot,' muttered Robert, stirring his coffee.

'This is a dreary subject of conversation,' I said. 'I've no idea what happened, apart from the gossip going round. As you'd expect the police are saying very little. It's certainly disrupted the film schedule, that's for sure. '

'Sorry, sorry, I had no intention of being so inquisitive. You are quite right, let's talk about something else.'

The rest of the evening passed pleasantly. Robert was an engaging companion, but whatever problems Simon and I were having at the moment, anything more than friendship with him wouldn't help matters, so when it came to paying the bill, I was very firm about dividing the cost.

'But I asked you out for dinner,' he protested.

'Even so, that's not the point. Besides, we might want to meet up again and this makes everything so much simpler.'

Very reluctantly, seeing how determined I was, he agreed to my suggestion.

We walked out into the cool evening air and wandered in the half light over to where I'd parked my car on the grass verge a short distance from the Mount Stuart restaurant.

'My bicycle is chained up over there at the end of the path,' he said, pointing to the far end of the car park.

We stopped for a few moments, enjoying the last of the light, watching the stars come out, before I said brightly, 'Well, that was a very pleasant evening, but I must be getting back,' in case he made any suggestion of a walk through the grounds of the estate.

As we parted, I held out my hand to shake his, but he leaned forward and gave me a kiss on the cheek. 'It would be good to meet again soon, Alison. I'd be most interested in visiting the film set if that could be arranged.'

Mumbling a vague reply, I jumped into the car and drove off, watching the red eye of his cycle lamp in the rear mirror as we headed down the long, unlit driveway on to the main road before he peeled off at Ascog to head up Mill Lane towards his cottage, while I kept to the main road, heading for Rothesay.

We'd had such an enjoyable evening, our non-stop chat confirming we'd a lot in common. Perhaps any attraction I felt was to do with my present worries about Simon.

Robert was good company, might be the only decent company I'd have during this spell on Bute. I didn't see myself becoming bosom buddies with any of the actors or the crew, that was for sure.

I drove into Port Bannatyne and headed up the hill towards Castle Street. Decisions could wait until tomorrow. Tonight I'd pour myself a glass of wine and sit out on the terrace, watching the star speckled sky in the quiet of a summer evening.

8

There was only one topic of conversation: Franklin had been taken in for questioning. Not that anyone was particularly concerned about him, but they were worried the shooting schedule might have to be re-arranged yet again, as continuing was almost impossible without the leading man.

We'd been instructed to turn up on set bright and early as usual, even those of us with minor parts. It had been agreed shooting could resume and the plan was to do a read through in the Port Bannatyne Hall to make sure everyone was familiar with the most recent changes to the script. Originally a church, the hall retains all the architectural features of one, but is now used for a variety of activities in the village from the local choir to regular keep fit classes and Sol had hired it for the duration of the film as a base for rehearsals.

There was a tension in the air, a buzz of noise as little groups of actors and cast members stood around outside the main door, chatting aimlessly. Occasionally one would break off to head down the street to the café on the front for yet another snack. At this rate they'd all find fitting into their costumes difficult.

As I came down the road Tracy was standing outside the Coronet Hotel, hopping anxiously from foot to foot in her strappy gold sandals, tightly clutching a pile of papers.

'What's the news?' Though my part was a small one, I'd visions of the project being abandoned.

'Franklin's been released.'

'So soon?'

'Mmm…yes. He was detained for questioning but they let him go when they found out he had an alibi.'

'That must be a relief. Where was he?'

She ignored this question and said, 'Have you seen Sol anywhere?' Today she was wearing a pair of very tight Capri pants in a lurid shade of pink and a low-cut sleeveless top in gold.

'No, isn't he in the hotel?'

She shook her head and without another word turned on her heel and went indoors.

Once more I felt a pang of regret at accepting the small role of Harriet's maid, but it was too late now. The woman originally cast for the part had phoned to say she planned to stay on the mainland for a few weeks until her granddaughter had made a full recovery and, while she was very sorry about the inconvenience, it was most unlikely she'd be back any time soon. It sounded like an excuse to me.

'That's what comes of t…t…trying to bring in amateurs, give them a chance of the spotlight,' grumbled Matt, ignoring the fact that one of the reasons for Derek doing so was because their rates would be a lot less than those of professionals.

And I would hardly call the tiny role of Harriet's maid being "in the spotlight".

He turned to me. 'You'd have thought Sol would've tried to find someone to replace Derek but, no, he claims the casting has been done and there's no need to bring in a r...r...replacement. Ridiculous.'

As though on cue, Sol came round the corner. 'Come on, guys,' he said waving his stick at us, 'you're all supposed to be at the hall.'

'But Franklin's been released,' said Tracy, 'so there won't be the need for so many changes.'

Sol frowned. 'I'll decide that, thank you very much,' and he stomped off, leaving Tracy and me to follow in his wake.

Given the choice of sitting in the hotel, engaged in idle chatter, waiting to be called and watching the run through in the hall, I'd decided it would be much more entertaining to find out more about the production, or if any of the suggestions I'd written had made it to the final script. When I thought of all the hours I'd spent in script meetings in a dingy room in a cheap hotel in Glasgow I could feel my blood pressure rise.

Once again Matt had tried to talk me down as he said, 'Your suggestions weren't bad for a first attempt, Alison, (at least he got my name right this time) but you have a lot to learn about the craft of scriptwriting. Not that I'm blaming you...and you were h...h...helpful on some of the historical facts, but the dialogue in particular had to be opened out.' This all said in a voice which made it clear he thought little of my talents, but even so, he watched nervously for my reaction.

About to reply, 'Well, if it hadn't been for my original book about James Hamilton of Kames and his disastrous marriage to Harriet Wynne there might have been no film at all,' I quickly thought better of it. There was no point in antagonising him.

It would be some time before the film was 'in the can' and I kept reminding myself there was no option but to remain on Bute. I could have started writing something else, but somehow wasn't in the mood for putting together a proposal for another book.

Eventually Sol seemed pleased with the preparations and said, 'Right, that's fine, guys. You've got it spot on. Costumes and make-up for those in the next scene.' Though he could be incredibly grumpy when things were going wrong, he was equally swift to praise if the actors were performing well.

Obediently the cast and crew moved from the hall down to the caravans to be transformed into character. There was no word about my next appearance and glad to escape for a while, I headed down to the front to enjoy the warm weather.

Quentin Quizling was sitting on the bench in the bus shelter. I'd seen him around, but hadn't been introduced and it seemed rude not to pass the time of day. For a moment, as I sat down beside him, it looked as if he was going to ignore me: his shoulders sagged and his whole demeanour suggested an air of defeat. Someone had told me he wasn't happy with his role as Daniel, the older brother of James and I searched for a neutral subject of conversation.

'The seagulls seem to have quietened down. That will please Perry.'

He half turned to look at me, as though he'd only just noticed I was there.

'I guess so.' His voice was flat, dull.

Another silence until I said, 'How's the part going?'

This was probably the worst thing I could have chosen to say. It was like setting a match to dry tinder as he blazed into life.

'My part isn't the one I should've had. I auditioned for the part of James Hamilton; my agent promised me it was as good as mine. It went to that smart-Alec, Franklin Todd. He couldn't act his way out of a paper bag.'

'But isn't he a well known actor? Apart from the current soap, he's had parts in...' Sadly I couldn't recall any other appearances so I ended lamely with... 'so many programmes.'

'He's certainly a star, or rather thinks he is, but his days are numbered. Imagine asking me, a good few years younger, to play his older brother. Even with the best make-up in the world, who's going to believe that?'

Quentin did have a point. On the other hand, perhaps Franklin was a bigger name, a bigger draw, though the gap of several years as claimed by Quentin (if true) did seem more than a little bit of an oversight. Underneath his facial hair he did have that kind of smooth baby face whose plumpness keeps the years at bay.

'This was to be my big chance, you know. Screwed up by that fool, Derek. They even made me grow this set of whiskers to make me look older.' He stroked the decidedly wispy beard partly covering his chin.

This was only one of the many puzzles about this production, but there was no way I wanted to become involved in a discussion about Derek, not in the circumstances.

'Why did you take the part then?' All said innocently enough, but he stared at me as if he thought I was trying to wind him up.

'Don't you know anything about acting? Parts are scarce. My agent says you can't get the reputation for turning any part down, no matter how much you may want to. When the police arrested Franklin I thought I'd be in with a chance of my part being re-written, enlarged, but no, it appears he had an alibi.' He smiled slyly. 'Though whether the alibi holds up remains to be seen.'

This whetted my curiosity. 'So what was his alibi?'

Quentin tapped the side of his nose. 'Ah, you only have to ask who might want to help dear Franklin, no matter what the cost.' It was clear he wasn't going to tell me.

He gazed off into the far distance, out across the bay, no doubt pondering his bad luck and I said, 'I'll see you later,' being in no mood to listen to more of his complaints.

'I'll have to head for costume and make-up,' he replied, standing up and stretching. 'Else Sol will be sending out a search party for me.'

I wandered down along the seafront towards Kames Castle, past the boatyard, noisy with activity as sailors repaired and painted their boats for a season of sailing in the Kyles of Bute and beyond, past the North Bute Primary school, eerily silent at this time of the morning.

As I reached the end of the boatyard, a little distance from the castle, a pony and trap was being made ready, so it would seem that filming had started.

Eager to see this outdoor take, I moved as close as was permitted. The scene being shot was starting by the playing fields. Unfortunately this was the spot where the public toilets were, but someone had had the bright idea of disguising them with a frontage resembling an old farmhouse. The concrete of the parking bays and the bus terminus had been heavily covered with dirt and straw and the midget Submarine Memorial garden hidden behind a collection of carts and old style farm implements, probably on loan from the Bute Museum.

As I drew nearer there was the sound of a great commotion and Sol shouting, 'Whose idea was it to have all these goddam chickens on the loose?'

Matt and Perry were running about trying to shoo a number of hens and geese back towards the "farmhouse" with little success.

'I don't like to speak ill of the dead, but it was Derek's idea,' Matt shouted. 'He t...t...thought it would help with the atmosphere.'

'When I asked him to get the cast together I didn't expect him to bring in these animals.' Sol was almost incandescent with rage. 'Get 'em out of here.'

With some difficulty, but aided by others from the crew, Matt at last succeeded in cramming the hens into various baskets, except for one large white hen that had flown up onto the roof of the "farmhouse" and was sitting there, flapping its wings and screeching defiantly.

'There's n...n...no way I'm climbing up there,' muttered Matt. 'With a bit of luck the seagulls will get it.'

Sol had by now moved towards a pony and trap, waiting beside the roadway. 'Where's Franklin?' he said, looking round.

'I'm here, I'm here.' Franklin came strolling over, nipping his cigarette out. Now that he'd been released by the police he looked more smug than ever.

But Sol was having none of this casual approach.

'Let's get on with the scene,' he said in a calmer tone of voice. 'Franklin, get yourself up onto the trap and we'll do the shots as you head towards Kames Castle. Perry, frame the shot so you get him passing the farmhouse.'

Perry did a mock salute as he set up the camera and fiddled with the lens. 'All ready, Sol, whenever you are.' He nudged the bored looking trainee beside him. 'Watch and learn.'

Sol moved back. 'Action,' he called and the clapper boy ran forward.

At least that's what would have happened if the pony, Diamond, had been willing to co-operate. I recognised the owner, Bobby, had seen him about the island often, driving round in a leisurely fashion or making an appearance at one of the many galas and events.

Today, however, nothing was going according to plan, if indeed there was a plan. Whether it was all the hustle and bustle with the chickens or the general noise, Diamond was decidedly skittish, refusing to be harnessed to the cart, neighing and tossing his head up at every attempt to bridle him. It didn't look like a problem that would be resolved any time soon.

'Cut, cut,' yelled Sol. 'Hell, no, that's not the way.'

Perry sighed, standing back with the air of someone who has been through this many times before.

'What are they shooting today?' I asked him, watching the spectacle with interest while Harry Gothwick fiddled with the microphone mounted on the end of the boom that was swinging dangerously back and forwards as he worked.

Perry grinned and said, 'There's going to be a couple of outside shots as James Hamilton comes back to the castle and then we're going to the inside set for the showdown between him and his wife. At least that's what they'll do if they can sort out the pony. Doesn't look as if they're having much luck at the moment. ' He grinned again. Why did I have the impression he was enjoying this diversion from the usual film histrionics? 'This scene should be good. I'm looking forward to it - I've seen the rehearsal, if you could call it that.'

He dusted down the remains of the straw clinging to his jacket, adjusted the camera on the rolling platform, and he and the boy began moving it further down the road ready to begin shooting as soon as the pony could be prevailed upon to behave.

I was disappointed. This scene was one I'd had nothing to do with, hadn't even thought about and it was unlikely I'd be allowed inside to watch the filming: the space was limited and by the time the director, the lighting crew, the sound crew and Linda, the dresser/ make up/props organiser, were crammed in, there would scarcely be space for the actors, never mind spectators.

Before starting this project, I'd had no idea there would be quite as much hanging around, waiting for something to happen. Everything seemed to depend one thing on another, and the way the scenes were shot, out of sequence, made me wonder why anyone chose this as a way of making a living.

The pony had finally been secured to the trap and calmed sufficiently for Franklin to take his seat beside the owner, who was dressed for the part in an old fashioned riding coat and three cornered hat, beneath which peeped a white wig. The costume looked as if it had been made for a much bigger man - I wasn't the only one with wardrobe difficulties. In spite of her promises, Linda hadn't succeeded in altering my costume and I dreaded having to squeeze myself into it yet again. I really shouldn't have been so greedy with the meal at Mount Stuart.

This was becoming tedious and I was on the point of leaving when suddenly everything became much more interesting as Sol appeared, walking as quickly as he could from the direction of Kames Castle.

'Have you got that horse sorted out? I thought you told me it was easy to deal with, would be no trouble. Time lost costs money, guys. Let's get it together, like right now.'

Bobby muttered something under his breath which I'm sure Sol didn't hear, because there was no reaction. But to me it sounded like, 'It's not the poor horse's fault that this is a shambles.'

Franklin was sitting straight and rigid, decidedly ill-at-ease, holding on tightly to the sides of the seat, his face contorted with fear. 'Are you sure this animal is under control?' I heard him say. 'I don't want any accidents.'

But Sol had now decided everything was ready to shoot the scene and this was not the moment for Franklin to admit he was terrified of horses.

Sol lifted his hand to indicate to Perry that he should stand by, then looked over at Franklin. 'Stop fussing, man – you're being paid enough for this role. Let's get going.' He was in no frame of mind to placate Franklin, who wasn't so easily cowed.

'I'm not being paid danger money,' he retorted as the trap and pony set off along the sea front, Perry and the camera rolling along beside them on the platform on wheels.

Delighted to be free at last and heading away from those who had been causing him so much grief, the pony moved from a trot to a canter in a matter of moments and was with some difficulty finally brought under control by Bobby, before pulling up short at the entrance to the castle to throw Franklin forward so suddenly he had to grab on to the front of the cart to prevent himself falling.

'Bloody hell,' shouted Franklin, 'can't you control this thing.'

I was sure that wasn't in the script.

Franklin came down slowly from the trap, saying, 'This is nonsense. Why would someone of James Hamilton's status be coming along to Kames Castle on a cart?'

There was something else disturbing about this production. Low budget as it was, I suspected many of the costumes had been amassed from other productions on a need rather than an accuracy basis. Bobby's costume of riding coat and rough trousers was surely seventeenth century, while Franklin's was a mixture of early eighteen hundreds in his waistcoat and breeches and nineteen twenties in his very foppish cravat. Not that any of this seemed to trouble either the cast or the crew.

A wind had sprung up across the bay, threatening rain and Sol was encouraging everyone to keep going, get the scene right before the weather changed. On the last take, Diamond obviously decided he'd had enough of all this bother and trotted meekly along, performing the scene like a professional and stopped quietly outside the castle as though to say, 'What was all the fuss about?'

As happens when people are under pressure, nothing was going right and Juliet, now in her role as Harriet Hamilton coming out to the gate to greet her husband, kept fluffing her lines as Franklin stood to one side, tutting every time the director called 'Cut'.

Sol hurried over to where Juliet stood, her eyes averted.

'It's not that difficult, honey. Have you looked at the script at all? It doesn't require much, Juliet, but if we go on like this we'll never finish the film.'

Juliet bit her lip, looked as if she was about to burst into tears and Linda came rushing over to apply yet more powder to hide the sheen of sweat on her forehead.

Sol patted her on the arm, seemingly ashamed of his rough treatment of her, saying, 'Just keep it together and you'll do fine.'

Franklin walked over to hiss in her ear, 'Do you think you could get it right this time? I'd rather be indoors filming than standing around out here.'

Juliet took a deep breath and said, 'I'm doing my best, darling,' and this time managed to complete the scene without a hitch. There was a collective sigh of relief as the director said. 'Cut! That's a take, folks. Good work, Juliet.'

The crew began to move along nearer the castle, some walking to take the opportunity for a cigarette, others struggling to load the heavy equipment on to the minibus, but all were in a much happier mood. Even Diamond was standing quietly, snuffling into a nosebag of feed. It was as though everyone felt the run of bad luck had ended.

As they drifted past, chatting and laughing, I caught sight of Juliet. She looked anything but cheerful: she was downcast, not far off tears. For a moment I considered going over to her, asking what was wrong. No one else seemed to have noticed she was still upset.

The moment passed as Tracy came up and linked arms with her, muttering something about, 'Oh, do cheer up, Juliet; it's not as bad as it appears. That take went well - you know Sol was pleased.'

Juliet's reply, as she drew away slightly, was impossible to catch, but if anything she looked more upset than ever at Tracy's words.

There was something bothering Juliet, something serious and it was much more than concern about her performance.

9

Juliet's behaviour intrigued me, especially the way she bristled every time she and Franklin met off-set. Did she harbour suspicions he had something to do with Derek's death, in spite of his alibi?

We'd all been upset by the murder in different ways, but it was out of our control now, in the capable hands of the police, and until there was more information about what had happened, who was responsible, we were urged to continue as normal.

'Time is money, guys,' Sol said yet again. It was his stock phrase, repeated so often no one paid any attention. On the other hand, everyone was eager to continue with the film. It's not that they were heartless, not completely, about what had happened to Derek, but so many people had invested in this production one way or another. It was Franklin's first screen part and for Juliet it was an opportunity to make her way back into films after a very empty period with nothing more than a few episodes of a radio serial. In the cold light of day, it was clear she was past the first flush of youth, in spite of Linda's skills with make-up.

Some of the team had other commitments after the end of this shoot. If the film overran there would be serious difficulties of availability and even Quentin, with his unconcealed dislike for Franklin and his grudge at not having the part of James Hamilton, knew the importance of making the most of his character of Daniel.

The next morning when I arrived on set bright and early, in spite of not having been called at all the day before, Juliet was sitting on her own on the bench beside the large stone flowerpot at the slipway leading down to the shingle beach. The number of boats at the moorings appeared to be increasing daily, a sure sign high summer was on the way and they bobbed at anchor on the tide, the sound of their clinking in the light breeze strangely comforting.

'Enjoying the peace and quiet?' I said, sitting down beside her.

She turned and smiled at me, but it was a very half- hearted smile.

'Yes, for a little while at least, before everything goes wrong again.'

'I suppose it gets very hectic while you're filming? It seems as if there are periods of absolute mania then times when nothing happens.'

'Exactly! You'd think I'd be used to it, though.'

'I don't think I ever could get used to it,' I sighed. 'The early mornings are a nightmare for me. I need at least three cups of coffee before I'm fit for anything.'

She laughed and turned away to look out again over the bay.

'And,' I continued, uncomfortable with the silence, 'there's so much waiting about. Don't you find that incredibly boring?' I regretted the words immediately, this implication her chosen profession was less than exciting.

She didn't seem in the least offended. 'Yes, a lot of people have something to do on set when they're not actually working – crossword puzzles, or knitting, or,' with a sideways glance at me, 'even writing. You need something to pass the time between takes, darling, or else it all becomes terribly dreary.'

Taken aback at the implication writing was nothing more than a way of passing the time, I said, 'I've no commission at the moment, but working on this script has been enough to convince me I'm not a fiction writer.'

'Don't worry, all good experience. Though heaven knows if we'll be here much longer. The police might have let Franklin go, but someone killed Derek. '

Another silence, each of us occupied with our own thoughts and I was tempted to jump in and say, 'Is everything okay - you seemed very upset the other day. Was it to do with Derek's death?'

Before I could find a way to frame the question without sounding too nosey, she stood up and said, 'I've not had breakfast yet. I should join the others in the hotel. Come along if you want. There's always plenty of food.'

About to reply, 'Thanks, but I've already eaten,' but something stopped me, made me decide to take up her offer. There was little point sitting here on my own and another cup of coffee would be most welcome for the day stretching ahead, even if my days seemed to be punctuated with endless cups of coffee. Besides it would give me the chance to find out if there was any more information, or more likely gossip, about Derek's murder, in the light of Juliet's remarks.

'Sounds good to me,' I replied and stood up to cross the road with her to the Coronet Hotel.

The tempting smell of bacon met us as we went in to the dining room where the rest of the cast and the crew were enjoying the local fare. Linda and Tracy were together at a small table for two, their backs to the rest of the company, engrossed in conversation. In the far corner Sol sat on his own, tucking into a full Scottish breakfast.

'Do you mind if we join you?' said Juliet. 'These seem to be the only free seats.'

Sol scarcely looked up, but motioned to the empty seats. 'Not a problem,' he said, between mouthfuls of bacon and egg, but I was sure he was only being polite.

The waitress came bustling over to take our order, Juliet opting for toast and tea while, unable to resist the tantalising aroma, I opted for bacon sandwiches and a pot of coffee.

Sol made no attempt at conversation, concentrating instead on cramming as much food as possible into his mouth in the shortest time.

Juliet ignored him and chatted to me as we waited for our order. 'How are you enjoying the experience of working in films?'

'It's all a bit strange,' I replied cautiously, careful not to upset either Juliet or Sol. I didn't want to say it seemed to me the most boring way imaginable of earning your living, not at all the glamorous life people imagine.

She laughed, nodding her head to show she understood the subtext perfectly.

'As I said, I guess that's why so many of us have a hobby to keep us busy while we're hanging around waiting for the action to start.'

'What kind of hobby do you have?' I said.

'I crochet,' she said. 'Everyone in the family has at least one item I've crocheted during filming.'

Visions of every member of Juliet's family swathed in multi-coloured crocheted garments sprang to mind and I looked down at the table to hide my amusement.

As we chatted, members of the cast and of the crew came in and out of the hotel. There appeared to be no sense of urgency, a reminder not to take too seriously the order to be on set early in the morning, at least not with this company.

'We'd better move, darling,' said Juliet at last, though this comment was probably for the benefit of Sol, who had now reached the stage of coffee and toast and still hadn't said a word. 'I've yet to costume up and subject myself to the ministrations of Linda and her make-up skills.' She raised her voice as she made this last comment, directing it at Sol, but even then there was no response.

It was strange how make-up could completely transform these ordinary people into something very beautiful or very ugly, depending on the requirements of the plot. As we walked out into the sunlight I caught sight of the tiny frown lines on Juliet's face. There were only a few here and there, but in this highly competitive field I could guess she was worried about time catching up with her.

We left the director to finish his breakfast and headed for make-up and props before catching the minibus down to Kames where the whole team had been instructed to assemble.

As we approached the bus shelter Franklin came rushing out of the props caravan. 'You'll have to do it,' he was yelling at someone we couldn't see. 'You promised me.' He shook his fist, unaware we were watching this display open-mouthed. 'It's all nothing to do with me. Everyone's got the wrong idea.'

He slammed the door behind him and started to walk away, stopping when he saw us standing there, astonished at this exchange with some unseen person.

'Well,' he glared at us, 'come along to see the action, have we? Can't help wanting to know everything that's going on, can we?'

'Actually, darling,' replied Juliet in a sugar sweet voice, 'we've come to work. There is a film being made and I do have an important part in it.' She waved her arm languidly towards the caravan entrance. 'And this is the place where we're fitted out with our costumes.'

Franklin turned on his heel and went off towards the minibus, muttering to himself. Another instance of the mood swings I'd heard he was subject to. Not an easy person to work with, even in the febrile world of film making. Pity the poor person who'd been on the receiving end of his wrath.

Juliet went up to the caravan, opened the door and looked inside while I stood on tiptoe behind her and peered over her shoulder, undecided about following her in, but curious to discover the cause of his anger.

Tracy was sitting in the far corner, snuffling into a damp tissue, pausing occasionally to blow her nose, throw the tissue in the overflowing bin beside her and pull out another from the large box on the table.

Juliet went over to put an arm round Tracy while I remained on the top step, craning forward for a better view. 'What's the matter, Tracy? Has Franklin been upsetting you again?' she said.

Ah, so this wasn't a one-off occurrence? There seemed to be some problem between Franklin and Tracy, and, if my guess was correct, part of the difficulty was she was more than a little in love with him. Sometimes you would glance over and see the adoring look on her face, quickly disguised when she realised she was being watched. The worst of it was, Franklin knew how she felt about him and took advantage when it suited him.

This turn of events wasn't a surprise: things had been brewing up for some time and the anxiety over Derek's death hadn't helped. Everyone, no matter how calm and disinterested they pretended to be, was on edge, especially as there had been no more news about the killing. We'd all been interviewed twice, but with no arrests, nor suspicion of arrests, though everyone had an opinion. If the police had any idea about who was responsible, they were keeping the information close and in this tight-knit community rumours continued to grow.

'It's nothing, it's nothing.' Tracy turned away to avoid our gaze, hiccupping as she did so. 'It's Franklin being his usual high-handed self, making a big thing out of nothing.' She didn't sound convincing.

'Come on, now, darling,' said Juliet in her usual kindly way. 'You mustn't let him get to you. He's one of these temperamental artists who think only of themselves. You've been in the business long enough to be able to deal with people like him, surely?' She straightened up and patted Tracy awkwardly on the shoulder.

'I suppose so,' replied Tracy, still snuffling into her tissue, 'but it's harder than you think. I can't take much more of this. This isn't what I signed up for.'

Nor did any of us was my immediate thought, but before I could offer my commiserations, Juliet glanced round, as if only just remembering I was there, then held up a hand to Tracy, a signal to say no more in my presence.

'Oh, I didn't see you,' said Tracy, following the direction of Juliet's gaze. She wiped her eyes, still red from crying. 'Sorry about this. I'll have to get on. I'm wanted on set.'

She stood up and blew her nose noisily one last time, before pushing past me as she left the caravan. Given her size, I had to flatten myself against the door to let her through.

As Juliet followed her out, she shrugged and smiled as though dismissing the incident as of little consequence.

'This is what it's like on a film set, Alison. We all get wound up, edgy, particularly when things aren't going well. And you've seen what it's like dealing with actors like Franklin, who think because they've a part in some soap opera, that they're megastars.'

Mmm…it might indeed be no more than a problem of when you have a temperamental actor. Or when someone has been murdered. Juliet was being rather too protective of Tracy.

There had been no more news about Derek's death, but there was a tension in the air. It might have been a random killing, or a vicious act by someone who knew him from elsewhere, but if not, the person responsible for his murder had to be in the cast or the crew of Pelias Productions.

Even allowing for the huge egos in this line of work, there was something not quite right, as though everyone had closed ranks. It was to be hoped the police would soon find out who was responsible. Perhaps that was the problem. They did have a good idea who'd done it - proving it might be the difficulty.

Juliet linked arms with me as we walked towards the minibus.

'Linda must be somewhere around with the cast. Let's go and join the others, darling. I'm sure you'll find today interesting. More material for a book, perhaps?'

While her attempt to cheer me up was appreciated, I was more interested in the row between Franklin and Tracy and what Juliet was determined I wouldn't find out. There was also the perplexing question about Tracy being in the props caravan on her own when we knew Linda guarded her territory like a mother hen.

Perry came walking towards us, minus his shadow of the trainee. 'We'll be starting again shortly,' he said, 'as soon as I've managed to sort out the problem with the trolley.'

'What's happened?'

'Nothing major - one of the spindles has to be replaced. It will only take a few minutes.' He sauntered off, whistling in a tuneless way.

It was only a momentary distraction and once again my thoughts turned to recent events. What was going on between Franklin and Tracy …and what did he want her to do that had so upset her?

10

As can so often happen on the West coast of
Scotland in summer, a relentless drizzle began the
next morning and persisted all day, the light too
poor for outdoor work. Sol decided it would be
best to shoot some of the interior scenes.

'That way we can be ready to move on as soon
as the weather improves,' he said.

Even so, it was a long and tedious day.
Increasingly I could understand why so many
actors took up some kind of hobby, something to
while away the long gaps between takes.

Scene after scene was repeated, Sol dissatisfied
with one or other of the actors, though Franklin
and Juliet appeared to be well suited to the parts of
James and Harriet. Their off-screen antipathy came
over well on set, lent an extra dimension to their
fictional relationship.

Robert had phoned me to ask if he could come
along to "see the action" as he put it and I had to
apologise for forgetting his earlier request. The
decision wasn't mine, but with a number of scenes
in the can, Sol was amenable.

'I've a friend staying on Bute at the moment,' I
tentatively approached him, 'and he'd very much
like to see the film being made. Would that be a
problem?'

'Hell, no, as long as he keeps well away and doesn't interrupt,' he replied.

 Knowing only too well how the idea of having lots of time to write seems great in theory, but is daunting in practice and any distraction welcome, I guessed Robert was feeling lonely.

'So, you're having a break from writing your book, then?' I whispered as he came up to join me in the gloomy corner of the room well away from the glare of the strong lights on set. Sol was busy moving the actors into place on the criss-cross tape.

For a moment Robert looked puzzled, then said in a very off-hand way, 'Yes, yes. Writing this book is not as easy as I thought it would be.'

'I can sympathise with that,' I replied with feeling, thinking of the hours I'd invested in the script of *A Man Alone*, with little result.

Sol turned round, shading his eyes as he looked in our direction. 'Quiet on set.'

Once the clapper boy had run off, everything went smoothly for the scene where Daniel decided his brother James was a lost cause and that he had to leave him to his fate at Kames Castle and return to Edinburgh. This was a part Matt had written into my original story and it could only be because they had to make something of the role of Daniel. Perhaps Quentin's agent had more clout than he gave him credit for.

The next big scene was in the castle where James told Harriet he'd had to sell the bedroom furniture to meet some of the debts she'd incurred living the high life in Edinburgh with her profligate friends and Harriet denounced him as a miser and said she'd leave him.

This was one scene I'd had a hand in writing, one of the most important episodes in the real life story of James Hamilton and I was anxious to find out how much of my contribution remained. While Harriet was off the island, having her portrait painted in Edinburgh by Raeburn, James was struggling to keep them out of debt, as various bills of sale from the castle would bear witness. I'd felt really sorry for him, but had tried not to let my sympathy for him show through in the dialogue.

Matt had evidently had other ideas and Harriet was portrayed as a real gold digger, something far from the truth: as her family were extremely well-to-do and it was more than likely she was only trying to maintain the standard of living she considered herself entitled to.

The more I saw of this film being made, the less I wanted to see my name in the credits. No one expects a historically-based drama to be one hundred percent accurate, but there are limits, even for poetic licence.

Fortunately for my continuing curiosity, Sol had decreed I should be in this particular scene. Not that I had any more dialogue, the problem with *Equity* proving impossible to sort out. Or so they said. My suspicion was that they could pay me at the lowest rate possible if I didn't have a speaking part. Sol thought Harriet might faint and "It'll be much better if her maid is on hand to help".

Matt wasn't happy with this continuing interference, but he said nothing, contenting himself with brooding from the sidelines, a permanent frown on his face.

In spite of the planning meetings in Glasgow, the talks before shooting began, there seemed to be a lot of on-the-spot decisions made during the production.

From my limited knowledge, the usual procedure for making a film was to have an agreed script, mastered by the actors and delivered in accordance with the director's instructions. But Sol kept changing, adding here and deleting there with very little warning, leaving the actors increasingly irate at this high handed treatment.

'For goodness sake, Sol,' growled Franklin, 'why can't we stick to the script. We're not able to cope with all these last minute changes and act as well.' A long spell on-set without the possibility of a cigarette break was making Franklin decidedly tetchy.

Sol ignored him and continued with his idiosyncratic style of directing. It was perfectly clear he thought he'd a plan, but sadly no one else was in on it.

We'd all arrived at the set hoping any changes would be minor, that on this occasion Sol would keep to the original script and the scene could go through with the minimum of fuss.

This scene was being shot in the mock up of the dining hall: the high ceilings and beams of the original barn making it the ideal location.

Franklin looked round. 'Is this the best Linda could come up with?' his sweeping gesture taking in the two benches, the wooden settle and a little carved desk arranged round the set.

Sol growled, 'We don't need much in the way of furniture. Remember he'd been selling it off to pay the bills.'

Franklin sniffed. 'I believe it was the bedroom furniture he was selling off and I refuse to accept even an impoverished nineteenth century aristocrat wouldn't live better than this.'

Matt jumped in, his voice quivering with suppressed anger at this slight on his work.

'H…h…haven't you read the script? H…h…he wasn't an aristocrat, he was a poxy lawyer. Now, are we going to stand around all day or are we going to shoot the scene?'

Sol nudged Juliet into position and wagged his finger. 'Let's get-go. Remember, honey, you've been in the big city of Edinburgh, enjoying all that social stuff with your friends. You're obligated to come back to Bute, you're a married woman. You're excited about having your portrait done by Raeburn, one of the leading painters of the day, but know your husband will be angry at the way you've gotten through his money. Try to show that mixture of elation and disappointment.' He waved his stick wildly in the air to illustrate the point.

Juliet looked over to where I was standing in the far corner beside Robert and rolled her eyes.

Sol whirled round to Franklin, whose facial expression made me think he was still upset about the lack of furniture on the set.

'And you're angry, very angry. You've been stuck here on your own while your wife has been living it up on your money, or what little's left. You have to get across that suppressed rage, the desire to give her your two cents worth as she starts to tell you about sitting for Raeburn while you've been trying to sell off the furniture.'

The air was fraught with anxiety as they did take after re-take and at one stage Juliet seemed to dry up completely.

'This sucks,' I heard Sol mutter, but he went back to urge into yet another repeat in a calmer tone of voice.

It was a puzzle why so much of the production seemed to be impromptu, what I would call under-rehearsed, when Matt was the chief scriptwriter, but now all was becoming clear. Not only was this such a low budget production a number of roles had been doubled up, but Sol was of the school of directors who advocated an element of realism through spontaneous action. So while there was a script, and there had been rehearsals of a kind, he was encouraging the actors to involve themselves in the action to give the production an extra cdgc. Somehow this wasn't quite going as hoped.

Sol advanced to the set, his walking stick abandoned for the moment, making me think my original guess was right and it was no more than an affectation.

'Juliet, honey, you did have even a brief look at this script before we started? I know we want some input from the actors, but some of this is crap. And keep to the marks. There's no point to the scene if we can't see your face.'

Juliet swallowed hard. 'Sorry, Sol, but I don't seem to be able to get anything right at the moment.' She fiddled with the bodice of her costume, looking as if she was on the verge of tears, but Sol merely patted her on the arm and moved back to his seat.

'That's an understatement,' muttered Franklin from the chair at the corner of the set where he was waiting for his cue, and as Juliet heard him she whirled round. 'Did you say something, darling?'

'Okay,' said Sol with a sigh. 'Let's go again. And try to get it right this time. Every time we re-shoot the scene I can see the bucks draining from my checking account.'

'Money you're not likely to get back, if this continues,' muttered Franklin.

Sol whirled round to face him. 'What was that, Franklin? I wouldn't say your own performance is so great. You'll need a teleprompter if you muddle any more lines.'

It seemed that Franklin was about to reply, but instead he slumped back down in his chair, muttering to himself as Sol turned to face Juliet. 'Now give it your best shot, honey. Let's wrap this scene up.'

The clapper boy ran forward and shouted, 'Scene Five, take Eight,' before hurrying out of harm's way.

This film had all the makings of a disaster. Derek dead, the film well behind schedule, tensions among the cast and a disgruntled director were not making for a happy or professional production.

I could see Juliet steeling herself, taking a deep breath before entering again from the far side of the room and watched her with some trepidation, willing her to get it right. This time she was word perfect and the scene went without a hitch, if you didn't count the little pause where Franklin seemed almost to be taken by surprise when he was cued in.

The next scene should have involved me, but Sol again changed his mind. 'Better to keep the tension going with just the two of them in the room,' he said, dismissing me with a wave of his hand, 'but don't go too far. We might need you later.'

I grew bored and wandered away, leaving Robert continuing to watch avidly. He was showing a much greater interest in the production than I was: he was even taking notes. As I left I mimicked my exit to him, but all he did was wave and smile and continue to watch the action.

Besides, apart from the friction on set, the glare of the lights was giving me a headache. Though everything seemed to be back on track, watching umpteen takes of the same scene wasn't exactly enthralling.

In spite of my early belief I'd contributed to the script, there wasn't much I recognised, confirming my suspicions about the reasons for engaging me in the first place. Matt had carefully edited everything to suit his own requirements, or those of Sol, and it was hard to spot any contribution I'd made in this version.

I wandered out of the room into the quiet side room of the barn. Some of the later scenes were planned for the 'day room' and the 'walled garden'. That was if the weather improved. A glance out of one of the side windows confirmed the drizzle had slackened off and I considered going outside for some fresh air, but I was still in costume and I wouldn't be able to walk far.

Mindful of Sol's command not to leave, I sat down on one of the chairs, then jumped up thinking it might be some kind of antique and strictly not for use. A closer inspection confirmed it was old but not valuable, so I settled down, moving this way and that to find a comfortable position as I reflected on the various problems in my life: my role in this production, my friendship with Robert and, most importantly, my concerns about Simon.

The year in America wasn't turning out as exciting as he'd anticipated: he gave every impression of finding it difficult to cope. His last phone call had been brief and he'd dropped the strongest hints about coming back soon.

'But what about your contract?' I'd said.

'I can arrange that,' he replied. 'I honestly think I've done all I can, and there's no shortage of consultants here.' There was a bitter edge to his voice.

'But I thought the idea was to give them a different perspective, show them how things were done in another country.'

'The truth is it's not only the job, or the people – in general it's all fine on a day-to-day basis. But

I miss you, miss the children, even if they are all grown up. I even miss the food. It's impossible to get a decent meal here - it's all hamburgers and steaks.' He chuckled at this joke.

There was a pause. What I said next would be critical, might persuade him either way, but somehow I couldn't put how I felt into words, not at this distance.

Simon jumped in with, 'How are you doing on Bute? Making friends with the film stars?'

'I know a few people here. I'm not short of company,' I chattered on nervously for a few moments, deflecting further questions about my social life by describing the flat I'd rented, the quirks of the cast and crew of *A Man Alone*, the unpredictable weather of the past few days. Anything but allow him space to make plans to come home, until eventually he said, a note of impatience creeping into his voice, 'I'm glad it's all going well. I'll have to ring off - I'm due at a meeting in a few minutes. I'll give you a call at the end of the week and let you know my decision.'

I must have been sitting there in the quiet for a good five minutes, pondering this, about to leave and return to the house and slump in front of an afternoon television programme: with the rain now coming down heavier than before, there were few alternatives. I'd a vague idea for a new project, so perhaps I'd be inspired to do some work on that, though I doubted it. I wasn't in any mood for new projects at the moment and had lost any enthusiasm I'd once had for helping with the script.

Suddenly there was the sound of muttering close by and for some reason, instead of calling out 'Hello,' I stood up, went behind the floor length curtain put up to screen off part of the entrance, pulled it over and shrank back into the corner, trying to make as little noise as possible as I peeped out.

Tracy had come in with Matt and they were standing over by the door, whispering. Their voices were low, but I could just about make out what they were saying, though not every word.

'You have to do something about it,' muttered Tracy. She tugged at Matt's sleeve.

He shook her off, his tone of voice indicating how upset he was. 'D...d...don't be stupid. What can I do? In fact it's nothing to do with me. It's Franklin's problem. D...d...don't get involved. I think you should tell the police. Better now than that they find out later. Then you'll really be in trouble.'

They moved across the room a little way, out of earshot and I couldn't hear more than a few words, none of which made sense. Then Matt raised his voice in anger and said, '...and it won't only be Derek who ends up dead if you d...d...don't speak out.'

Again, most of Tracy's reply was lost to me as they headed back for the set, but I caught, '... breath a word of this please, Matt. I'm begging you. There's no proof.'

I didn't hear Matt's reply, but his body language indicated he wasn't happy about Tracy's decision to ignore his advice. Matt was someone who couldn't cope with any difficulties, who took fright at the slightest problem... and there were plenty of those at the moment.

In the empty silence I sat for a moment, considering what I'd witnessed. It was clear Matt and Tracy knew something about Derek's death, something they didn't want to tell the police and even worse, they were worried another death was about to take place.

11

Back at Castle Street I decided, in spite of my earlier plans, that it would be too slothful to waste an afternoon in front of the television, a decision confirmed by a quick flick through the programmes on offer.

Instead I set up my computer and began to make some notes for a short book on St Blane's. This is one of the most famous areas on the island and there is a wealth of legends associated with this saint, alleged to have been set adrift with his mother in a coracle to fetch up on Bute some time in the sixth century.

The church and the monastery he founded are ruins now, a favourite walk on the island, but the legend of how Blane and his mother, Ertha, were set adrift in a coracle and landed in Ireland, only to return to Bute late in life, has always intrigued me.

If I could put together enough material, I might manage something that would sell well to tourists. After my success with the story of James Hamilton and Harriet Wynne, someone might be willing to pick it up and make a film. Though I wasn't sure that was a good idea, judging from my recent experience.

But even as I typed the first few words of introduction, my mobile rang. Unwilling to be interrupted, I was tempted to ignore it, but on checking the number realised it was my son, Alastair. His phone calls are rare: as an academic he seems to lose all track of anything that doesn't concern his latest research project and I'm usually the one to make the first connection.

'Everything okay,' I said, trying not to sound like an overanxious mother.

'Fine, fine,' he replied in that vague way he has. There was a pause as I searched for some topic of mutual interest to keep the conversation going.

'Everything's well with the new research project?' while frantically trying to remember exactly what it was. Something to do with his subject of environmental bio diversification? Or was it bio environmentalism? I could never quite remember.

He saved me from a difficult situation by continuing, 'Fine, fine.' Another pause. Then he said, 'I'm actually in Edinburgh at the moment. I'm at a conference here for a week so I thought I'd come over to Glasgow to see you, catch up.'

'I'm not in Glasgow at the moment,' I replied, 'I'm sure I told you.'

Yet another pause. 'Oh, I do remember something about that. Where are you again?'

I explained as briefly as I could, re-told the saga of my stay on Bute, my involvement with the *A Man Alone* production.

'That's not a problem. I could do with some sea air after sitting in a stuffy conference hall for three days. I'll come down on Monday once my presentation is over.'

'Well, remember to text me from the ferry and I'll pick you up there.'

'I'm sure I can manage to find my way, mum.'

'Even so, it'll be quicker if I meet you.'

He agreed to my suggestion and rang off.

This was an added complication. Though Alastair is perfectly capable of amusing himself for a couple of days, I'd want to spend some time with him, given how little I see of him.

It looked as if my plans for the day to make some inroads into the story of St Blane were to come to naught as my mobile beeped again. This time it was a text message from Robert.

'Hello, Alison, are you busy today? I thought we might meet up if you have nothing special planned?'

Robert hasn't quite got the hang of texting. He has a very formal way of speaking that carries over to his text messages, so they tend to be very long. This one was, thank goodness, mercifully short and I could legitimately reply I was indeed busy, but I found myself agreeing to get back to him about meeting for coffee the next day at the Ettrick Bay tearoom, once I knew whether or not Sol would need me on set.

Why didn't I ask Sol what he was planning? He must have some idea about the sequence of the scenes he was going to shoot. If my memory served me correctly, there was a recognised format - a storyboard, that was it- where the scenes were laid out one by one, so that even if they were shot out of sequence, there was an overall view of the plot.

Perhaps I could persuade him to include me in the next scene if he'd nothing lined up, make some suggestion useful for the script. That was if Matt didn't interfere.

It was becoming increasingly clear Matt had concerns about being outdone, wanted all the plaudits for himself. Changes or additions I suggested were dismissed in the most cutting of terms. Well, I wasn't going to sit back and let that happen much longer.

A quick look at my watch – five o'clock. There was still time and determined on this course of action, I marched down to the Coronet Hotel, hoping to catch Sol. It was here in the lounge that Sol gathered the main actors every evening to talk through the next day's shooting schedule and to make the final decisions on who would be needed on set and for how long, though he was every bit as likely to change his mind at the last minute.

I'd been excluded from this for too long, had to show more determination, instead of letting these people push me around.

When I reached the hotel, Franklin was standing on the steps, smoking.

'Not in at the meeting? I thought everyone had to be there.'

He blew a couple of smoke rings and watched as they disappeared on the breeze, then threw the cigarette down and ground it out with his heel. 'Everyone needs a breather from Sol,' he said. 'I thought this would be a chance to move on, make my name that would lead to better things, but the whole film will be a disaster.'

'Move on? I thought you were only doing this as a way of broadening your portfolio? Surely you're well established in *Heart and Home* with a huge following. Why would you want to change?'

He laughed mirthlessly. 'Oh, why indeed? What happens when the looks fade, Alison? Or the fickle public becomes bored? It happens all the time. Besides, since this is an historical piece, or claims to be, it seemed a good chance to make my name in another field. What a bad decision.'

With my own reputation to protect, I was about to say, 'Oh, that's nonsense, of course it will all be fine,' but instead I muttered something non-committal.

'There's something strange going on,' continued Franklin, almost as though I wasn't there. 'Every production I've worked on has been much slicker than this. Oh sure, there have been problems, but it's almost as if Sol isn't interested. Oh, well, better find out what he's up to now.'

He was right. Sol's style of direction was a disaster. He might want to be known as a follower of the school of realism or some such, but sadly he'd very little talent for this, for getting the most out of the actors. All he seemed to do was to antagonise them.

'I'm going in to speak to Sol,' I said, having no wish to listen to yet more grumbles about the production. I'd enough problems of my own. Franklin shrugged and turned away and I followed him into the hotel.

My chat with Franklin had helped me make up my mind. Somehow I had to protect what I'd contributed to this production, had to find out how Sol was proposing to continue. If he didn't have plans, I'd suggest some to him.

12

Sol was nowhere to be seen inside the Coronet Hotel.

'He was h...h...here earlier,' said Matt, looking round as if the director might suddenly materialise in a corner of the bar. 'He muttered something about a phone call.'

He shrugged and went back to gazing morosely into his pint of beer, drumming his fingers on the table, making it clear he had no intention of engaging in further talk. This project was falling apart, the air of despondency contagious.

Franklin had come in and sat down on the bench by the window. He lifted the newspaper lying there, making a great show of ignoring Juliet and Tracy at the next table, deep in conversation, their heads close together. From time to time Tracy let out a shriek of laughter, causing Franklin to rustle his paper to express his annoyance. There was no point in interrupting them – it was obvious Sol wasn't around.

As I turned to leave, the door opened and in came Robert.

'What are you doing here?' I said in surprise.

'Thought I'd come and seek you out, since you've shown no interest in getting back to me about coffee as you promised,' he said.

Caught like this, what could I do but offer to buy him one here in the Coronet? 'Or perhaps you'd rather have a drink?' I said.

'Bit early in the day for me,' he replied. 'Coffee will be fine.'

We settled down at one of the vacant tables with our cappuccinos and I skimmed the froth off with my spoon as a way of avoiding talking. In spite of my reservations I had to confess to liking Robert more and more – he was kind and funny and good company, but whatever troubles Simon and I were having, becoming involved with Robert wouldn't help. So what was the little niggle of concern that made me avoid mentioning him to Simon?

'How is the film doing? Are you enjoying your starring role?' There was a twinkle in his eye as he spoke.

'It's certainly not that,' I shuddered. 'While it's interesting, it's not something I would want to do as a career. Everything is such a muddle, I'll be surprised if the film is ever finished.'

'No chance of seeing your name up in lights, then?'

'I'll be lucky to get a mention in small print in the closing credits. I'm not sure even that would be a good idea. It would probably be better if any contribution I made wasn't recognised.'

'What's the problem? I thought you helped write the script and surely Sol is a well established film director? Things not going well?'

'I've no idea,' I replied. 'When I got the contract it looked fine and Sol does seem to have a list of credits to his name. The details of the film are nothing to do with me.'

Robert wagged his finger. 'Didn't you get someone to check it out for you?'

'Nooo... actually I didn't. I thought it all seemed above board,' I said. 'Anyway,' more defiantly, 'the problem is I don't know much about making films. That's all there is to it.'

I silently dared him to say any more about my laxity in having the contract checked, but he must have guessed I'd been so flattered it didn't occur to me to ask the right questions, or any questions.

We chatted for a few minutes about the film in a casual way and I'm ashamed to say in the light of Robert's sympathy, I couldn't but help unburden myself about my suggestions being so often ignored, about the fiasco of my supposed job as assistant scriptwriter.

He listened but said nothing, merely nodding from time to time. Strange how someone who shows a genuine interest in you and your problems can make you feel better, encourage you to talk. Of course it was easier for Robert, given his background. In his career he'd most likely had to deal with some very difficult clients.

'So you'll have dinner with me tonight? It doesn't appear you'll be needed here.' He arched his eyebrows to make it plain any excuse would be a poor one and I heard myself say, 'Yes, of course, that'd be fine.'

Robert stood up. 'How about the Kingarth Hotel? I could meet you there about eight.'

'That suits me,' I said meekly.

He bent over and kissed me on the cheek. 'See you at eight, then.'

He turned to leave, still smiling and almost bumped into the man coming in through the door to the Lounge Bar.

'Sorry,' said Robert, making to hurry out.

The man put a hand on Robert's arm. 'What are you doing here?' he said.

It was Sol. For a moment Robert appeared startled by this encounter before quickly regaining his composure.

'I might ask you the same thing,' he replied, but he made it clear he wasn't stopping. 'I was catching up with Alison.'

Sol frowned. 'I've got every right to be here – I'm directing the film about James Hamilton.' Then he glared at Robert. 'Saw you on set the other day. Thought I recognised you.'

'Yes.' Robert shrugged. 'Passing the time. You know how it is.'

By now everyone in the bar had stopped whatever they were doing and looked in the direction of the two men, standing face to face.

'Well, yeah, as long as that's all it was,' Sol said. 'It's in the past, anything you knew. Leave me alone.'

For a moment it seemed that Robert was about to reply, but instead he shook his head and elbowed Sol out of the way as he left. 'See you at eight, Alison.' And with that he left.

'Seen enough?' said Sol, waving his stick at the assembled group. 'I suggest you get on with whatever you were doing. We meet in fifteen minutes to discuss the scenes for tomorrow's shoot.'

No one else seemed to have noticed, but in the exchange with Robert, Sol's American accent had slipped more than usual, confirming my suspicions. Perhaps he thought adopting this accent gave him more authority as a director.

He went up to the bar and ordered a double whisky, deliberately ignoring the unspoken questions. He brought his drink over and said to me, 'How do you know Robert Broughton? What was he doing on set the other day?'

'If you didn't want him there you should have said.'

'I didn't really notice, honey, I was busy if you remember,' and he moved off to sit at a table in the far corner without waiting for a further explanation.

My mind was in turmoil. It was clear Sol and Robert knew each other and there was bad blood between them, which was odd enough. But even stranger was Robert's comment. Why had he not said he knew Sol? There would have been no harm in telling me when I'd first mentioned the director's name.

Suddenly I realised how little I knew about him. Certainly we'd chatted, caught up on the intervening years, or so I thought, but how much could you learn about someone you hadn't seen for such a long time? Sure, he'd told me about his job at the University, that he'd never married ('not after losing you, Alison,' he'd said jokingly). I'd assumed Robert was genuinely on holiday here on

Bute, enjoying his retirement, toying with the idea for a book. Perhaps it was a good thing we were planning to meet for dinner. There were a lot of questions I wanted to ask.

As I was about to leave, Sol stood up and addressed the group in the bar, his American accent in place once more. 'I guess you guys are wondering what that call was about?'

Disappointment crossed his face as it was clear no one had remembered he'd gone out to take a call, being too intrigued by the exchange between him and Robert on his return.

'So what was it about?' said Quentin, yawning deliberately, coming through the group to sit down on the chair beside Sol and put his feet up on the table as he absentmindedly stroked his wispy beard, his tone indicating a complete lack of interest in anything Sol had to impart.

There was a pause for effect and then Sol said, 'Our sponsor, Zach, called me on my cell phone. He wants to come over and find out how the film he's invested his money in is going. Let's hope he's happy with the result.'

There was a hush in the bar. This was a serious business, much more worrying for the cast and the crew than Derek's death. It concerned them all.

Sol smirked, as though pleased with the atmosphere he'd created, ensuring he was now firmly back in charge.

13

Alastair had already disembarked from the ferry when I screeched to a halt and reversed none too successfully into one of the parking bays on the pier.

I jumped out of the car and waved and shouted to him, trying to catch his attention, but he was engrossed in looking at the boats in the Marina and my words drifted away on the wind. I slammed the car door shut and ran over.

'I'm here, Alastair.'

He looked round for the source of the voice and smiled as I joined him.

'Great to see you, mum,' he said, enveloping me in a bear hug. He looked well, if somewhat sturdier than when I'd last seen him, but I suppose his job entails a lot of sitting in front of a computer, not the best career for maintaining a lean physique. All those irregular meals, no doubt. Sadly it looked as if he would take after mc in thc weight department as much as in his fair hair and complexion.

We sauntered back to the car, exchanging news as we did so. Or rather I talked and Alastair chipped in a word or two. He's not the most talkative of people, but I'm used to that by now.

He was interested in the film, asked some questions, especially about the technical side – though I didn't have all the answers. 'We can chat to some of the film crew,' I said. 'They'll be more than delighted to have someone with a keen interest in what they're doing.'

Fortunately the next day was free of any film commitments, and it was one I was going to enjoy. I planned to take Alastair round the island, show him some of the sights, take him to Scalpsie Bay for a walk and with a bit of luck we might even see seals basking on the rocks. The weather had turned warm enough for them to make an appearance, one of the highlights of any visit to Bute and, as this was his first trip, I was anxious for him to see the island at its best.

It didn't take long to settle Alastair in the tiny spare room in the house at the Port. 'How long are you planning to stay?' I said, standing at the door to his room and watching him unpack his few possessions and put them away in the chest of drawers in that methodical way he has. Alastair believes in travelling light.

'Just a couple of days. The conference lasts a week and these two days are nothing to do with me,' he said. 'They try to cram in as many papers as possible to attract lots of delegates, but there's no point in sitting through something that's of no interest.' A moment's hesitation, then a frown. 'Did I tell you I've a meeting at Edinburgh University next week immediately after the conference ends?'

'No. I thought life in Canada suited you very well. I'd no idea you'd any intention of returning to Scotland.'

He grinned, looking somewhat sheepish.

'It's a temporary post. They need someone with my expertise to help with the current research project ...or at least to help get it off the ground. Then I'll return to Canada. The department there have been really good in giving me the time off...though I suppose it will benefit them in the long run. They'll be paid well for my services.'

'Well, it will be good to see more of you,' I said. 'Now what would you like to do?'

We agreed a quick car trip round the island would be a good start, let him see something of Bute and we could have lunch somewhere along the route. With no calls to the set for the rest of the day, I'd have a leisurely time of it with Alastair and enjoy the sunshine, now making an appearance after several heavy showers.

'Give me half an hour to pop down and remind Tracy I won't be around this afternoon,' I said. 'There have been so many changes and I wouldn't be surprised if Sol suddenly decided I was absolutely necessary for some scene or other.'

'That's fine,' he said. 'I'll just do a quick check on my emails.'

Given recent form, a call to the set was extremely unlikely as I soon discovered and I hurried back up the hill to the house, very much looking forward to an afternoon out.

Alastair was sitting in the living room, hunched over his laptop when I came in. 'Ready?' I said.

'I've cleared it with Tracy and if we go now, we can make the most of the afternoon.'

He looked up, a puzzled expression on his face. 'Where are we going?' he said, evidently having completely forgotten our arrangement.

'Over to Scalpsie Bay, remember? We decided it would be a good idea to have lunch out and then a walk?'

I tried hard not to let my impatience show. Alastair becomes so wrapped up in whatever he's doing that the real world sometimes fails to make any kind of impression on him.

He stood up and struck his forehead in a very theatrical gesture.

'Sorry, mum, I completely forgot. I've arranged to Skype with a couple of colleagues this afternoon. I was setting it up when you came in.'

I tried to hide my disappointment, not to mention my annoyance at this change of plan, but didn't succeed because he sprang to his feet and said, 'I really am sorry I forgot about it, but a problem has come up back in Canada and I do have to get it sorted out.'

Remembering all too well the times I'd been in a similar situation in my previous teaching post, I said, 'I'll leave you in peace. I'm going to make the most of the day.'

'Perhaps we could do that walk tomorrow? I'm sure once this is sorted out there won't be any more calls on my time before I leave.'

No point in saying he had only one day remaining before he headed back to the mainland:

if he chose to spend his holiday working, that was his loss.

He turned back to the laptop where a decidedly fuzzy and shaky image had appeared on the screen and I left, heading down to the front with no clear idea about what to do. No point in driving to Scalpsie Bay if Alastair wanted to go there tomorrow, though I hoped he understood any trip would be weather dependent. I looked in at the Coronet Hotel, but the lounge bar was empty. Filming must have started again.

I strolled along the seafront, stopping from time to time to have a look at the latest boats in the bay, and by the time I reached the set the level of noise indicated some action was indeed taking place, the sound of Sol's voice raised to its loudest volume as he shouted at the actors.

'No, no, no,' he was calling as I crept in, 'you gotta put a lot more passion into it. Remember the script is only a vehicle, a vehicle for your own expression of your most intense emotions.'

Juliet was intensely emotional all right: she was looking furious, obviously trying to control her anger.

'Now go again.' He turned to the cameraman. 'Roll them.'

The clapper boy ran forward. 'Scene Twelve, Take Six,' he shouted, clapped the board and ran back out of sight.

Juliet moved towards Franklin who was standing beside Quentin, engaged in a furious argument. As I listened to the dialogue, I became more and more determined my name wouldn't appear on the credits. I'd never have written anything like this.

'You are only a messenger, forsooth,' Franklin as James Hamilton was saying. 'You have no right to counter my demands, sirrah.'

'This letter is my responsibility,' was Quentin's reply in the guise of the messenger whose costume bore a remarkable resemblance to the one he wore as Daniel, except for a missing adornment or two and a differently coloured wig. I had some sympathy for Quentin, having to double up this part of the messenger with that of Daniel Hamilton.

Sol sprang forward from the far side of the room where he was sitting with Matt in front of two monitors, one black and white and the other coloured, waving his hands about frantically and almost tripping over the thick black cables from the floor mounted lights. 'Stop, stop,' he called. 'This isn't what we want. Didn't I tell you there had to be some changes? For goodness sake, can't you get anything right? Let's go again.'

The actors moved forward to the taped crosses that allowed them to hit their marks, but Franklin kept wandering from his, possibly because he thought he wasn't in shot enough in this scene.

'We'll be in tight all the time,' said Sol, 'so be careful about the overlaps in dialogue. No more mistakes, got it?'

Juliet looked over at him, waiting to be cued in.

'We'll do the shooting first and then the close-ups and lastly a couple of over the shoulder shots to get Franklin and Quentin together.'

The clapper boy ran forward and the scene sprang into life. It was amazing how these actors could stand around looking incredibly bored one minute and the next assume the manners, the actions, the very nature of the characters they were playing.

'This is nonsense, sire,' Juliet said, tossing her head. 'This man is nothing to me. He is a friend of Eugenia, my sister, and has come here to seek our help.'

'I do not believe you,' Franklin shouted. 'You think I am a fool. Well, I will show you.'

He produced a pistol from his jacket and waved it about in the air. The film crew, who had been standing around not trying to conceal their boredom at what was obviously a well-worn scene, perked up visibly and even Sol was grinning.

'Leave my land forthwith,' Franklin said, edging menacingly towards the other man, who stood his ground.

'Sire, I have no wish to do you a discourtesy, but my instructions are to hand over this missive only to milady and to no other.'

'You will hand the missive to me, sirrah, or I will not be responsible for my actions.'

Standing on the sidelines, I could only wonder how much of this dialogue had been written by Matt, and how much was spontaneous. None of it sounded too good. If Sol was pleased with this version, goodness knows what the earlier takes had been like.

On the set, the action was hotting up and I looked back in time to hear the messenger say, 'It is more than I can do, milord. I must hand this to milady.'

'Do that, and I'll shoot.' Franklin waved the pistol in the air wildly.

Out of the corner of my eye I caught the sight of Sol's face and he certainly wasn't smiling. Perhaps this was a direction he hadn't expected the script to follow and he edged forward, with every appearance that he was about to shout, 'Cut!'

Before he could do so, Franklin shouted, 'Get away or I will shoot. This is no idle threat.' He moved menacingly towards the messenger and there was the sudden sound of the pistol discharging. Quentin slumped to the ground, clutching his chest.

Sol jumped up out of his director's chair. 'Cut,' he shouted, running towards the set. 'Brilliant, you guys, that's a wrap.'

There was a collective sigh of relief. At least something was going right. Juliet looked no happier, but Franklin appeared mightily pleased with himself as he waved the gun around to dispel the very realistic smoke coming from the nozzle.

He went over to the messenger, still lying slumped on the ground. 'You can get up now,' he laughed, extending his hand. Quentin didn't move, continued to lie still in the position where he'd fallen.

'He's fainted,' shouted Juliet. 'Help him someone.' Several people rushed over and began trying to move him.

She turned to Sol. 'Didn't you warn him this would happen? That it would sound so realistic? He must have got a terrible fright, poor man.'

'I'm not surprised - more likely he's had a heart attack at hearing this terrible dialogue,' muttered Harry, who was standing beside me and starting to pack up his equipment. 'I've worked on any number of films and none as dreadful as this one. It'll be a wonder if it ever makes it to DVD let alone the big screen.'

There was a little knot of people now gathered round the unfortunate messenger and Franklin was bending down over him frowning, ready to loosen his collar, undo his shirt. There was a moment's silence as we watched him then saw him recoiling in horror as he pulled his hands away and looked at the blood on his fingers. Those standing around him moved back and there was a sharp intake of breath.

'Someone call an ambulance,' he shouted, 'and quickly.'

14

For a few moments no one moved, then there was a great explosion of noise.

'What's happened?'

'Is he all right?'

'Has he been shot for real?'

Several people pulled out their mobile phones, while Harry came forward to Quentin who was lying absolutely still, crumpled up at Juliet's feet.

'Anyone here know any First Aid?'

Matt pushed Perry and the camera aside as he came running over to the stricken man. As he leaned forward the flap of hair fell across his eyes and he pushed it back impatiently.

'D...d...don't attempt to lift him, for goodness sake.'

All I could do was stand and watch as Franklin made efforts to stem the blood dripping on to Quentin's shirt. How had this happened? The only possibility, the only answer was that the gun Franklin had been using had real bullets instead of blanks.

Linda was standing on tiptoe on the edge of the crowd, moving this way and that for a better view, and I sidled up beside her whispering, 'Surely Franklin was using a prop gun, one that wasn't loaded?'

'Well, of course it was a prop gun. Why would we be using real weapons on set? It's a genuine pistol, but we use a flash instead of bullets. Everything's checked.' She sounded frightened, was visibly shaking, her face drained of all colour. 'I'll get the blame for this, but honestly, Alison, it was checked before it was released to Franklin.'

'I'm sure no one will accuse you, Linda. How could it be your fault?' I replied, patting her on the arm, but I wasn't convinced. Some of the blame must lie with Linda. There wouldn't have been enough time for someone to tamper with the gun in the short interval between it being issued to Franklin and discharged in the last scene.

There was the sound of the ambulance racing along the road towards us and we moved back a discreet distance as the paramedics flung open the doors and came running in to tend the injured man, unpacking their equipment as they went.

Franklin was standing as though turned to stone. The gun, the cause of the accident, lay on the ground beside him and I saw Linda creep over quietly to lift it and push it into the large make-up bag she always carried on set.

Should I say something? Even if this was an accident, the police would want to see the gun, examine it closely. Quentin was now moving, groaning, but he might have been killed.

One of the paramedics looked up.

'Don't worry; he's going to be fine. The bullet, if that's what it was, only just grazed his neck. A little blood goes a long way, you know.'

As if on cue, Quentin made an attempt to sit up. 'What happened?' he said, gazing round as though he didn't recognise where he was.

'Stay where you are,' replied the paramedic briskly, in a tone of voice not to be challenged. 'You're fine. You had a fright and fainted. It's only a superficial wound to your neck.'

Quentin gingerly put his hand up to touch his collar and looked in horror as it came away bloodstained. For a moment it appeared as if he was going to faint again.

'Steady, steady,' said the paramedic, motioning to his colleague to assist him. Between them they helped Quentin to his feet and outside into the waiting ambulance while many of us crowded after them, excitedly trying to make sense of what we'd witnessed. Franklin was shouting to be heard over the din, 'It was nothing to do with me, I tell you. I didn't know the gun was loaded.'

Linda was nowhere to be seen in the crowd gathered at the entrance and assuming she'd gone back inside, I slipped away to find her.

It took a few moments for my eyes to adjust to the gloom of the interior and then I spied her sitting on a seat at the far end, staring sightlessly ahead.

She edged along to make room for me.

'What's wrong? Why are you so upset? I think Quentin's going to be fine. It appears to be a superficial wound.'

'Of course I know he's not badly injured, but that's not the point,' she said scornfully.

117

'No one will blame you.' I tried again to re-assure her.

She stood up suddenly, shaking with anger. 'Of course they will! I'm responsible for the props after all. Everyone will wonder how on earth real bullets ended up in Franklin's pistol. They'll say I was careless.'

'Are you sure the bullets you put in were duds?'

'Absolutely.' She sat down again. 'I check everything carefully. Especially on a low budget film like this where we have to comply with all the Health and Safety regulations and there's no room for error. There's no way we can risk being sued.'

'Well, there's an easy way to check, surely? Where do you store the fake bullets?'

'Even though they're fakes, they're kept under lock and key together with all the other potentially dangerous props.'

I stood up and pulled her to her feet. 'If it'll help, why don't we go along together and have a look. The police will want to question everyone and best be prepared, find out exactly what happened.' Then I added, 'If you have the gun, you'll have to hand it over to the police.'

'I know, I know,' she replied. 'Lifting it was an automatic reaction.' She pulled the weapon from her capacious bag and held it carefully at arm's length as though it might suddenly fire of its own accord and then put it back, closing the bag with a snap.

Before I could say anything about tampering with the evidence, there was the sound of a siren and then the slamming of car doors. 'I think the police have arrived. Best give this to them at once,' I urged her.

She hesitated, but only for a moment. 'Okay. Let's do that,' she said, sounding calmer and we walked out together to the vestibule where the police had started questioning those who'd been on the set.

One of the officers approached to ask us what we'd seen, about Linda's role in the company before closing his notebook, saying, 'Fortunately it seems as if he's going to be fine. The word is it's only a graze. But we'll have to take statements from everyone, so please don't leave the area.'

In all the confusion, the noise and the bustle it took me a few minutes to realise Linda hadn't done as promised and handed over the gun. It was on the tip of my tongue to remind her, but something made me hesitate.

'Let's go, Alison,' she hissed as the police officer turned his attention to Matt, loitering at the entrance.

As we left, walking hurriedly past the little crowd of actors and crew being interviewed, Linda whispered, 'I'll explain everything in a minute, Alison - there's something I must find out first before handing the gun to the police.'

Sol was standing speaking to one of the policemen and Linda ignored him as she walked past, but he grabbed her arm. 'What's going on - what happened with that gun?'

There was a note of hysteria in his voice, but she shook off his hand and said, 'There's something I have to check out. We'll talk later.'

With that she quickened her pace and I had to scurry to keep up with her as we hurried along the seafront to the caravan where the props were kept.

There was no one there, nor anywhere nearby, if you didn't count those enjoying a cold drink and the sea air at the Post Office café tables.

Even so, Linda looked round nervously before ferreting in her bag for the key to unlock the caravan and her hand shook as she fumbled about with the lock, before she finally managed to open the door. 'Come in,' she said, pulling me towards her and closing the door behind us.

How anything was found in this colourful crush of costumes and props was hard to imagine. Racks of costumes were ranged round three of the walls, squashed in together, shoes of all colours stacked in boxes underneath, hats and other accessories piled up perilously on the shelves above.

Linda made straight for the far end of the caravan where a large wooden box sat, heavily padlocked. 'We keep all the dangerous props in that box,' she said, pointing to it.

She reached through the rack of costumes nearest the box and moved her hand around, causing the costume rack to sway in a most alarming manner.

'Careful,' I said, making a grab for it before all the costumes tumbled in a heap onto the already cluttered floor.

'It's here somewhere,' she muttered and a few seconds later pulled her hand out, triumphantly clutching a small gold coloured box.

Inside was the key for the padlocked box. 'Is the key just left lying about?' That seemed a very dangerous procedure to me, after all the talk about Health and Safety.

'Several of us must have access,' she said by way of explanation, 'and we've learned from bitter experience that giving out more than one key is a recipe for disaster. Only those who need to know where the key's hidden.'

She swiftly unlocked the box and with some effort lifted the heavy wooden lid. Peering over her shoulder I could see a number of daggers, a small sword and a lethal looking knife, all hopefully realistic fakes, but Linda ignored these and pulled out a long silver case.

'That's strange,' she said frowning as she opened it. 'Everything's correct. There should be two blanks missing, the two used for Franklin's pistol, and the other four should be here and they are.'

'So who was responsible for putting the dud bullets into the pistol if it wasn't you?'

Linda shook her head. 'I was. At least all was well when I left it here for Franklin to pick up. I can't understand what's happened.'

Thinking over what she'd said, I wondered, 'Do you use real pistols?'

She nodded. 'Yes. It's very expensive to have good replicas made so we tend to buy real ones at auction and adapt them.'

'You'll have to tell the police about this, hand over the gun,' I reminded her, but she didn't respond, remained staring at the contents at the top of the box. How could she have made a mistake over the dud bullets and the pistol? It was her job to check everything carefully.

'Let's go back and find out if there've been any developments,' I urged her. 'Perhaps they've managed to find the bullet - it must be somewhere in the room. And,' a reminder to her, 'you can hand the gun over to the police.' Though you'll have to have a good reason for not doing so earlier, I thought.

She put the box containing the dud bullets back, secured the padlock and after she'd hidden the box with the key, we left the caravan.

'You must tell the police the full story. They'll want to see all of this. Where have you put the pistol?'

She gave me a sly look. 'I don't think the police need to be involved, do you? After all, there was no harm done. Quentin wasn't badly injured.'

'I don't think you can keep this quiet,' I replied. 'The paramedics will have filed a report, apart from anything else. And of course the police will want to know what caused Quentin's accident. They're already involved.' I didn't mention Health and Safety officials would be next to make an appearance and that might hold the production up even more, if not close it down entirely.

She shook her head and we left the caravan. Various members of the crew had also deserted the Castle, most making for the hotel and the bar.

'There's Franklin,' hissed Linda as he came towards us. 'I wonder what he has to say for himself?'

Franklin ignored us and hurried past.

It was increasingly hard to understand how something that had started out as an interesting assignment, a new challenge, was becoming so complicated. Was someone trying to disrupt this production or cause more problems for Franklin? If so, why?

15

I hadn't seen or heard from Robert for several days. I wasn't deliberately avoiding him, it was more that with so much going on there was little time to think about him. It certainly simplified my life. That's if you didn't count the fallout from the latest episode on the film set.

'There's someone trying to put this production out of business,' Franklin muttered, daring anyone to contradict him. 'If this keeps up there's no way we can carry on.'

Now that filming had again been suspended, the bar at the Coronet Hotel was busier than ever. With so much time on their hands, the cast and the crew seemed to gravitate there. Shame really, as the island was benefitting from a long spell of warm summer sunshine, but no one seemed in a mood to take advantage of it. Goodness knows it would have been a good idea for most of them, who were looking pale and drawn after the most recent incident.

My suggestions to Juliet and to Tracy fell on deaf ears. 'I don't think fresh air will help the situation, Alison,' said Tracy. 'I'm not really an outdoors person.' She turned back to the celebrity magazine she was reading, or at least gazing at the pages, giving me the feeling her mind was elsewhere and reading was a way of avoiding further conversation.

Juliet was even more blunt.

'Go for a walk? Are you mad? We have to stay here, together. Goodness knows what will happen if we go off on our own. There have been plenty of problems already. There's someone determined to cause mayhem.'

The item she was now crocheting seemed to be some kind of top, in lurid shades of pink and yellow. I couldn't imagine who might want to wear such a garment, but perhaps someone in the family would be glad to receive it. She was wielding the crochet hook as though it was a spear, her fingers darting in and out of the wool in fierce concentration.

Her phone rang and she answered it, frowning all the while as she said, 'If you think it will help, then fine. Give me an hour.'

The call ended, she put her phone down and resumed her relentless crocheting, ignoring our unspoken interest in the caller.

'Well, I think I could do with some fresh air,' I said and left.

A walk seemed the best option, given that Alastair would still be hunched over his computer back at the flat. We'd managed no more than a swift trip round the island by car, in spite of his declaration of "being on holiday" and when I went up to the house to collect a jacket, it was to find my guess had been correct, but he abandoned his task long enough for us to chat over a cup of tea and agree where we'd go for dinner that evening.

It was my intention to have a short walk out at Ettrick Bay, but rather than take the car, I opted to walk along the Tramway route. This was the way the tramcars had run in the early 1920s, now refurbished as a convenient walkway out to the bay, past fields where only a few cows appeared the least bit interested in a human presence.

Opposite the old ruined church a Cnoc-an-Rath, at the start of the Tramway, I stopped to search for the rectangle of Victorian iron railings marking the grave of James Hamilton. 'Lone Man's Grave' was unkempt, the headstone broken and lying to one side, the grave hidden by such a tangle of lush summer vegetation you might not spot it, unless you knew where to look.

I stood for a few minutes, thinking about the story, about how James had asked to be buried here in the green shade of this little copse and even more strangely, buried standing up, so that on Resurrection Day, when the Just were called, his first sight would be of his beloved Kames Castle and the sweep of Kames Bay beyond. The story was that by the end of his life he and Harriet were so estranged that he couldn't bear to be buried in the same grave as her, but whether that was fact or later embroidery was difficult to know.

With a sigh I turned away to resume my walk. Whatever the truth, Matt seemed to be under orders to sensationalise the story, my book no more than a jumping off point for the film. Each scene I watched made me regret more and more my decision to sell out. How naïve I'd been to believe this seductive promise about being an assistant scriptwriter, how it would allow me to retain some control over my work.

Far from helping with the script, it would appear I'd had that role taken away from me and was now firmly established as one of the extras. How I wished I hadn't let out the house in Glasgow, could cut my losses with the rental of the flat on Bute and head home.

I left the quiet of the little copse where James Hamilton was buried and resumed my walk, past the stone circle, past the old Blacksmith's forge, now a comfortable cottage and paused for a break at the Ettrickdale Road which led up to the site high above the bay where my friend Susie, who'd recently married an American and gone to live in the States, had once owned a Victorian house that had long since been destroyed by fire and the land sold off.

Susie and I have been friends since our days at college, have been through the highs and lows of life together and I missed her. Memories of happier times crowded in and I was glad to reach Ettrick Bay.

The tearoom was busy. Cars sat squeezed together on the gravel and a large tour bus occupied the remaining space along the side wall, an indication how popular the island was as a holiday destination, in spite of the often unpredictable Atlantic weather.

It was warm enough for a couple of young men to be swimming in the waters of the bay and as I watched they came running out, shouting and laughing and snuggling into their beach towels, to the accompaniment of hoots from several others sitting amid the remains of a picnic. Perhaps the water was colder than they'd thought or they'd gone in for a dare.

I pushed open the door to the tearoom, hoping there would be a free seat, but if there wasn't, I'd buy a cold drink and some cake and head down to the far end of the bay along the Kirkmichael road where there were plenty of quiet spots, well supplied with benches.

For a moment it was hard to focus as I came in from the light but as I'd guessed, the place was very busy, the noise of chattering and laughter loud. Realising my only option would be to head for one of the quiet coves, I joined the queue at the counter, leaning over to make my selection from the chill cabinet then gazed round as I waited.

Then in the far corner, at a table for two by the side window, I spied Robert. He was sitting with a woman who had her back to me and they were deep in earnest conversation as if they'd known each other for some time, though I didn't recognise her.

'Can I help you?'

I turned back to the counter where the waitress stood ready to take my order. As she bustled about preparing the drink, wrapping up the cake I'd selected, I couldn't resist another look at where Robert and his companion were sitting.

Then in a blinding flash, I realised that, even from this restricted view, I did indeed know the woman he was with – it was Juliet.

16

If Robert knew Juliet why had he not mentioned it the day he'd visited the set? Surely there was no harm in telling me if he'd met her before. This was the reason she'd refused to join me for a walk, had pretended to be engrossed in crocheting. She'd planned to meet Robert.

Whatever they were talking about, it was very serious. Robert was stony-faced and they were too wrapped up in their discussion, or each other, to notice what was going on around them.

After paying, I hurried out, sure they hadn't spotted me and then stopped by the side of the little play park where a toddler and his mum were having great fun as he yelled 'Higher, higher,' as she pushed him on the swing. This was so stupid. It would only have taken a moment to go over and say hello. What harm would there have been in that?

Too late now. My plans for a leisurely walk spoiled, I headed for one of the benches along the pathway beside the beach, out of sight of the Ettrick Bay tearoom, and settled down.

I'd brought a book with me, but every time I started to read, my mind drifted to the sight of Robert and Juliet, heads together, deep in conversation.

Although no expert on the world of films, so much had gone wrong on this production, there were so many loose threads, I wanted some answers. First with Sol and now with Juliet, it would appear that Robert wasn't quite what he seemed. What was he really doing here on the island? Was the story about writing a book no more than a cover? Strange that whenever I'd mentioned it, asked him how it was progressing, he was evasive, vague.

I drained my can of juice and threw the remains of the cake to the seagulls squawking around my feet, sat watching them for a few minutes as they squabbled for the crumbs, before reluctantly starting back.

It was so peaceful sitting here in the sunshine, with the smell of new mown grass from the cottage across the way drifting towards me on the light breeze, the water lapping on to the rocks below, but I had to head for home.

As I made my way up and along the Kirkmichael Road I began to regret not bringing the car, fearful I'd be spotted by Robert or Juliet on the walk back to the Port. They'd guess I'd seen them together and that I didn't want to happen, not until I knew more about what they were up to.

I needn't have worried. There was no sign of either of them as I walked briskly towards Kames, though I took the unnecessary precaution of keeping close to the hedge with my head lowered.

Some twenty minutes later I'd reached the entrance to a deserted set. Even if he'd been cleared by Health and Safety, Sol must have decided to postpone filming for the rest of the day. With the light fading over the bay, he wouldn't want to start at this late hour, yet this was more time lost, another chunk of money spent on nothing. The sponsor would have plenty to complain about.

Weary of it all, wishing I could turn the clock back and refuse the contract I'd so eagerly accepted, I reached Port Bannatyne and headed up the hill, just as my mobile rang. I glanced at the screen – it was Robert. Curious to know what he had to say, I said, trying hard to sound normal, 'Why, hello Robert. How are you?' If he said he'd seen me out at the Ettrick Bay tearoom, wanted to know why I hadn't spoken to him, I'd no answer.

'At a loose end, to be truthful. The peace and quiet are fine for a while, but I am beginning to miss city life and thinking of returning to Glasgow for a week or two.' So he hadn't noticed me or, if he had, wasn't going to mention it.

There was a pause. Was he waiting for me to persuade him to stay on Bute? Now was the opportunity to encourage him to reveal his connection with Juliet, so I replied, 'You must know some people on the island, surely.'

'A few, but most of them are working during the day.'

Another pause and I pushed for an answer.

'Don't you know any of the actors? I would have thought you'd get on well with them. You've met Sol before?'

'How on earth would I know any of the actors?' Now he sounded cross, refusing to pick up on the reference to Sol. 'Really, Alison, you have some strange ideas. Anyway, one of the reasons I phoned was to ask if you would like to meet for a drink tonight, or even better, a meal.'

'Sorry, I have Alastair staying with me at the moment - he's only here for a couple of days before he goes back to a conference in Edinburgh.'

'Bring him along. It would be good to meet him. And,' as a way of persuading me, 'it may be my last night on Bute for a while. Let's paint the town red.'

A most unlikely event on Bute, I thought and laughed to myself, imagining the very staid Robert letting his hair down.

'I'll ask Alastair, find out what his plans are,' was as far as I was prepared to commit myself.

If he intended to leave the island and if Alastair was with us, what harm would there be in accepting his invitation. It might be the last decent company I'd have for some time. These actors and the rest of the company weren't any more my kind of people than they were Robert's.

We said goodbye and I shut off my mobile and wandered up to the flat, mulling over the conversation with Robert.

It was stifling indoors. The heat had built up through the large picture windows and after opening up the door to the terrace, I turned to find Alastair exactly as I'd left him, hunched over his laptop.

'Have you been here all day? Did you not go out for a walk? Or at least open the windows?'

Alastair looked up, a puzzled expression on his face. 'I've been trying to set up a conference call but the line keeps dropping.'

A look of alarm crossed his face. 'Why? Was there something you wanted me to do?' It was clear the notion of opening the windows hadn't crossed his mind.

'No, no,' I assured him and told him about Robert's phone call inviting us to dinner.

To my surprise he agreed readily.

'Sounds fine. Celebrate a bit.'

If there's one good thing about Alastair's concentration, or rather obsession, with his work it's that he's not the least bit interested in anyone's personal life. Maura or even Deborah would have been full of questions, wanting to know all about Robert: where I'd met him, how long I'd known him, what Simon thought about it all. As it was, since Robert had absolutely nothing to do with Alastair's work, he expressed no interest.

'I'll let Robert know,' I said and went outside to the balcony to call him as Alastair turned back to his computer.

Truth to tell, going to dinner with Robert would be very helpful. Much as I loved my son, sometimes I found him more than a little difficult. He's so wrapped up in his various projects general conversation can be hard work. Having both Alastair and Robert there would be an advantage and as academics they might even have some topics of conversation in common.

'That's it then,' I said, coming back into the room, 'we'll meet him at the Mariner Bistro at eight o'clock.'

Alastair suddenly seemed to realise what he had committed himself to.

'I suppose I should know something about this man, if we're going to have dinner with him.'

'His name's Robert, Robert Broughton. He was a lecturer in Accountancy before he retired. I knew him when I first started teaching, but after a few years he went out to Canada.'

A puzzled look crossed Alastair's face.

'Robert Broughton? Was he at the University of Maple Ridge?'

'Yes,' I said, surprised. 'Do you know him?' - thinking it was most unlikely given the vastness of Canada.

'Mmm. I know him…or at least know of him. He was well respected in his field. He decided to retire early.'

'Yes, that's right,' I replied, wondering what else he knew about Robert.

Alastair appeared to be trying to recall the detail. 'Yes, he retired from that post, but if I remember correctly he went on to do something else. Now what was it?' He frowned, then stopped and shook his head.

'As far as I know he's retired, might be writing a book, but that's all,' I said.

Tapping his fingers on the desk in concentration he said, 'No, I've heard something about him, something he was involved in, though I can't recall what it was exactly. Something about him working

134

independently? It might come back to me when we meet.' He turned back to his computer.

This was so like Alastair - to remember half a story. If Robert was now freelance, he certainly wasn't working at the moment - he was on holiday on Bute. Or was he?

17

Now there was the added complication about meeting for dinner, given Alastair's sudden revelation about Robert. On further questioning it appeared he didn't know Robert, merely knew of him '... because the academic world is very small now, especially with the internet. Besides his university is one I've a lot of dealings with.' Then, seemingly puzzled by my reaction, he hurried on to say, 'Of course I don't know the details, only that there was some reason or other he decided to leave his post early.'

He gazed at me, an anxious look on his face, as if he hoped this explanation would retrieve the situation, but my natural inclination was to be sceptical of the story.

Already I'd dismissed the sighting of Robert with Juliet, knowing there could be any number of reasons for their meeting, none of them suspect. They could have met unexpectedly at Ettrick Bay and Juliet could have recognised him from the interchange with Sol. She'd be only too happy to make a friend of anyone who had a grievance against the director, especially someone like Robert who was good company...and still a very handsome man.

When we met up later that evening Robert was already waiting for us by the Albert Pier, leaning over the railings, watching the ferry, the *MV Bute*, swing in to berth in the bay.

We'd parked further along the road, near the Discovery Centre, once a favourite place of entertainment and now the tourist office, surprised to find how busy the island was with visitors. We walked the rest of the way to the bistro, enjoying the cool evening air and the burgeoning display of summer flowers in the carefully tended flower beds. The fountain in the middle of the tiny square was in full flight, the jets of water rising and falling, glittering in the evening light.

At first Robert didn't spot us, so intent was he on watching the ferry, but as I called out, 'Hello,' he turned and his face broke into a smile as he hurried forward to greet us.

Introductions made, we crossed the road quickly and were lucky to secure a table by the window where there was a good view of the Marina and the boats tied up beside the pontoons, their names and countries showing how far some of them had travelled to berth here on Bute.

Once we were settled, Robert leaned back in his chair and said, 'Now, Alastair, tell me about this latest research project of yours. I still have an interest in what's going on in the world of academia.'

This was not a good idea so early in the evening and I groaned inwardly. If encouraged, Alastair could talk for ever about his work, something I'd seen happen often and cringed as I watched interest fade and eyes glaze over.

To my surprise, on this occasion Alastair was unusually reticent. 'I don't want to bore you,' he said and turning to me, 'I know mum has heard plenty about it and it's not her favourite topic of conversation.'

Given this opportunity to divert the conversation, I broke in.

'When are you thinking about going back up to Glasgow, Robert?'

He looked at me as if he didn't understand the question.

'Glasgow? I think I might stay here on the island for a bit longer, enjoy the good weather.'

What on earth was he talking about? Last time we'd discussed this he'd been determined to return to the city. Had something happened to make him change his mind?

In most circumstances I wouldn't have pressed him, but the memory of seeing him with Juliet in the Ettrick Bay tearoom made me say, 'Found something, or someone, interesting on the island since last time we spoke, then?' Only just in time did I stop myself from mentioning Juliet directly.

He shrugged.

'No, not really. But the weather is so good at the moment and it could change at any time. I intend to wait a few days, see if it continues to be sunny. I might even manage the ...' he paused. 'What do you call that walk you can do round the island?'

'Oh, the West Island Way, starting out at Kilchattan Bay.'

'That's it…though perhaps walking all of it might be over ambitious.' He lifted the menu from the table. 'Now, what are we having to eat? I hear the seafood is particularly good.'

'It all looks very tempting.' There was nothing further to be gained from Robert, best to relax and enjoy the evening. It was of no concern to me what was going on between Robert and Juliet.

The evening passed pleasantly enough with general chat and several funny anecdotes about life at university that made even the usually serious Alastair laugh loudly.

As the waitress came over with the bill, Alastair stood up and stretched.

'Gosh, all this sea air has made me tired. And I have to check my e-mails tonight.'

I swirled the last of the ice cubes round in my glass and finished off my drink as Robert said, 'Do you never switch off? It is so important not to overwork.'

His question was good-natured, but sadly Alastair has little sense of humour as far as work is concerned. He frowned. 'It's not easy trying to balance what's happening on my project in Canada with the demands of the conference and the work starting soon in Edinburgh.'

Out of the corner of my eye I could see Robert bristling, about to make some nippy reply, so I said, 'I'm feeling pretty tired too and I'm due on set tomorrow morning early.' I yawned to give more credibility to my performance. Perhaps a career as an actor wasn't so far fetched.

'As you wish.' Robert looked disappointed. Perhaps he really had intended to make a night of it.

'Let me pay,' he said, motioning me to put away my purse. He held up his hand. 'This is my treat. I invited you.'

Alastair had wandered outside across to the railings and was looking out over the lights of the bay reflected in the calm water. The ferries were berthed for the night, their lights shining, dancing, making shimmering reflections. He turned as I approached. 'It's so peaceful here,' he said. 'No wonder people come here and never leave.'

I nodded.

'Mmm. That's one of the best things about it. You feel so relaxed. Nothing matters. It's a different pace of life.'

Robert turned away, but not before winking at me to let me know he wasn't upset by Alastair's comments. As a university professor he'd no doubt dealt with plenty of people like Alastair, with their self- absorption and lack of engagement with the real world.

'I'll give you a call tomorrow.' Robert bent to put on his bicycle clips and swung into the saddle like some latter day cowboy. 'Thank you for a lovely evening...and it was good to meet you, Alastair.'

'What? Oh, yes, good to meet you.' It was evident my son's mind was on other things, the evening's entertainment already a distant memory.

I smiled and waved to Robert as he wheeled round to head for Ascog. There was no point in chiding Alastair about his lack of social skills. It wasn't deliberate and he'd be horrified to think he'd been rude.

Now I was more intrigued than ever about Robert. Alastair's vague dismissal wasn't enough for me. There was more to this man than appearances suggested, confirmed by his deliberately avoiding my questions over dinner.

As we drove back towards the Port, I broached the subject with Alastair again, leading in with a cautious, 'That was a good evening. Did you enjoy it?'

'Yep.' He was gazing out of the car window, possibly once again absorbed in thinking about his project.

'Did you have the chance to check out Robert with any of your colleagues?'

'Oh, that?' He suddenly seemed to realise I was asking him a question.

'So what was it you found out about Robert?' I repeated.

He turned to look at me, as though weighing up what to say,

'He was well respected in his field but there was a problem of some kind about a piece of research. One of his researchers was accused of fiddling the figures on a major piece of work and Robert felt it was his responsibility, that he should have supervised the work more carefully.'

Oh dear, it all seemed like a storm in an academic teacup to me. 'It doesn't sound like something that would cause a lot of concern,' I said. 'All over a piece of research.'

Alastair frowned at me as though I'd said something outrageous.

'Of course it caused concern. In universities you live or die by your grading. What could be worse than spending hours supervising research, testing your findings, losing sleep, only to find you were being duped by one of your researchers? All academic work these days is teamwork, and sadly this kind of fraud isn't unusual. Believe me, lowly researchers have to fight tooth and nail for their spot in the sun and to find one of their own has been feted for something that involved cheating would not sit well with anyone in the university.'

This was a long speech for Alastair, leaving me feeling suitably rebuked. Even so, Robert was retired so all that must have been long in the past, over and done with. And there remained a suspicion there had been more than a little exaggeration in the story, so I changed the subject.

'Are you looking forward to the job in Edinburgh?'

His face lit up as it always does when we move back to the subject of his work. 'Yep. I'm working with Laura France. I haven't seen her in ages, not since we were at university together.'

Was that a blush I spied on his face as he quickly turned to look out of the window, making me think there was more to this job at the University of Edinburgh than first appeared. If there was a romance in the air, the likelihood of Alastair telling me was slim.

The Port was quiet, the streets deserted. Even the local pubs, the Port Inn and the Anchor Tavern, showed no obvious signs of life at this time of night.

Perhaps most people were indoors, watching television or surfing the net, rather than meeting their neighbours in the local bar, though the hall at the top of Stuart Street had had a new lease of life of late, as well as being used as a rehearsal hall for the production company. The sound of singing came drifting out on the still night air: possibly a local group was performing, or a wedding reception was being held there.

Light from the streetlamps shimmered in puddles of rain; signs there had been a shower or two while we were in the restaurant. A light breeze had sprung up, ruffling the water, sending the wires on the rigging of the boats anchored in the bay ringing and singing, like so many bells. A pleasant sound to doze off to and I was certainly sleepy, trying to stifle a yawn as I got out of the car, careful to close the door quietly. It seemed rude to disturb the peace of the village, even if it wasn't so very late

'I'll be sorry to go back to the mainland tomorrow,' said Alastair, quite unprompted.

'Really? I thought you were much more a city person.' My son was full of surprises.

'Yes, but it's so peaceful here - you can think clearly.' He got out of the car and stretched. 'How long are you considering staying here? I might come back over and join you for a weekend.'

'That would be great.' I was too astonished to say more. It had never occurred to me that my son might be captured by the charms of Bute.

Indoors, I yawned again, slipped off my high heels (a bad choice as my feet were suffering) and said, 'I'm off to bed. I have to be on set early tomorrow.'

Alastair grinned and nudged me.

'This might be your big opportunity, mum. We'll see you at the Oscars soon.'

Even as a joke this wasn't worth a reply. All delusions about having a pivotal role in this production had long since faded, and even yet I could scarcely believe I'd ended up as an extra, someone I'd heard Franklin refer to disparagingly as a "live prop".

Everything had this strange dream-like quality, as though it was happening to someone else. If I'd had more spunk, I'd have told them what to do with the part, but a bit of me sneakily hoped something urgent would come up and Sol would be desperate for my help with the script.

'I'm staying up for a while,' said Alastair, sitting down at the table and switching on his laptop.

About to say, 'Oh, give yourself a break, you'll be back to work tomorrow,' I stopped. It was no business of mine how he organised his life.

As I said goodnight and headed for bed, he looked up saying, 'I'm going to log on and see what more I can find out about Robert. There's bound to be something on the internet with details of his career and what he's up to, now I know more about him.'

'How will you find out? Surely that business with the researcher is ancient history?'

He laughed.

'You can find almost anything these days if you know where to look. And no, it's not that old stuff about the researcher I'm looking for. I told you there was some story about a new job and something he had done.'

Trying to disguise my curiosity, I nodded. What would Alastair find out? And would I want to know?

18

With Alastair safely embarked on the first ferry back to Weymss Bay, complaining loudly at such an early start, I hurried back to the Port.

Having to be on standby until the production had been given the all clear was becoming tedious and, in spite of my reservations, I hoped there might be something happening on set today.

Alastair had spent a good hour or two trawling the internet after I went to bed, but his searches had produced little in the way of results. 'It's strange,' he'd said as we sat together having a quick breakfast, 'I'm sure I heard something, but I can't find any record of it. All that's available is the usual stuff about his career at the University of Maple Ridge and the papers he's written, the conferences he's been involved in.'

'Well, unless he's committed a serious crime, I don't think I'm interested.'

The mystery of Franklin's dagger hadn't yet been solved. The police had interviewed everyone again but, in spite of the stories circulating, there had been no news of progress. There was no doubt the dagger was the one Franklin had been allocated for his role as James Hamilton, but he claimed to have no idea how it had gone missing.

The latest rumour was that Tracy had provided an alibi for him, that he'd been with her all night, but the casual way he treated her didn't confirm there was any great love affair. If anything, he went out of his way to avoid her.

In the meantime there remained the problem of the shooting of Quentin in the role of the messenger. There was a lot of talk and more than one murmur of suspicion the shot was supposed to kill Quentin, rather than merely wound him, but that might have been wishful thinking by those he'd upset in one way or another.

Fortunately for Quentin - and for Franklin - he'd made a quick recovery and was refusing to press charges, but he was relishing the attention he was getting.

'It was no more than a surface scratch,' he said. 'It only grazed my neck. I'm sure it was all a mistake.'

Franklin was only too ready to agree with this version of events and almost grovelled to Quentin when they met. This change of fortune suited Quentin very well and he took every advantage of it, especially as Linda was also keen to please him. 'I'll get on to our supplier. There must have been some mix up.'

Health and Safety inspectors had been crawling all over the set, demanding details of every aspect of the filming, insisting risk assessment forms be filled in for every action, every move. Sol followed them round, but I could see he was at breaking point as they produced yet more forms, colour-coded in vivid shades of blue, green and purple.

At last Pelias Productions was given the all clear and with stern admonitions and warnings about safety locks, staff training and safety notices they departed, leaving us back in business.

I'd been assured that there'd be some work for me today, providing all the new requirements for Health and Safety could be met in time and I'd no choice but to present myself at the props caravan to struggle once again into the costume of Harriet's maid.

In spite of all the promises about adjusting it to fit me, little had been done and I wasn't looking forward to being squeezed into the corset deemed necessary for an authentic nineteenth century outline. Not to mention the prospect of a long day ahead, especially as a spell of hot weather was predicted.

'I'm sorry, Alison,' Linda had said at our last encounter, 'there's not enough let out in the seams of this costume to help you.' She visibly brightened. 'As long as you don't move about too much it should be absolutely fine.'

This was in theory a solution to the problem, but though my part was small it did involve a certain amount of movement. Besides which, I'd a sneaking suspicion all this good eating on the island hadn't helped. Even if that was what she thought, Linda was too tactful to say so as she pulled and tugged at the lacing on the back of my dress, while I tried in vain to hold my breath to make her task easier.

'Isn't there anything else to fit me among all these costumes?' A last ditch attempt to secure something more suitable. If there was little concern for historical accuracy with the costumes surely finding something to fit me, even if it wasn't the right period, was a possibility.

She laughed.

'I don't think so. All the costumes remotely relevant to this period have been allocated. We've no spares. And let's face it, you are an unusual fit.'

A kind way of saying I was too plump for any of the few costumes still available. In the time I'd been on Bute my own clothes had begun to feel a little too tight - the result of a lot of sitting around and too many meals out, alas.

When I was finally squashed into the costume, laced up tight, I could scarcely breathe, let alone speak and I slowly made my way to the minibus for the short ride to the set.

Now filming had re-started, there should have been an air of jubilation, but Sol gave every appearance of being deeply unhappy. No one could do anything right. He kept darting back and forwards between the actors and the monitors, now set up in the far corner, calling out instructions.

Matt was nowhere to be seen. Perhaps he'd given it all up as a bad job, was lying low well away from Sol's displeasure. There had been so many changes to the script at Sol's insistence and last time he'd been on set, I'd overheard him say, 'I d...d...don't know why Sol didn't write the whole script. He's changed almost everything.' He was more nervous than ever and I wondered how on earth he'd managed to be taken on as scriptwriter. I could only guess it was the usual reason - he was cheap to hire.

'What's wrong?' I whispered to Tracy, who was standing to one side, clutching a clipboard. 'Sol seems even more tetchy than usual.'

Tracy put a finger to her lips.

'Careful. Don't let him hear you. It appears one of the sponsors has decided to bring forward his visit and he'll be on the set tomorrow with the producer. Basically Sol is freaking out. The film isn't nearly as far along as he's been telling them. So prepare for fireworks.'

'How do you know that?' From everything I'd seen so far, the film was well on its way to completion. 'I thought the sponsor's visit wasn't for some time yet?'

She tapped the side of her nose.

'I heard from Harry. You can't keep things like that secret, not on a film set.'

'Why should he want to keep it secret?'

'To surprise us all at the last minute of course. That way there's less chance of us getting in a flap.' She shrugged. 'As if we would. It's a bit late to be worrying now. What with Derek dead, and still no arrest, and poor Quentin narrowly missing death, goodness knows what the sponsor will say.'

This might explain why Sol was so worked up, although not all the difficulties were of his making. With so much going wrong anyone who'd invested money in this production would be far from happy. Even so, discussing it with Tracy wasn't appropriate. There was enough gossip on the set as it was. Yes, Derek had been murdered, but the notion Quentin had narrowly escaped death was a typical Tracy exaggeration.

'The marks are quite clear.' Sol had re-emerged and was tapping his stick towards the criss-cross of tape on the floor. 'Surely you guys can manage to stand within them. I know we've had a couple of days without filming, but your memory can't be that short.'

Franklin was having none of this bullying.

'I thought the whole point was for us to be inventive, to use the script as a starting point.'

'There's a whole bloody difference between artistic input and complete anarchy,' yelled Sol. 'Else how is the cameraman supposed to be able to follow the action?'

In the background I could see Perry nodding vigorously.

Juliet raised her eyes skywards. 'Let's go for it, darling,' she said. 'The sooner we get a wrap the sooner you can get back to the bar in the hotel.'

Franklin shrugged and moved forward, ignoring this slur on his character, possibly because he knew there was more than a grain of truth in it, and then made an elaborate display of standing exactly on the spot marked out for him. 'Will this do, Sol?' he said, striking a pose.

There was no reply and the boy ran forward with the clapperboard. 'Scene Eight, Take Nine,' he shouted and slid back into the gloom of the corner.

This time, at last, the scene appeared to go to Sol's liking. He veered between watching Franklin and Juliet act out an elaborate quarrel about her desire to move off the island and shifting back to the black and white monitor. The scene only lasted a few minutes and I sensed much of the problem was to do with the clash of personalities, rather than any real problem about the film.

'Cut! That's a wrap,' shouted Sol, appearing from behind the monitors, but rather than stay to talk to the crew, he turned on his heel and stalked off the set.

Tracy shrugged. 'There's no pleasing him at the moment,' she said.

'I guess he's pretty wound up about the sponsor coming tomorrow,' I said. 'That's understandable.'

'He's good reason to be worried,' said Tracy gloomily. 'I've seen some of the rushes and believe me, there's not much to be happy about.'

Perhaps I could ask them to give me a pseudonym for my part in the film. It wasn't a big part and under the heavy make-up and the wig it was unlikely I'd be recognised even by close family or friends.

Without waiting for Juliet and Franklin to come off the set, I hurried back to the dressing room as fast as my uncomfortable costume would let me. As expected, I hadn't been required. There had been so many re-takes the day had slipped away. Even worse, no one had had the courtesy to let me know what was to happen next. It was a bubble of a world, with so many large egos, each one striving for the big chance. Not that any of them was likely to achieve fame through a part in this particular movie.

Linda was busy doing some repairs to one of the costumes when I arrived back at the props caravan, trying hard not to let my frustration with what was happening, or rather not happening, show.

She looked up and smiled. 'All finished? How did it go?' She seemed more cheerful somehow.

About to say, 'It was a complete waste of time. I wasn't called,' but I hesitated. 'I'll be glad to get out of this costume,' was my only comment, beginning to unfasten the many buttons before twisting round to try to unloosen the laces at the back.

'Careful.' She stood up. 'Let me help you. This costume is under enough strain as it is and you're not quite the contortionist you think you are.' I willingly abandoned my efforts to struggle out of the gown, as a sudden pain in my shoulder caught me unawares.

She helped me pull it over my head, and placed it on a padded hanger before restoring it to its place on the rail.

Now that we were alone in the caravan, it seemed a good opportunity to ask her the question that had been bothering me for some time.

'The gun that wounded Quentin? Did you hand it over to the police?'

'Oh, of course. I explained everything to them. They seemed perfectly happy with what I said.' She seemed cheerful, not in the least upset.

'Tell me, Linda,' I said as I pulled on my own clothes, 'What's the problem with this production? Everyone seems to be at loggerheads and there doesn't seem to be enough money to do anything properly. Is it always like this when making a film? Or is there some other reason for what's happening?'

She sighed.

'I know, I know. You would think there's some kind of a jinx on this one. Sol apparently thought this would make a really good script, be the kind of thing that would be a big box office hit, but at the last minute the sponsorship fell through and the money the producer was able to pull in wasn't nearly enough to do things the way Sol wanted. Perhaps the story wasn't sufficiently interesting to take a trick with backers.'

Ignoring this put-down of my hard work, I said, 'So the original sponsor pulled out? And that's why this visit tomorrow is so important?'

'Exactly. I'm glad of the work, if I'm being honest. And yes, the visit by the new sponsor is more than important. He wants to see the rushes, see what Sol has done so far and as you know, that's not very much.'

'He does have an excuse,' I protested. 'Derek's murder for one thing. And then that episode with Quentin.'

Linda shook her head.

'I think there are other problems.'

She broke off the thread and shook out the costume she'd been working on and I sat down on a nearby chair to put on my sandals. In spite of all she said, there was something unconvincing in her story, almost as if she was giving a performance. To my way of thinking she'd dismissed the episode of the gun far too casually. Would the police really take her word for what had happened?

As I was about to leave, her phone rang. 'Yes, yes,' I heard her say, a note of impatience in her voice. 'I'll come along straight away.'

She stood on tiptoe and lifted a small blue box from the shelf. 'One of the children has torn her costume quite badly and I'll have to go along and make a running repair. Sol's in the middle of finishing off the scene so it has to be done now.' She rolled her eyes. 'Everything has to be done yesterday. There's always some crisis or other.'

'Don't rush,' she said. 'Just give the door a good bang behind you. It's self locking.' She searched inside her blouse and pulled out a long silver chain with a key dangling on the end. 'I always keep this here now, saves any problems about it getting lost.'

She almost ran out as her phone rang again. 'Coming, coming,' she muttered.

I sat down on the bench at the large make-up mirror to put on my shoes. As I lifted my head I caught sight of my reflection in the glass and behind me the prop box where all the 'dangerous' items were stored.

Had Linda forgotten I knew where the spare key for these items was kept? There would surely be no harm in checking.

Feeling about behind the costumes as I'd seen Linda do, I pulled out the container with the key for the large padlocked prop box. Still unsure if I should be prying, with some difficulty I pulled the box over, staggering for a minute under its weight, remembering three pistols were originally kept here apart from the other 'dangerous' props: the one Franklin used and two others. So if Linda was telling the truth, Franklin's pistol was with the police and there were two remaining.

I lifted the lid. Good, there were only two pistols here; Linda must indeed have given Franklin's pistol to the police. I was about to close the box up quickly, fearful she might return at any minute. But as I did so, something made me hesitate. Yes, there were indeed two pistols here, but there was something not quite right. I examined them more closely: one of them was the elaborately decorated pistol Franklin had used on set.

So what had happened to the missing pistol? There could only be one explanation. Linda must have given the wrong prop gun to the police. Why would she do that?

19

On set next day tempers were frayed, the slightest comment seized on. For a brief moment I considered opting out, driving myself to the other end of the island, pleading ignorance if asked later why I hadn't turned up for the sponsor's visit. With all these very important people about, it was unlikely he would want to speak to me.

Unfortunately, as I came down to the Post Office to pick up the morning paper and the most recent copy of the local paper *The Buteman*, Matt was standing outside, peering in through the window.

It would have been a sensible course of action to dodge him, slide into the shop before he noticed me, but I wasn't quick enough and he turned away from the window as I reached the front door.

'Ah, Alison,' he greeted me like a long lost friend. 'Am I p…p…pleased to catch up with you. I wondered when you'd put in an appearance.' He smiled, baring his teeth, as a shark would. Today he'd taken action to keep his combed-over hair in place and it looked as if it was glued to his head.

'I'm only popping in to buy the paper,' I said. 'I won't be needed today I'm sure. I'm planning to…' I racked my brains for a convenient excuse. '…I'm planning to catch up on some other work.

Do a bit of research on the island for my next project.'

He continued to beam at me, a smile so false it seemed as if his face would crack. 'That's where you're wrong. Zack Kissack has said he's r...r...really looking forward to meeting you, to hearing all about the book that inspired the film. He'll want to ask you a lot of questions.' He took off his glasses and wiped them on the sleeve of his thin jacket.

'He's on the island already?' A quick look at my watch confirmed he must have caught the six thirty ferry from Weymss Bay if he was here in Port Bannatyne.

'Ah, no ...n...not quite.' Another beaming smile from Matt, more nervous than genuine. 'He won't arrive until after eleven o'clock, but I'm sure he's really interested in the story of James Hamilton and Kames Castle. You'll want to meet him, chat to him about it. You know so much about this period of history on Bute. You might even be able to t...t...take him round some of the sights.'

Matt's enthusiasm puzzled me. Surely the sponsor was more interested in what was happening now, how much of the film had already been made, seeing the rushes, rather than chatting about my book or having a tour of the island.

But Matt was not to be dissuaded. He peered at me through his thick glasses. 'Make s...s...sure you're here when he arrives. We're meeting up in the Port Bannatyne Hall. Sol has said it's important we're all there, at least at the beginning.

The sponsor wants to see us in action, h...h...how we work out the scenes.'

He gave me yet another smile, then to my great surprise he hugged me. 'We're h...h...hoping for a great result here, Alison. We all have to play our part. And you'll be a big contributor to the meeting.' The breeze whipped at his hair, lifting it and he tried to smooth it back, but it was a futile task.

He quickly disengaged himself as though suddenly regretting this display of affection and headed for the hotel, leaving me staring after him, too surprised to speak. Should I be flattered that Matt thought I could contribute so much to the meeting with the sponsor? This wasn't like him. Since I'd arrived on the set, he'd been at great pains to say on several occasions that, while my "little story" might have been the starting point for the film, it was only that and no more. Why would he now be so eager to include me, make certain the sponsor had time with me?

As I stood there, perplexed by his sudden friendliness, it dawned on me what this was about. How could I have been so stupid? Matt was worried that the script wasn't up to scratch, that he might be in trouble, so much better to give the impression the script was mine, my responsibility. Then Matt could plead his efforts had been curtailed by what was available.

In spite of an initial feeling of anger at this subterfuge, I couldn't help but laugh. Anyone could see the script left a lot to be desired. With so many alterations, so many changes to the original, it was almost unrecognisable as being sourced from the book I'd written.

There was no time to brood. Committed to joining the others at what promised to be a disastrous meeting, I hurried in to the Post Office.

Copies of the latest edition of one of the national dailies were piled up on the counter and I glanced at the headlines: 'Franklin Todd Shock Over Film Death' and underneath was a photo of Franklin in full costume, glowering at the camera.

Intrigued by this banner headline, I read on. Franklin had been released without charge so why was he talking to the newspapers and with the sponsor's visit imminent, what would Sol have to say about this less than welcome publicity?

20

Zack Kissack arrived in some style - in a vintage Rolls Royce no less, accompanied by the producer, Noel Winter. If he'd wanted to attract lots of attention, he couldn't have chosen better. The word went round the village in no time and people appeared from all corners to have a look, under the pretext of shopping or having a walk along the seafront or even waiting for a bus, one that was very unlikely to appear as the bus stop was still out of commission.

Before any of us could even say, 'Hello,' he was whisked off by Sol with, 'Howdy, Zach. We can have a chat first, buddy, if that's okay.'

Franklin growled at this attempt by Sol to take Zach off. 'He wants to get his excuses in before Zach has a chance to meet us,' he said, lapsing into a fit of coughing. Day by day Franklin's cigarette consumption had increased until now he was chain-smoking, pacing up and down in front of the Coronet Hotel, not even trying to disguise what Juliet had called "that filthy habit".

I'd walked in on a terrible row with Sol before Zach's arrival. 'Are you trying to end this production deliberately?' Sol was shouting. 'If so, you're going the right way about it.' He waved a copy of the newspaper in Franklin's face.

It was stupid of Franklin to write this piece, claiming he was the centre of gossip, wrongly identified as being involved in what had happened to Derek and to Quentin. We'd heard the police from the mainland were investigating Derek's past in the hope of finding some clue there, but from all accounts they'd drawn a blank. In spite of appearances, Derek seemed to have led the most blameless of lives.

Franklin had replied sulkily, 'There's been no formal accusation, that's true, but you all think I had something to do with it, just because I was taken in for questioning. Why should I have all this gossip and innuendo hanging around me. Better everyone should know the truth.' With that he'd turned on his heel and gone outside, his face suffused with rage.

Juliet came up to me as I came through the bar. In spite of the commotion going on around her, she was as cool and elegant as ever. 'Come and sit here with me, Alison, away from all this testosterone. It's all too much.' Close up, her face looked pinched.

I would gladly have dissolved into the shadows, but that wasn't what Matt had in mind for me. He came rushing over, almost wresting me from Juliet's side.

'You n...n...need to be with me,' he whispered. 'We need to stick together on this.' He held on tightly to my elbow as he pulled me to my feet and through the thin material of my cardigan I could feel him trembling.

It was on the tip of my tongue to say, 'You should have thought of that earlier when you were telling me my help wasn't required,' but there was no point in complicating what promised to be a difficult morning.

Sol had briefed us earlier. 'Remember this is a very important visit. Be upbeat. Zach wants to see what he's getting for his dough.'

While he was off at the private meeting he'd engineered with Zach we made our way to the Port Bannatyne hall, where we hung around chatting, reading and in Juliet's case crocheting. Finally they returned, with Noel trailing in their wake. Somehow, from what everyone had said about him - his rise to fame, his great wealth achieved through his own efforts - I'd anticipated Zach would be a giant of a man. Instead he was small and thin, casually dressed in jeans and a checked shirt and, when he spoke, his voice was soft and melodious. 'Hello, everyone,' he breathed so softly those of us at the back of the room had to lean forward to catch what he was saying. 'I'm pleased to meet you all at last and find out how the film is going.'

'We're glad you could spare the time to come over to see our little film,' said Sol.

'My "little" film,' said Zach a touch icily. Mmm, perhaps there was more to him than first appeared, but then he couldn't have reached the dizzy heights of success he'd achieved without having a core of steel.

'Well, you've chosen a great day for it, guys,' said Sol, ignoring this comment. 'It would be a pity to waste it all indoors. I thought we might take the Bute bus tour - it goes right round the island, let's you see the place, hear something about the history of the island. I'm sure you'd enjoy it...' So Matt wasn't the only person who'd come up with this idea to distract Zach from the business in hand.

Zach cut him short, a note of astonishment in his voice.

'Why would you think that's the reason for my visit? I've come over to meet the cast and the crew, find out where you are with the film, watch some of the scenes being shot. And to have a look at some of the rushes.'

In spite of Sol's attempts to steer him away from the film, trying to persuade him he'd be better off doing the tour, Zach was determined. 'I've come to meet the cast and the crew and see what you've got so far,' he stressed again, this time in a tone of voice that brooked no argument.

Sol visibly crumpled and clutched on tightly to the table in front of him. 'Okay, okay,' he said.

Why was Sol behaving like this? We'd all worked hard over the past few weeks and though the production hadn't been without its problems, surely there was enough of the film, even in an unedited state, to keep Zach happy?

Zach turned away from Sol and moved over to where we were all sitting, and started chatting to us, asking what we were doing, but he showed no special interest in the script. 'It's the action I want to see, not the script, a movie is all about movement,' he said, waving it away as Sol came forward clutching a copy.

I looked over at Matt, firmly ensconced in the far corner. There was a look of relief on his face. So my guess had been correct. Well, he didn't need to worry: Zach wanted results and as Sol finally led him through to the back room where the monitors were set up in the makeshift editing suite, I only hoped there was enough to make sure this sponsor didn't decide to withdraw his money.

As they walked off with Noel, who hadn't said a word since his arrival, in tow, Tracy sidled up to me. 'Let's hope Sol can carry it off,' she said. In deference to this important occasion, today Tracy was wearing a glittery silver top, a little too short for decency and a skirt that was a frou-frou of lace.

'I'm sure at least some of the film will be good. We've all worked hard.'

'That's not the issue, Alison. There's not as much been filmed as you think.'

'But we've been going for several weeks. I thought all the main scenes had been completed to Sol's satisfaction.'

She stared at me and then said abruptly before moving quickly away. 'If you want to shoot a scene you have to make sure there's a magazine in the camera.'

She couldn't fail to spot my astonishment as she turned on her heel and left me staring after her, open mouthed.

21

After what seemed like an eternity, Zach Kissack finally departed and the grim set of his face showed he wasn't pleased. We crowded at the door of the hotel to watch his Rolls Royce speed off towards Rothesay and the teatime ferry back to the mainland.

In the end everyone had rallied round, tried their best to make the visit what he wanted, but he made no attempt to conceal his disappointment.

He kept saying, 'I thought you'd be further along than this,' as Sol showed him rush after rush. The fact that everything was being shown on a black and white monitor - 'We can't afford a colour one,' Sol said pointedly, - didn't help, even though everyone else knew full well that Sol had been using both a colour and a black and white monitor on set.

There was some game going on here, something very odd. It was difficult to know if the rest of the cast and crew, or only some of them, understood what was happening.

There was a collective sigh of relief when Zach's car finally disappeared from view. 'A drink for everyone, you've worked hard,' said Sol, his good humour restored. He appeared least troubled of all of us by the visit, or perhaps he was relieved it was over.

There was a sudden hubbub of excitement as cast and crew members jostled to the bar to take advantage of this opportunity before he changed his mind.

With so many unanswered questions, I was in no mood for a drink and instead of joining the others went to the front door of the hotel for a breath of fresh air, away from the febrile atmosphere.

Juliet came out and stood beside me. 'Never let a sponsor loose on the set before you've plenty to show for his contribution,' she said. I marvelled at how she remained resolutely calm in the midst of this chaos.

'Sol could hardly tell Zach not to come – it's his money after all,' I protested. 'And what about Noel - what is he supposed to be doing? Doesn't he have some role in all of this.' I could scarcely believe I was defending Sol, but it did seem he was getting a raw deal on this one.

'There are ways, Alison. We're all wondering how this is going to turn out. Let's hope we're paid for our work.'

With no idea what she meant and with less inclination to continue to discuss it, I said, 'Well, at least he's gone and Sol can get on with the filming.'

'If Zach doesn't decide to pull the plug.'

'Surely he wouldn't do that at this stage in the project?' I was horrified at the suggestion.

She shrugged. 'It wouldn't be the first time a sponsor had pulled out at a late stage, let me tell you.'

This latest piece of gossip was nothing to do with me. I'd been paid for my story and besides, I was fed up with my role as the lady's maid. All my part seemed to involve was a lot of standing about, waiting for instructions, rehearsing moves I didn't get to put into practice.

Then there was the unresolved problem about my costume. Linda had tried again, this time by putting in a number of inserts, but to no avail and in the few scenes involving me I had to stand at a peculiar angle so that the tight waist wouldn't display my spare tyre. Worse still, I was beset with aches and pains from having to adopt the most uncomfortable positions.

Meanwhile Robert had been phoning me again, leaving notes at the house. I couldn't put him off for ever, but I'd no idea what to do, especially given the latest call from Alastair.

'Exactly as I thought,' he said. 'There was something odd about Robert leaving his post. It was all very sudden. More than that I can't find out.'

'Don't tell me he was sacked, had his fingers in the till, or rather the grant money.'

'No, no,' said Alastair hastily, 'I don't think it was anything like that. But everyone was taken by surprise when he announced his departure.'

My thoughts were interrupted by Sol as I went back into the bar. 'Well, now that Zach's gone, we can crack on with the next stage of the film.'

'So I guess he was pleased with what he saw?' said Juliet, a wicked gleam in her eyes as she came slowly walking towards us.

Sol refused to rise to the bait.

'Pleased or not, we gotta get this film wrapped up. You'll all have to put your backs into it, make sure you know your lines. I want no more messing around, guys. Understand?'

He glared at everyone, daring anyone to contradict him, but no one had the energy for a fight with Sol, even if we did believe he was the one responsible for the delays and repeat takes.

'We're ready when you are,' said Quentin, stroking his beard, twisting it into a little coil of hair.

'I've just to sort out the matte box for the camera and then I'll be with you,' said Perry. 'Won't be long.' He hurried out, as anxious as anyone else to get back to work.

While the atmosphere so far hadn't exactly been dynamic, we knew it wasn't only a matter of finishing off the film, making sure the rest of the project went according to plan, it was trying to convince the distributors the final version would be worthy of general release, rather than going straight to DVD or worse, not released at all.

'I hope you know how you're going to handle the rest of this, Sol.' The voice from the corner belonged to Franklin. He stood up, swaying slightly, the glass in his hand at a dangerous angle.

'I think you'd better sober up,' said Sol through gritted teeth. 'You'll be wanted on set first thing tomorrow morning.'

'To do what?' Franklin sneered. 'Trouble is, Sol, you're no better a director than I am.'

There was a deathly hush in the bar as everyone waited for one or other of them to make the next move, but Sol merely shrugged, like a deflated balloon.

'I'll expect you to be in costume and ready along at the set first thing in the morning, Franklin. Like it or not, you've a contract, buddy.'

'How I wish I hadn't signed it,' Franklin blustered, downing the last of his drink. 'Why I thought this would help my career, I've no idea. This isn't the kind of thing my fans expect at all.'

'Probably because you realised that your days as the lead in *Heart and Home* were numbered,' replied Sol coolly.

Franklin lunged forward, fists clenched, but suddenly he pushed past the director and headed out, muttering to himself. Juliet rushed out after him. 'I'll try to calm him down,' she said, looking back at Sol.

'I wouldn't bother, honey,' replied Sol. 'He knows that this is his last chance to make it big. He's not getting any younger and making it to the big screen is his only hope of success. He's all washed up as far as his television role is concerned. I've heard he's about to be dropped in the next series. Meet a grisly end, in fact. Yes, sirree, a very grisly end.' He accompanied this last remark with a titter.

Juliet didn't hear the end of this speech, but the rest of us did. You could have heard a pin drop as Sol, with all the appearance of someone who had everything under control, sauntered out of the door.

'What do you think he meant by that?' said Tracy, turning to me. 'I thought Franklin was the star of *Heart and Home*, that they couldn't do without him?' She gnawed at her finger. 'Franklin makes the show; he's the best actor in it.' Then as though realising this remark made her adoration of Franklin too obvious, she hurriedly added, 'Or so people say.'

'No one, but n...n...no one is indispensable,' said Matt, tapping the side of his nose and knocking his glasses askew. Matt was looking extraordinarily pleased, having got off lightly during Zach's visit. 'I've heard r...r...rumours they want to write his character out, bring in someone younger.'

This was Quentin's opportunity to pipe up. 'I've been saying all along how ridiculous it is that I'm supposed to be the older brother.' He smiled and then a smug look crossed his face.

He'd made a remarkably quick recovery from being 'shot' and had given every impression of enjoying the attention he'd received as a result. 'Besides,' he swivelled round to make sure he had everyone's attention, 'I've heard there was some bad blood between him and Derek. All is not as it seems.'

He lifted his drink and went over to sit at the table by the window, refusing to answer any of the babble of questions following his outburst.

Was Quentin so determined to get the star out of the way he'd kill Derek and try to pin the blame

171

on Franklin? That didn't make sense unless Sol was prepared to re-shoot the whole film and besides, Franklin had an alibi.

And yet, and yet he would have had access to the props. In spite of all Linda's assurances, the place where the props were kept wasn't secure. It would have been easy to get the key and steal the dagger. But why Derek - unless Quentin really hated him for offering the part of James to Franklin.

And what about Quentin's accident: could that have been rigged to throw suspicion on Franklin again, when the first ruse didn't work? A dangerous strategy - he might have been killed if the bullet had been an inch higher.

Or perhaps I was wrong about him, he had nothing to do with it and there was indeed some problem about Franklin's starring role in the long running soap. If that was the case, it might just have something to do with the current difficulties on the set of *A Man Alone.*

22

Later that evening Sol gathered us together in the lounge bar of the Coronet Hotel. 'Derek's body has been released to the family,' he said. He looked round. 'That leaves us with the tricky problem about who should attend the service, folks.'

No one spoke. Several people shuffled their feet, or found something of extraordinary interest in the far corner of the room.

'Well?' said Sol. 'Someone has to represent the company. He did work with us.' There was still no response and now clearly annoyed, he said, 'Some of you guys have good cause to be grateful he hired you.'

'I don't see how I could go,' blustered Franklin, 'I mean in the circumstances.' He gazed round for support.

'You mean because it was your dagger that killed him?' Quentin spoke from the far end of the bar where he was propped up on one elbow, sipping at a pint of lager.

'No, I bloody well don't mean that. Don't keep calling it my dagger. It was a prop, or we thought it was a prop.'

'Oh, I see,' said Matt, raising his eyebrows. 'You're t...t...too important to leave the cast.'

Franklin clenched his fists. He was so on edge these days, ready to take the slightest comment as an insult and it took very little to set him off. It was all becoming very wearing.

As she so often seemed to do lately, Juliet moved between them, her voice calm. 'Let's not get into all that, both of you.' She turned to Sol. 'I know someone has to go, but Franklin's right. It will mean a couple of days off the island and lost production time, if it's any of the major players. I don't suppose you can spare any of the crew.'

'You've got it, that's the problem,' he said. As most of the crew were already doubling up, any one of them away from the set for two days would cause serious disruption.

Matt, who'd ostentatiously opened his newspaper and made great pretence of reading it, suddenly lifted his head. 'W...w...what about Alison? She doesn't have any scenes for a while, does she?'

Before I could protest he went on, 'She would be good on two counts - she's part of the cast, but she's also w...w...written a little bit of the script.'

Too astonished to say anything about this further demeaning of my contribution to the script and to the cast of this film, I tried to sink back into the shadows.

Now that Zach had gone, Matt had evidently decided to drop all pretence to my being in any way a serious contributor to the production.

But Sol was having none of my reticence. The relief was evident in his voice as he said, 'Gee, of course, of course. Alison, you're the very person.

You live in Glasgow, don't you?' His face lit up and he rubbed his hands together, delighted to have a solution to this problem.

'But I've nowhere to stay,' I protested. 'The house is let out for the summer while I'm here on Bute. I can't go and turf the people staying there out onto the street.'

'Nonsense,' said Sol, 'you must have a friend who'd put you up for one night,' indicating this couldn't possibly be a problem.

'Now, guys,' said Sol briskly, turning away, making it clear it was all settled and everyone could move on, 'where were we? Let's roll.'

Resigned to doing as requested, or rather ordered, I couldn't help but feel peeved everyone thought my services could be dispensed with so easily.

'You'll have to give me the details about the funeral,' I whispered to Tracy, who was seated beside me.

'See me later,' she hissed, conscious Sol was glaring in our direction.

As the director talked on, listing the changes he wanted made, the details he was most concerned about, much of it went over my head and my mind began to drift off.

Perhaps it wouldn't be such a bad idea to go off the island for a while. It would give me time to think, away from the difficult atmosphere of this film production.

It was all becoming terribly claustrophobic, something I never thought I'd say about Bute, and as I'd hardly known Derek, the funeral wouldn't be the problem for me that it might have been for some of the others.

So it was almost with a feeling of relief that I prepared to leave the island for a short while.

And it would save me from deciding what to do about Robert.

23

The journey back to Glasgow the next afternoon was trouble free: no ferry cancellations, no hold ups on the road through Greenock, no road works on the Erskine Bridge. It was a pleasure to drive along by the seafront and through the green countryside. The recent rain had encouraged plants to run riot and amid the shrubbery wild roses intertwined with the purple rhododendron bushes that crowded along the verges where rogue saplings had seeded.

As I drove along the Clydeside Expressway on the final lap of my journey home, it was good to see once again all the familiar landmarks: the vast shed-like Exhibition Centre, the Armadillo - so-called because of its resemblance to the South American mammal - and close by, the new Transport museum beside which the elegant tall ship *The Glenlee* sat berthed at the quay, its flags fluttering in the breeze from the River Clyde. At the very top of the Hydro Centre, still under construction, several workmen clambered about, resembling so many ants from this distance.

How pleasant it would be to have one of the penthouses in the new blocks of flats along the waterside, with those wonderful views down the river, though the days of the Clyde bustling with ships were long past. The *Waverley*, the last sea-going paddle steamer, lay anchored at the Broomielaw, ready for another of its summer journeys taking tourists round the coast of Scotland, but in the huge expanse of the Clyde it cut a lonely figure.

I'd arranged to stay overnight with my next-door neighbour, Ella, who was looking after our cat, Motley. I phoned her on a regular basis. The American family had come with good references, but you could never be sure and when I told her I'd be coming to Glasgow and why, she insisted I stay with them.

'It will be no trouble, Alison. We've plenty of room and I'll enjoy your company. Fred goes to the bowling club tomorrow night, so we can have a chance to catch up on all the gossip.'

'My only worry is the people renting our house might think I'm spying on them,' I said doubtfully. 'Perhaps I'd be better putting up in a hotel. It is only for one night and we could meet up for coffee.'

'Nonsense,' she'd replied. 'Why would you do that? Besides, it'll give you a
chance to see Motley and have a sneaky look at the house to set your mind at rest. You know the council is talking about closing the library? You can sign the petition when you're here.'

Several reasons to stay with Ella. I also suspected that since her only son left to work in London she's been more than a little lonely and it would be good to catch up with the local news.

As anticipated, we spent a pleasant evening gossiping and even managed to fit in some shopping the next morning before it was time for me to head for the afternoon funeral.

It was a hot day, one of the hottest we'd had in the West of Scotland so far and as I made my way through the afternoon traffic to the crematorium, my mind drifted to the little flat on Bute, thinking of the sea breezes of the island, the possibility of a picnic on the sands out at Kilchattan Bay, a walk along the shore at Ascog.

Almost immediately I rebuked myself for being so selfish. Derek's death had been such a shock and the least I could do was pay my respects on behalf of the company, especially as no one else was keen to do so, though Sol had said, 'Tracy will arrange for flowers to be sent from all of us, honey, so you don't have to worry about that.'

I parked at the far end of the crematorium, and walked the few yards to the entrance, hoping I'd know no one, could slip out quietly at the end, avoiding the line of grieving relatives and make the teatime ferry back to Bute.

All was quiet and there was no sign of any other mourners. I glanced at my watch. It was almost four o'clock, the scheduled time. Surely I hadn't got that wrong? Or even worse, the place? I wandered over to the first row of headstones, each telling its own poignant story of a life lost and then looked in my handbag for the instructions Tracy had given me, conscious it wasn't beyond the bounds of possibility she'd made a mistake. No, the details were correct and I was in the right place.

No sooner had I put the instructions back, than there was the soft purr of a car engine as a sleek black hearse came up the hill and I moved smartly inside the low-rise wooden building just ahead of several people coming in from the car park.

Thank goodness I wasn't the only mourner, but now it dawned on me I knew nothing about Derek, hadn't thought to enquire if he'd any family.

My intention had been to sit inconspicuously at the back among the lesser mourners, but there were so few people, scarcely enough to fill one of the pews at the front, I'd no option but to join them, to sidle in at the end of the row.

The woman beside me glanced round, gave me a faint smile. She was dressed from head to toe in black: black suit, black tights, black shoes, black bag, making me feel aware my navy jacket was my only concession to the occasion being a funeral.

'I'm representing the film company, Pelias Productions,' I whispered to explain my presence.

'I'm Derek's cousin,' she said. 'We weren't really close, but I felt I had to make the effort as I was one of the few family members he kept in contact with. It's so long since I've been to a funeral, I didn't realise the protocol had changed. I expected everyone to be in black.'

Any further conversation was impossible as the pall bearers entered with the coffin and we rose to the strains of *The Lord's My Shepherd*.

The service itself was brief: a minister who'd obviously been brought in for the occasion, though

I suspected Derek didn't have a religious bone in his body. The minister spoke on and my attention wandered as I watched the motes of sunlight dancing in through the stained glass window, thinking about how Derek had died and wondering if Franklin's protestations of innocence were no more than a smokescreen.

Surely the police must have suspicions about him, in spite of all he said. Could he really be having an affair with Tracy? You would have thought now it was out in the open, now Tracy had given him an alibi, there'd be no need for secrecy. They didn't give the impression of a couple in love.

There was no doubt Derek's death had a curious air of unreality about it, given the cast and the crew of *A Man Alone* had moved on so quickly. A few moments of apparent grief, some kind words and then the show had to go on, the casting director and the circumstances of his death completely forgotten in the need to finish the film.

I came to with a start, realising everyone was standing and singing a final hymn as the curtains closed on the coffin.

Derek's cousin turned to me.

'We're going along to the local hotel for a cup of tea. You're welcome to join us.'

'I've a few things to do before heading back over to Bute tonight,' I blustered. 'I've promised to meet up with my friend, Robert Broughton.'

Why I mentioned his name I'll never know, but her reaction was swift, taking me completely by surprise. 'Robert Broughton?' she said with a frown.

'Yes, do you know him?' A small world indeed.

'His name is familiar. It's an unusual name and I'm sure Derek mentioned him.' She paused, then said quickly, 'Of course. He said he'd asked Robert Broughton for help. Something to do with the production Derek was working on. He was the casting director and he was unhappy about the film, said there was something very odd going on.'

24

Dispensing with the formalities of offering my condolences, I left the crematorium as quickly as possible. This news about Robert was totally unexpected: he hadn't mentioned knowing Derek, but now it appeared he'd been asked to help him in some way. While Robert was under no obligation to tell me what he was up to, it seemed strange he hadn't mentioned it.

As I drove off at a reckless speed, almost colliding with the next hearse making its slow and stately way up the hilly drive, I was cross I hadn't taken the opportunity to ask Derek's cousin more questions.

The sensible course of action would have been to join the other mourners for tea in the local hotel. While mulling over the failings or successes of the dead doesn't appeal to me, especially when it was someone I knew only slightly, this would have been the chance to find out why Derek had enlisted Robert's help. Now my only course of action would be to ask Robert directly.

At the junction with the main road the traffic lights suddenly went to red and I had to pull up abruptly, much to the annoyance of the driver behind me, who'd evidently anticipated I'd drive through.

Ignoring the toot of his horn, I sat patiently waiting for the lights to change, all the while trying to work out Robert's real motivation for being on the island.

Another toot, louder this time, from the driver behind me, to remind me the lights were now at green and I jerked forward, stalling the car in the process and moved off just in time before another change of lights as the driver roared past, turning round to glare at me as he did so.

For the rest of the journey to Weymss Bay, I focussed on the road and the traffic, turning the radio to an intricate discussion programme requiring total concentration and put all thoughts of Robert out of my head.

In the passenger lounge on board the ferry, I joined the queue at the café, tempted by the aroma of fresh tomato soup, suddenly realising I hadn't eaten since early morning.

The ferry was crowded with tourists, eagerly anticipating long summer days on the island and there was an unusually large crowd at the café. I soon discovered why. A line of tea cups sat on the counter as a new recruit struggled to use the large tea and coffee machine that beeped and pinged in a most disconcerting way.

As I waited in the slow moving queue, a voice behind me said, 'Why, hello Alison.'

I turned round to see Linda standing behind me and, food and drink purchased, we went to sit at one of the tables at the far end of the ferry.

'Were you at Derek's funeral? I didn't see you there.'

'No, I was over in Glasgow looking for costumes in the second hand shops in the West End.'

'But weren't all the costumes bought before the film started?'

This seemed an odd way to go about things, buying new costumes half way through filming.

She made a face.

'We had most stuff, but Sol has decided he'd like to set up some of the scenes with more of the local children in the background and we didn't have enough costumes for everyone. Most of those I managed to find are adult sizes, but I can cut them down.'

'A lot of work, surely?'

'Yes.' A sigh. 'But there's no alternative. The budget is so tight and altering these will be a good deal quicker than trying to make everything from scratch. I can always sew any members of the cast into them if necessary.'

Memories of being stitched into my own costume surfaced and while this didn't bode well for the remainder of the production, all I said was, 'Rather you than me, with my sewing skills, or rather lack of them.'

'How was Derek's funeral? Did many people turn up?'

'A few,' I said, 'but not as many as I'd expected.'

It was on the tip of my tongue to tell her about my encounter with Derek's cousin, but something made me hesitate. No need to add to the gossip factory. There was enough of that on this production already.

Linda gazed out of the window as we passed the bobbing buoy marking the Skelmorlie Heights, the mid point of the journey, absorbed in her own thoughts, before suddenly appearing to remember I was there, saying, 'There's been no arrest for Derek's murder, you know, though the police must have their suspicions.'

She stared at me as though hoping I might have some news on the subject.

Sorry to disappoint her, I said, 'I've not heard anything either. I guess Franklin has been cleared, even though the dagger was his prop?'

'Strange that. You'd have thought he'd have missed it, but I suppose he wasn't in costume at the time, so there would be no reason to do so. Besides Tracy has given him a cast iron alibi.' Something about the way she said it struck me as odd, making me think she knew more than she was willing to reveal.

'Ah, the dagger was taken from the props caravan?'

'What do you mean by that? I hope no one's implying I was careless. I made sure everything was securely locked up.'

The usually cheerful Linda sounded prickly, defensive.

'No, no,' I replied hastily. 'There's no way you could be blamed for the dagger going missing. Whoever stole it had planned it well.'

This seemed to appease her and she smiled again.

'Yes, I'm sure the police will find the culprit. And I'm sure it was nothing to do with anyone in our cast or crew.'

'What about Quentin? Has he recovered?'

'Ah, of course, you won't have heard about that.'

'Was it worse than we thought?' Visions of another death came to mind.

'No, not at all. No one is certain, but the story is that he wasn't injured at all.'

'But we all saw the blood.'

She gave me a sly look.

'Fake arterial blood can be very effective, especially at a distance. Even the paramedics were fooled - well, for a short while.'

'Why on earth would he want to do that? How can you be sure?'

'I've no idea why he'd do it, but no bullet was found after several extensive searches and one of the paramedics is friendly with the receptionist in the Coronet Hotel. He told her what had happened - Quentin hasn't admitted it of course.'

'That's strange. What could possibly have been his motive? Won't he be charged with wasting police time?'

She turned away to gaze out of the window, as though regretting she'd passed on this information.

'I don't know for certain - it's only what I heard. I daresay we'll find out soon enough, but I told you it wasn't my fault about the pistol.'

It was as though this film was jinxed. Derek's death, Robert's involvement with him, attempts to set Franklin up for the murder and now Linda was telling me the 'shooting' of Quentin had been a fake.

Then there was the business of her handing the wrong gun over to the police - needlessly it would seem, if Quentin's accident had been no more than another bit of play-acting. At least it explained why she'd swapped the pistols.

My inclination was to head straight back to Glasgow on the next ferry.

25

Linda's curious tale about Quentin and the fake blood continued to nag away at me for the rest of the evening, but any questions would have to wait. When I reached the flat at the Port, there was a note lying behind the door and reluctantly I picked it up, thinking it could only be from Robert. I sighed, reminding myself to get rid of this notion Robert had an interest in me, especially now I'd learned about his connection with Derek. With my current concerns about Simon, I was imagining something that didn't exist.

My resolution wavered as I went through to the living room clutching the note, feeling a pang of guilt about Simon. I hadn't been in touch with my husband for some days, except for the briefest of texts and resolving to contact him later, I decided to find out what Robert wanted.

When I sat down and looked at the envelope more closely, the handwriting was unfamiliar. Now intrigued, I tore it open and a single sheet of lightweight paper fluttered out, the kind people once used for airmail letters in the days before email and texting made such ways of communicating redundant.

The message was simple, stark. 'Meet me at the Quay at eleven tonight.'

There was no signature, no indication who might have sent it. My first reaction was to laugh. This was surely someone playing a joke. I scrutinised the envelope, but there was no clue as to the sender.

I stared at the sparse text of the letter and mentally ran through all the people I knew on the island.

If it wasn't Robert, who else in the cast or the crew might want to play this cloak and dagger game? I'd met Linda on the ferry, unless she'd delivered it before leaving. It had to be Tracy. She was worried about something, the tension between her and Franklin increasingly evident. She hung around him at every opportunity, but he ignored her, saying as little as possible to her, leaving when she entered the room.

I re-read the note, now wondering if it would be sensible to do as the writer suggested and meet at the quay. With Derek dead and the 'accident' to Quentin, (even assuming Linda's explanation was correct and not some kind of cover story) would it be safe? On the other hand, surely no one would want to harm me: I'd no information that might pose a threat to anyone.

That decided me. If I didn't take up the invitation, I'd be forever curious.

At the hour suggested, many of the residents would be tucked up in bed, and while many of the cast of *A Man Alone* would most likely be in the Coronet Hotel bar, the more industrious would be in their rooms rehearsing their lines for the next day to try to keep Sol happy.

I looked at my watch. There were still several hours to kill before it was time to head out for this strange assignation and try as I might, I found it impossible to settle. My mind kept wandering, going through all the possibilities and after re-reading the pages of my current book several times, switched on the TV to find it offered no better fare to keep my mind occupied.

As eleven o'clock approached, fatigue began to overtake me and I must have dozed off, only to wake with a start as the clock in the village chimed the hour.

Grabbing a jacket from a peg in the hall to ward off any evening chill I rushed out, hoping the mysterious writer of the note would still be waiting for me.

Down in the village all was quiet, except for sounds of laughter and merriment drifting out from the Coronet Hotel bar: very likely there'd be a few late arrivals on set in the morning.

Away from the last of the streetlights, down at the end of the quay, it was difficult to see anything in the gloom. Darkness had settled and under a sky heavy with clouds, with no moonlight, I had to pick my way down carefully.

It was no more than a few minutes past the appointed time, but whoever had sent the note had either decided not to wait, or else not turn up. Perhaps the sender had developed cold feet, or the whole thing might be what I'd originally suspected - a hoax.

With mixed feelings of relief and disappointment, I was about to turn away, head back up to the house and bed, when suddenly a figure stepped out of the shadows at the side of the stone shelter.

For a moment it was difficult to make out who it was, then suddenly the clouds parted and the moon sailed out to bathe the quay in a pale silvery light.

'Hello, Alison,' said Juliet. 'Thank goodness you've decided to come.'

26

'Why all the secrecy?' I said as Juliet drew me back into the shadows.

She put a finger to her lips and motioned me to follow her. 'Let's go round the other side of the bus shelter, out of sight,' she whispered.

The stone bus shelter is a little cream-painted building, set back from the road and appropriately decorated with colourful paintings of sailing boats, a welcome refuge when the wind is blowing in off the bay.

We sat down together and I shivered as much from concern as from cold. Here and there anchoring lights glinted from the boats hitched to the buoys in the inky waters of the bay, the sound of the tinkling rigging carrying across the quiet of the late evening.

'What's this all about, Juliet?' I racked my brains to think of a reason she might have asked for this meeting. She was the last person I'd expected.

Steadfastly avoiding my gaze, she continued to look out across the water in silence, watching the moonlight making erratic patterns as it drifted in and out of the clouds.

At last she spoke, her voice so quiet I had to strain to hear. 'It's about the film...' she began hesitantly, screwing up her face. To see the usually cool and collected Juliet lost for words was enough to convince me there was something seriously wrong.

My inclination was to say I wasn't the person to give advice about the film, but something in her manner made me hesitate. Better to curb my natural desire to jump into the silence, wait for her to continue. She must have some reason for this subterfuge of arranging a meeting at the quay in Port Bannatyne.

She looked down at her feet as though finding the sandals she was wearing of great interest.

'It's to do with the film. Don't you think there's something strange going on?'

'You could say that,' I began cautiously, wondering how she would follow this up. I thought, yes, you could call a murder, an 'accident' and an attempt to confuse the police "strange".

She went on as though I hadn't replied. 'I was intrigued rather than anything else when I first was offered the part. You know the story, you wrote it initially.' She looked at me and smiled as I nodded in agreement. 'Harriet was a renowned beauty of her day... and young. I fit neither of those categories.'

'Well, perhaps you're being a bit hard on yourself, because...'

'Oh, for goodness sake,' she interrupted impatiently, 'I'm not young and most of the parts I've played have been what are politely called 'character' parts. I didn't even have to audition for this one. My agent called me up, told me it was available and that was that.'

'I don't know enough about how the casting process works,' I ventured, trying hard to think of a form of words that wouldn't sound critical.

'Anyway, what could I do but accept the part, even though when I heard who was playing James Hamilton, I was tempted to turn it down.'

If all she wanted was someone to listen to her frustrations that was fine, but why ask to meet here at this time of night? We could have talked more comfortably over a bottle of wine and a decent meal at the Kingarth Hotel.

'I'm sure it's been no more than a run of bad luck,' I said, reluctant to agree with her if she was going to disparage Franklin Todd. Okay, he wasn't the nicest guy, but he had to think of his own career, his own future, also very much waning, if rumours were to be believed.

'Run of bad luck, darling? It certainly was for Derek. And the police seem no closer to catching the murderer.'

'Perhaps it's because they are trying to gather enough evidence to make an arrest. I'm sure they'll catch him...or her.'

'In the meantime, we're all under threat. Look what happened to Quentin. Call that an accident?' She shook her head. 'No, there's something not right.'

I was about to tell her what Linda had suggested about Quentin's 'accident', but hesitated. After all, this might be no more than another piece of gossip.

'You surely don't think this is anything to do with someone from the cast or the crew? It must have been someone else, perhaps an outsider who had a grudge against Derek, who targeted him. Yes, surely the police will find there's been something in his past.' Already I'd constructed a scenario exempting the employees of Pelias Productions from blame.

There was a gleam of malice in her eye as she replied, 'So why was Franklin's dagger used to kill Derek?'

'You don't believe Franklin had anything to do with it? Why would he start to injure or kill members of the production team. From what I know he was as pleased as Punch to land the part of James Hamilton.'

'Can I trust you?'

'Yes...' I said, wondering what was coming next.

'Your friend Robert has spoken to me - he also thinks there's something peculiar about the set up.'

'Robert?'

'Yes, he asked me a lot of questions about the production, questions much more searching than someone casually interested in film making would.'

'Why do you think Robert was quizzing you?' Ah, this now explained the meeting between Juliet and Robert at the Ettrick Bay tearoom.

Juliet shook her head. 'I'm not sure, but he did ask me...' She stopped and held up her hand. 'Wait a minute,' she whispered.

'What's wrong?'

'Shhh!' She stood up very quietly, scarcely making a sound in the stillness of the evening. On tiptoe she moved round to the other side of the shelter, facing the main road.

A moment later she returned and sat down beside me again, breathing heavily.

'My nerves are so much on edge. I thought I heard someone.'

'There's no one there.' Juliet was imagining things. What's more, I was beginning to feel chilled through, sitting on the stone seat, in the direct line of the strengthening breeze from the water. I stood up. 'Juliet, I'm going to head home and I think you should get back to the hotel. It's another early start for us all tomorrow.'

She grabbed the bottom of my cardigan.

'No, Alison, you don't understand. I've worked on other films, some low budget, some with money to splash around, and this one is completely different. There are too many interruptions, too many changes. Changes cost money and Sol keeps saying we're on a tight budget, so what's that about?'

'I think you might be making too much of this,' I attempted to calm her while disentangling myself from her grasp. 'We're all upset about what happened to Derek. That's all there is to it. Robert was only being friendly - he's that kind of a person.' I stopped, having exhausted my supply of platitudes.

She laughed, but it was a mocking laugh. 'Do you really think so? I've been in some very strange productions, but I can assure you this is the strangest one of all.'

A terrible thought crossed my mind as I looked at her biting her lip, wringing her hands. Was Juliet having some kind of a breakdown? If so, it was professional help she needed, not my sympathy.

I moved away, but now she rose, grabbing at my arm and her next words took me by surprise. 'Have you seen any of the rushes?' she demanded. 'Have you seen any sign of the linear editing work?'

'Why would I? Sol isn't likely to consult me. He's hardly involved me in any script re-writes, so I fail to see why he would want my opinion on the progress of the film.'

A cunning look crossed her face, confirming my opinion that she was suffering some kind of breakdown. 'No one has seen more than a few rushes, not even the sponsor... and that's the problem. Whatever's going on, I think Perry has something to do with it. He's like no cameraman I've ever met.'

This was such a ridiculous statement I had to turn away to hide my laughter. 'Oh, come on, Juliet, that's nonsense. You'd have to have some proof of that.' Then anxious not to upset her even more, I added, 'Yes, I agree it's all very haphazard, but perhaps that's Sol's style, the way he works.'

'I intend to get proof,' she said, ignoring my last words. 'And I want you to help me, Alison. You're the only sensible person on this project.'

If she was attempting to enlist my help by flattering me, she wasn't succeeding. I'd had quite enough of all this, thank you very much. At the moment all I wanted to do was get home to bed and away from this draughty spot on the quay.

'I'll have to go, Juliet. It's late and I've still several things to do, including phoning my husband.' That seemed a good enough excuse.

'I'm telling you, Alison, it's not all over yet.' She shook her head and gazed out over the water.

'I'll see you tomorrow,' I said, patting her shoulder awkwardly. 'Try to get some sleep. Everything will look different in the morning.'

She remained motionless as I walked up on to the main road and crossed to climb the hill at Quay Street up to Castle Street. At the top I stopped to look back, but she was nowhere to be seen. I hoped she'd take my advice: we all needed our reserves of strength if we were ever to finish this production.

As I reached the flat, near the Port Bannatyne Hall, I heard someone cough and stopped, looked around, but there was no one in sight. Another figment of my imagination.

It was a perfect evening, tempting to linger outdoors, in spite of the relatively late hour. The clouds had drifted off leaving the sky clear and in the distance the sound of the waves rippling on to the shingle of the beach was soothing, comforting, as they lapped beside the tiny boathouse, freshly painted for the summer and glinting in a wash of pale moonlight.

As I was about to head indoors, I caught sight of a shower of bright lights streaking across the sky and for a moment I was mesmerised, until I realised it was the Perseids meteor shower, fast and bright on this short summer night.

I stood for a while watching this dazzling display of tiny fireballs before reluctantly turning towards the main door, casting a glance back every now and then to marvel at yet another show.

What was that? The sound of a cough again, nearer this time. I flattened myself against the wall and slowly, very slowly peered round. It wasn't my imagination. There was someone lurking in the shadows. I pulled back and waited, scared to move.

Whoever it was, from his furtive movements it was clear he was up to no good. There was a tapping noise and very cautiously I put my head around the side of the building.

He was moving slowly underneath the streetlight, the shock of white hair and the sound of the walking stick making it clear it could only be one person - Sol.

I breathed a sigh of relief and was about to call out, when something made me stop. Had Juliet been right about the film production? Had Sol been spying on us?

While I debated my next move, Sol moved away, the tap, tap of his stick receding down towards the hotel. Too late now. I opened the door to the flat, thinking about Juliet.

She had a lot to put up with. She must find being an actress no longer in her prime particularly difficult and finishing the film, re-establishing herself as a star a challenge in so many ways. I'd try to catch her in the morning, suggest meeting up for a coffee, show I was sympathetic to her problems.

Unfortunately by morning it was already too late.

27

Once inside the flat, I was too tired to think about Juliet, too tired for anything and headed straight to bed. My natural inclination was to dismiss what she'd said as so much fantasy. In my short (very short) acquaintance with the cast of this film, I'd come to realise how self-centred they were, obsessed with making sure they were always in the limelight.

Even so, I hoped next morning would see me in a better frame of mind to consider what she'd suggested. Someone had murdered Derek, Quentin's 'accident' was strange indeed and there was little doubt about Franklin's involvement, albeit peripheral, in both events.

Pausing only to brush my teeth, I undressed quickly in the dark and crawled into bed.

In that not-quite-asleep phase, my mobile rang, jerking me awake and I put my hand out to grab my phone from the bedside table. Damn. It wasn't there. It must be in my handbag, lying on a chair in the corner of the room and I stumbled out of bed, tripping over the rug in the process, stubbing my toe and hopped over to the chair, trying to ignore the pain.

Too late - the ringing had stopped, but I scrolled through the 'phone calls missed' list to check the caller before deciding whether or not to answer.

Simon's name came up on the display screen and for a moment I stood staring at it, trying to decide if I should return his call or wait until the next day.

Pulling aside the curtain, I squinted at my watch in the faint light of the streetlamp, but finding it impossible to see properly, moved over to put on the bedside lamp.

Almost midnight. Not so very late. Best to phone him now, in case his call was urgent.

'Hello, Simon, sorry I missed you. How are you? Is there a problem?'

He chuckled. 'No, no. I didn't think about the time difference when I phoned. It's nothing that can't wait till tomorrow, though it would be good to speak to you for a change instead of always texting.'

A mild rebuke about my recent lack of communication.

'I've been so busy,' I blustered, 'and there seems to be so much waiting about to be called, then being told to report back the next day, I've had no time to think about anything.'

'Well, anyway,' dismissing my excuses, 'I wanted to let you know I'm almost certain to be home earlier than I thought. The project is all but wound up and any odds and ends I can manage by e-mail and conference call.'

In the silence that followed I tried to think of an encouraging reply.

'Alison, are you still there?'

'Yes, of course,' I hurried in. 'But where are you going to stay? Remember the house in Glasgow is let and we can hardly throw the American family out.'

'Why, I thought I'd come to Bute, come over and join you. From what you've said the place in Port Bannatyne will be fine for two of us.'

'Yes, yes, there's no problem,' I said. But of course there was. 'You realise I have to be out all day, on set or hanging around the set?'

'Don't worry about that. I intend to stop by the house in Glasgow and collect my golf clubs. I'm sure your American friends won't mind. I've become very rusty, need the practice. Anyway,' more briskly, 'I'll be in touch when I've finished here, made the flight booking.'

'That's fine.' I could hardly tell him this didn't sound like a good arrangement.

'I do miss you, Alison,' he said and almost automatically I replied, 'I miss you too.'

As he rang off I put the phone on the bedside table, just in case, and sat for a moment on the edge of the bed.

This wasn't what I'd planned. We had to thrash out our differences, but now wasn't the time and Bute certainly wasn't the place. In spite of the assertion he'd be playing lots of golf, we'd have to face up at some stage to our problems. Did I miss him? In some ways, yes. He was so stolid, so sensible. But was that enough?

Robert came to mind. There'd been no communication from him since I'd arrived back from Derek's funeral and I'd no idea whether to contact him or not.

There were so many questions I wanted to ask him. Why had he not mentioned he knew Derek? And why had he been asking Juliet all those questions about Pelias Productions and the film?

28

Some time around four o'clock the dawn light filtered through the thin bedroom curtains and I wakened to the sound of birdsong and the call of oyster catchers down by the shore, only to fall asleep again and miss the alarm an hour later.

We'd been instructed to be on set by six o' clock and after the briefest of showers, without stopping for as much as a cup of coffee, I hurried to the Coronet Hotel, arriving fifteen minutes late.

The reception area was deserted, as was the breakfast room. There was a new girl on the front desk and she said, 'I think they've all gone over to the Port Bannatyne Hall. Sol was muttering about needing to rehearse some scene or other.'

As I walked up to the hall I wondered what to say to Juliet. With time to consider her strange outburst, I had to admit it did seem odd Sol had decided to go ahead with the option on this film. True, my book on James Hamilton was of interest to tourists and people who lived on the island, but it was a slight volume of limited wider appeal.

So why make the film at all, engage me as an assistant screenwriter, and arrange to make it in this sleepy corner of Bute where they'd had to make use of the old barn along at Kames for the indoor shots? The sets wouldn't be difficult to construct in a studio and there were plenty of places in Scotland with more extensive facilities for film-making.

Through the open door of the hall drifted the sound of voices rising and falling in anger, their identity impossible to make out, but I quickened my pace to push open the main door and hurry in.

The floor was clear, the chairs that usually filled the space stacked against the wall and on the stage Sol and Juliet were standing opposite each other, their voices echoing in the empty space.

The rest of the cast and the crew crowded round, enjoying this display of temper, intrigued to see who was going to win the battle of words.

'I'm telling you, Juliet, there's no way we can hold up the production while you go off the island on some whim. We're going to be in trouble if we don't move this film along.'

'It's not a whim.' Juliet glared at him. 'I've told you it's something important or I wouldn't ask.'

'Then why can't you tell me what the problem is? I can't have folk dropping out on a whim.'

'All I need is one day, and not even a whole day at that. It's something I have to do. You know that as a professional, I wouldn't ask for this unless it was something urgent, really important.'

At the mention of the word "professional" Franklin snorted and Sol turned to glower at him before swinging round and waving his stick at the crew, all seemingly dumbstruck by this display.

'I don't know why you're all standing there gawping. Surely you've got something to do? I gave you your call sheets - check 'em out.'

A few of the crew shuffled away, shamefaced, but Franklin remained where he was and addressed Juliet. 'Actually, Juliet, we all need to know what your plans are. There are other actors besides you in this film, you know.' He raised an eyebrow. 'Unless of course you're being auditioned for some big part in a Hollywood movie and are keeping it all to yourself? Naughty girl.' He sniggered and wagged a finger at her.

Juliet gritted her teeth and for a moment it looked as though she was about to retaliate, but she quickly recovered her poise and said in a strained but calm voice, 'If you believe that at the slightest chance of a proper part in a real movie, I wouldn't leave you all in an instant then you are very stupid. I think you all have to understand that this film would be nothing without me, darling. It's my name that's going to decide whether or not it's a box office success.'

Now it was Franklin's turn to look enraged. 'You're nothing but an old has-been,' he shouted. 'I'm the one with the fan following.'

'Your mother and your mother's best friend don't constitute a "fan following", Franklin,' said Juliet in a sweet tone.

Sol moved between them. 'That's enough, for sure,' he said. 'Stop right there, folks. We've wasted enough time arguing.' He turned to Juliet. 'I'll reschedule this once, Juliet. But only once. We're far enough behind as it is, and the rest of the cast and the crew have to be considered.'

Juliet nodded.

'Sorry about that, Sol,' she said meekly. 'I wouldn't have asked had it not been important. If I hurry to catch the next ferry I can be back by early evening.' She waved a piece of paper at him. 'It's so important.'

Sol turned to Tracy.

'How will this affect the continuity, honey?'

'Should be fine as long as Juliet is back when she says. We're almost there.'

It was clear that every single person on the team was more than a little interested in the reason Juliet had to go to these lengths to get time off the island, but equally clear she'd no intention of telling them.

As she came up past me at the back of the hall, I caught her by the elbow. 'Anything I can do to help?'

She shook her head. 'Not really. This is something I have to sort out, and sort out quickly.' She turned towards Franklin and glared. 'Some people would be only too pleased to see me come to grief on this production.'

'You're wrong, Juliet. The success of this film depends on everyone working together.' Then realising how pompous that sounded, I added hastily, 'Not that you aren't very important, being one of the main stars.'

She looked at me and I saw she was trembling, her hands shaking as she clutched the piece of paper she'd waved at Sol.

I had an idea and moved close to whisper, 'It's nothing to do with what we discussed last night? You've not found out more?' Was her trip off the island to see someone, the sponsors perhaps, and tell them of her suspicions about the production?

She shook her head. 'It's personal business,' she said. 'Forget anything I said last night. That was no more than frustration with all the delays and false starts. Sometimes I think this film will never be finished.'

She gathered up her jacket, her bag, her copy of the script and her empty coffee cup from the table by the door and rushed out, awkwardly clutching them to her.

She'd no sooner left than I noticed she'd dropped the piece of paper she'd been waving at Sol and bent down to retrieve it, before hurrying out after her, but she was nowhere in sight. Best then to put it in my handbag; give it to her when she returned. Whatever it was, it was clear she didn't want Sol or anyone else to see it.

Over on stage, rehearsals had resumed and as Sol said, 'Sorry, Alison, you won't be needed today,' my intention was to take my book and head for Ettrick Bay, well away from this tense atmosphere. But as I slid the piece of paper into the zip pocket of my handbag I couldn't resist having a peep at the contents.

Then I wished I hadn't read it. All I'd done was leave myself with yet another difficulty about what to do, who to tell, if anyone. The note was from Robert and he wanted Juliet to meet him on the mainland.

29

Nothing worked out as planned. Not that day, nor that evening.

With Juliet off the island, Sol had decided to shoot the scenes with Franklin as James and Quentin as his older brother Daniel. He was trying to persuade James to give up the castle, return to Edinburgh and a much more stable life as a lawyer.

As I passed the props caravan, Quentin came walking out, dressed for his part. He appeared fully recovered from the episode with the pistol and ready for action.

All was not well. The door was wide open and I could hear Linda saying as she came out behind him, 'It wasn't originally meant for you, Quentin. That's why there's a problem about the fit.'

Here was someone else with a costume difficulty and I felt a pang of sympathy. There's nothing worse than having to spend hours on end in a garment that's the wrong fit, especially one from an historical era where the main aim seemed to be to make the wearer as uncomfortable as possible in the interests of style and fashion.

Quentin muttered something I couldn't quite catch, but there was no mistaking his tone of voice and he wasn't happy.

Then he raised his voice as he turned to face her and she drew back into the caravan.

'There's no point in telling me we have to suffer for our art, Linda. Let's face it, this is a rubbish production. We'll be lucky if most of it doesn't end up on the cutting room floor. Sol will probably try to sell it to one of those wretched TV channels that specialise in compressing a century of history into a half hour slot. Oh, I forgot, a twenty minute slot after you take out the adverts.'

I crept past, deliberately looking out over the water as if the boats bobbing there were of supreme interest, hoping to avoid being spotted.

Quentin came storming down the road with Linda rushing after him. 'Wait, Quentin,' she was calling, 'Sol will go mad if you turn up on set like that.'

'Best that he sees exactly what we have to put up with,' was the reply as Quentin strode off towards the minibus, but suddenly he swung round and noticed me standing there, trying to look as if I hadn't a care in the world.

'You agree with me, don't you, Alison? This production must be the worst yet.' He leaned forward and whispered in a conspiratorial way, 'If I didn't need the money, I'd be out of here like a shot.'

An unhappy crew, a mutinous cast did not make for a box office hit. I suspected Quentin was right - there was no way this film would make money, whatever Sol tried to tell us.

Meanwhile I was counting the days till my house in Glasgow would be free. Another two weeks to go, though it seemed as if I'd been away for an eternity. In his most recent phone call Simon had said it was taking much longer than anticipated to 'tie up' all the loose ends, and it now looked as if he wouldn't manage to join me before I left Bute.

Muttering something non-committal to Quentin, I edged away, saying, 'I'm not needed at the moment, so I'm going to head back to the flat and get on with my next project.'

Quentin laughed.

'Good idea, Alison. Just make sure you don't let Sol get his hands on it, whatever you do.'

This was the best excuse I could come up with. I didn't have a new project in mind, except for the vague few notes about St Blane and the ruined monastery on the island I'd started to fiddle around with earlier and I was in no mood to work.

The note Juliet had dropped continued to puzzle me and I'd taken it out of the zipped compartment of my handbag several times to read it. There were no details, just a time, an address and Robert's signature.

A fine drizzle had started, and though it wasn't likely to continue for long, there was no point in standing around getting wet. I watched the minibus depart, Linda gazing after it, arms folded, and crossed the road quickly before she could catch up with me to unload her frustration with Quentin.

The afternoon passed pleasantly enough: I finished my book, listened to the news and, when the sun at last made an appearance, sat out on the terrace, watching the comings and goings down on the seafront.

By evening I was ready for a change, bored with my own company, yet uncertain what to do, knowing Robert was off the island. Perhaps I should call him, try to persuade him to tell me what was going on, what this meeting with Juliet was about, given she had involved me as an unwilling ally.

As usual I put off the decision. It would be better to speak to him face to face once he was back on Bute, arrange to meet for coffee (provided I wasn't wanted on set at short notice, which was what usually happened).

Decision now made, I headed in a lighter mood down to the Coronet Hotel. Juliet would be back from the mainland and I could quietly return the note she'd dropped. What I was less sure about was whether to wait until she broached the subject of the contents or confess I'd read it and ask her to explain.

It didn't work out like that. When I reached the Coronet and headed in to the bar, it was to see Sol sitting beside Franklin and Quentin, their heads bent together in an intimacy that took me by surprise. For people who were more often than not at loggerheads, they seemed very friendly.

Perhaps they had patched up their quarrel or perhaps this was the way with those of an artistic temperament. Enemies one minute and bosom buddies the next. No matter how long I worked in this industry (not that I intended to be a player much longer) I'd never understand it.

As I approached I heard Franklin say, 'It's not too late, Sol. There's still time…' He tailed off as I approached.

'Hi, there,' I said, pulling out a chair. 'Mind if I join you?' As they were the only people in the bar at the moment, it would have been ridiculous to do anything else.

They stared at me in unison as though startled by my presence.

'Not at all,' said Quentin, but the impression was of a polite response and no more.

Unable to cope with the ensuing uncomfortable silence, I said, 'How did yesterday go? Did you get the scenes you wanted done?'

'More or less,' said Quentin, 'though there are a few rough edges to the takes. Isn't that right, Sol?' A sideways look at Sol. 'Of course if Perry hadn't disappeared for a couple of hours this morning…'

The director sighed. 'Yeah, we were delayed in shooting the scene where James throws the papers Daniel has brought back in his face. That didn't work too well.' He looked at his watch. He ignored the comment about Perry's absence.

'Oops, sorry, did I interrupt something?' A sudden realisation struck me that perhaps this had been the purpose of this little get together, to go over the scenes they had to re-do, ready for the next morning. 'How stupid of me. I'll leave you in peace,' I said. 'I was only trying to find out when I might next be needed.'

Quentin waved his hand. 'Sit down, Alison. Sit down. We've been over the scenes plenty of times and I think we're all more than a little wearied of it all.' He stood up. 'What would you like to drink?'

'A glass of white wine would be fine, thanks.'

Franklin held up his empty glass. 'Same again for me,' he said.

Sol glared at him and waved Quentin away. 'I think I've had enough.' The remark was pointed, meant to include Franklin, but there was no sign of it being taken to heart. Sol looked at his watch again and muttered, 'Damn it,' under his breath.

As Quentin went off to the bar, I said, as a way of making conversation, 'And the film is going well? You're happy with what's happened so far?'

'What? Oh, yes, we're doing fine. It's always like this. You have a plan in mind, a storyboard, but it never turns out as you think.'

Franklin snorted. 'That's not true of every production. Most of the films I've made…' then he corrected himself, 'most of the productions I've been involved in have been a bit more organised than this.'

Sol glared at him.

'Much depends on the folk you have to work with, with how…'

He didn't finish his sentence as Quentin returned with the tray of drinks.

'White wine for you, Alison, double scotch no ice for you, Franklin, gin and tonic for me…and nothing for you, Sol.'

In spite of first appearances, they were all so tetchy, determined to needle one another, it would be best to finish my drink quickly and leave. I wasn't desperate enough for company to stay here.

216

Sol either didn't hear or chose to ignore this barbed comment. He was looking at his watch again, then he shook it and put it to his ear.

'Something wrong with your watch, Sol?'

Franklin laughed.

'It's not what's wrong with the watch. That's working perfectly. For goodness sake, Sol. Leave it be. She's either here or she's not.'

'That's all very well, but the last ferry has gone from Weymss Bay. It's too late now.'

'Don't fret, she'll be back in the morning.' Quentin sipped his drink.

'I don't know why you're making so light of it,' Sol replied. 'You try to help someone, give them a bit of leeway, and this is how they repay you.'

Ah, that was it. They could only have been talking about Juliet. She was due back this evening, but there was no sign of her.

'Quentin's right. She'll come on the first ferry in the morning,' I said. 'I'm sure there will have been a good reason she's been held up.'

'That's all very well for you to say, honey, but I've got to get the scenes with her and Daniel wrapped tomorrow. There've been enough flubs in this film.'

'Yes,' Quentin smiled and took a sip of his drink. 'I've had a call from my agent to say I've been offered a part in the new, big budget crime series *The Family Game* and I have to be in Edinburgh by next week to start shooting.' He stressed the words 'new' and 'big budget' all the time looking at Franklin, who studiously ignored him.

This reaction didn't please Quentin and he continued, 'I've been told this will be the crime series to beat all the others. The producers are expecting it will be a MAMMOTH hit and of course I'll be VERY famous.'

I had to turn away to hide my laughter at this display of ego, but he finally achieved his objective and Franklin stood up, shouting, 'You! Very famous? Don't make me laugh. They've only asked you because you're cheap.' He tossed back the rest of his drink. 'I'm off out of here. There's no point sitting around with this idiot who has a very exaggerated idea of his acting skills.'

'For goodness' sake, stop behaving like a couple of spoiled children, you two. We've gotta get the scenes wrapped tomorrow and that's it.' Sol motioned Franklin to sit down again.

Franklin glowered. 'It's your fault anyway, Sol, for not providing enough crew. When Perry did turn up he had to rush through the scenes. I thought at one point the crab dolly was going to topple over, the camera come down and kill one of us.'

Sol shrugged. 'Calm down, guys? It'll all be fine.'

'It won't be fine if Juliet doesn't turn up for her scenes. I mean who could fill in for her. Unless,' turning to look at me and sniggering, 'you were to ask Alison here.'

It was now my turn to feel annoyed. 'Don't be ridiculous,' I was about to say, but decided there was no need. There were enough egos around here without adding mine.

Our little group split up, with Sol saying, 'Make sure you're on set by six tomorrow in costume and made up. We'll re-shoot those scenes with the two of you and hope Juliet comes over on the six thirty ferry. If not...' a shrug of the shoulders said it all. If Juliet didn't turn up, there would be a real problem.

'Didn't you try her mobile?'

'Yeah, yeah,' said Sol, looking at me as if I was particularly dim. 'I've called her cell phone, left messages, but she's not got back to me. There's nothing more to do. I'm off to bed.' He headed for the stairs outside the bar and called over his shoulder as he left, 'Remember what I said about an early start tomorrow, guys. No excuses.'

'I'm going out for a ciggie,' muttered Franklin, leaving me standing with Quentin.

'Do you think there is a problem with Juliet?'

Quentin shrugged, looking not the least bit interested.

'Who knows? I'd have thought she was perfectly reliable, but this lack of contact isn't good. If she doesn't come back there's no one to take her place this late in the film.'

'I'm sure it's all been a mistake,' I said. 'She'll be here in the morning. You'll see.'

I said goodnight and wandered out, keeping close to the wall to avoid bumping into Franklin as I headed up to Castle Street. The red tip of his cigarette could be seen glowing in the darkness at the end of the quay, but I was in no mood for chat. Working with these people was tiring me out.

As I walked slowly up the hill, I remembered that note Juliet had dropped. Now it was all beginning to make sense.

And the more I thought about it, the less convinced I became that Juliet would be on the first ferry in the morning back to Bute.

30

There was an air of suppressed excitement among the cast loitering outside the Coronet as I made my way down to the props caravan the next morning.

In spite of all my protestations about my lack of interest in acting, I couldn't help but hope there might be some action for me today, that the promised part as Harriet's maid (to date amounting to three scenes, at least one of which seemed destined for the cutting room floor) might actually happen. But then, anything would be better than hanging around here with the cast and the crew, unable to settle to any other work, expecting at any minute to be called.

Linda was already in the caravan, concentrating on changing Franklin into the character of James Hamilton, both of them squashed in to the tiny space which served as the make-up table, framed by large well-lit mirrors.

'Come in, Alison,' she said as she saw me, 'I'm almost finished here. Then it'll be your turn.' She rooted round the bottles and cakes of various flesh tones, the liner pencils, the brushes and sponges crammed into the old ice cream boxes she used to hold the make-up.

Yet again I marvelled at her skill as she deftly applied the make-up to create light and shadow, to transform Franklin's very modern face into one of a man of the nineteenth century. As she adjusted the close-fitting grey wig, I said, 'Gosh, Linda, you make that look so easy.'

'Lots of practice,' she said, smiling. People seldom complimented her: it was more likely they'd be arguing with her, annoying her about some aspect of their costume or make-up, but she kept cheerful in spite of these difficulties.

The expression on her face changed as she said, 'Everything would be well if people remembered to lock everything up. I think I might make this the only key,' she gestured to the key hanging on a chain round her neck.

'What's happened now?'

'Someone hasn't replaced Bobby's wig. He swears he left it here, but there's no sign of it. Thank goodness we don't need it for the moment.'

'I daresay it'll turn up.' This seemed a trifling matter compared to everything else that had happened, the problems actors had with the costumes they'd been allocated, myself included.

Franklin stood up, admired himself several times in the long mirror on the wall opposite and then turned to me. He pulled a lace handkerchief from his pocket and sniffed, no doubt as a way of keeping in character. 'So, Alison, you were wrong.' There was a note of glee in his voice. 'Juliet hasn't arrived back yet. There's been no word and no sign of her. Sol is furious. We're having to re-schedule the whole of today's shooting until he finds out what she's up to.'

'Surely to goodness she wouldn't have left everyone in the lurch like that, without a word?'

I didn't want to reveal she'd told me how much she valued this opportunity to make her name well known again after a spell in the wilderness. The less Franklin knew the better. He was a little too fond of gossip.

'I've no idea what has been going through Juliet's mind. How should I know? She's certainly been cagey of late, not concentrating on her part. So unprofessional of her. Leaving the rest of us to pick up the pieces.'

With this parting shot he left.

'Anyway I can't stand around all day talking to you. Some of us take the job seriously and I have to check with Sol when he wants me on set.'

If the situation hadn't been so worrying I'd have burst out laughing, but as it was there was no cause for mirth. Not when I thought about that note Juliet had dropped. I was in a quandary. Should I tell Sol about it? He would want to know why I hadn't mentioned it sooner. And would Juliet want others to know? Most unlikely.

Any opportunity for action was lost as Tracy popped her head round the door.

'Oh, good, Alison, you are here. Sol has decided to press on with shooting some of the scenes even though Juliet hasn't come back. I've put out a cattle call for the extras.'

Stunned into silence, I gazed at her, trying to decide how to reply. Surely Sol didn't want me to take over Juliet's part? We weren't the same height nor the same size and even with a wig to cover my fair hair and the possibility of some extra high heels there was no way I could pass for Harriet, in spite of the technology at Sol's disposal.

This situation was difficult for Sol, for all of them, but I'd no intention of making a complete fool of myself. I'd been called on to do that too often of late.

'Sorry,' I said, shaking my head vigorously, 'but that's absurd. Linda is very skilled, but even she couldn't transform me into Harriet.'

Tracy stopped suddenly at the door.

'What? What are you talking about, Alison? The part of Harriet has nothing to do with you. Sol is going to use you in the scene where Daniel leaves for Edinburgh and tries to persuade James to leave Bute, to come along with him. As Harriet's maid, you're asked to summon her down to hear the news.'

Red with embarrassment, I muttered, 'Yes, of course I knew that. I'm worried about Juliet, that's all.'

A gleam of understanding dawned in Tracy's eyes. 'Oh, I see. You thought Sol was re-casting you for the main part.' She laughed loudly, throwing her head back. 'Alison, how could you?'

Now Linda joined in the merriment, at my expense. 'That is a good story. Sol may be in some difficulties, but he is an experienced director. The idea of changing the leading lady almost at the end of the film...' and she too went off into gales of laughter.

This would be a good story for them to spread around over a couple of drinks later that evening.

224

Their mocking prompted me into action and gritting my teeth I said, 'Well, if Juliet doesn't return soon, what is he planning to do? Perhaps she's had a better offer, better than this farce of a film.'

This stopped them. The idea that Juliet might not return apparently hadn't occurred to them.

'Surely she wouldn't let us all down,' said Tracy, wiping her eyes and looking serious again. 'I mean she's an actress of the old school - the show must go on and all that, even though she's only a few scenes left.'

'Mmm - that's as maybe, but you couldn't call this a major production, could you?'

Having started to put the knife in, I wanted to continue to twist it. They might think I was a soft touch - but let them find out there was a limit even to my patience.

'Not come back?' Linda looked fearful. 'But that would make nonsense of the production. In spite of what Tracy says, there are a couple of scenes where her appearance is vital. There's no way we could go on with the film without her.'

'That's why it's important to have a scriptwriter on hand, 'I said, 'especially one like me who knows the story and can suggest changes that might work if necessary.'

Now it was my turn to flounce out of the caravan, head held high. Let them deal with that idea, I thought. Then a little niggle of doubt. Was it possible I was becoming infected with the atmosphere of the production? And becoming every bit as much a diva as the rest of them?

31

Sol went ahead with the day's filming exactly as arranged, but there was an air of tension on the set, a feeling something wasn't quite right, and not only the performances. It was as though Juliet's absence had created a void, even though the scenes being shot didn't feature her, having been the subject of a hasty rewrite.

'It's no big deal,' he'd shouted when Matt complained. 'This is a global enterprise - in many ways the less dialogue the better. You want it to be understood from,' he waved his arms around, 'from China to South America.'

A most unlikely event, but Matt went off grumbling to do as he was bid.

Sol handed Franklin a couple of pages of dialogue as we went into the room. 'I'd to change this a couple of times last night when,' he glared round as though searching for a culprit, 'Juliet didn't return.'

Franklin flipped through the pages.

'You expect me to do this now?'

Sol ignored him.

'We'll put the camera to get your viewpoint, be in tight and close up all the time so no need to worry about any overlap in dialogue.'

Franklin continued to read through the pages of the script, but his face relaxed into a smile as he reached the end. 'I see you've increased my lines,' he said.

'Yeah, yeah,' replied Sol. 'Harriet will be kind of inferred in these scenes, rather than actually present.' He raised his stick towards Perry. 'We'll do a couple of over the shoulder shots, keep the camera focussed on you and Daniel before dissolving into you. That'll avoid any problems.'

Perry nodded to acknowledge Sol's gesture and began to adjust the camera. 'Ready when you are,' he said. Perry had an admirably relaxed attitude to the process: it was almost as if the camera worked itself, so little attention did he pay to it.

Linda fussed around, adjusting the costumes, pulling at Franklin's cravat. 'That will have to do, in the circumstances,' she said.

'What's wrong now?' said Tracy.

Linda made a face.

'Franklin's original cravat seems to have gone missing.'

'For goodness sake,' replied Tracy. 'Not something else. How am I supposed to arrange the continuity if items keep going missing?'

'It's not my fault,' sniffed Linda. 'Anyway what's the problem? Surely James Hamilton would have more than one cravat.'

'N...n...not if he worked here,' muttered Matt, but no one paid any attention to him.

There was of course, no mention of what I would be doing or where I would be, but I'd resigned myself to being overlooked by now.

Matt wasn't happy. He adjusted his glasses then said, 'I really don't see why you asked me to adapt the dialogue when you'd every intention of changing it. That's what I'm paid to do. I'm n...n...not sure my union would be happy at the notion work was being taken away from me by an amateur.'

Sol whirled round and banged his stick on the ground saying, 'Yeah, yeah, there'll be loads of chances for you to do your bit, Matt. This had to be done tootsweet. We all know you creative types and how long it takes you to come up with the goods.'

Matt cringed at this onslaught, his fear of Sol's temper choking off any reply.

The stick Sol was using was even more ornate than the last one I'd seen. It appeared he kept a good supply of them or perhaps he wore them out, with all the banging and waving about he did.

Matt slunk off, huffing and puffing, stroking down his hair. We all knew Sol was right. This was an emergency and if Juliet didn't return soon, there would be plenty of scope for Matt's creativity. Perhaps too much.

Uncertain if this was the right moment, I crept round to stand beside Sol. 'Will you want me on set at the moment?' and was startled when he swung round to say, 'Of course we do. You have to fill in as much as possible. Only a couple of alterations, but it'll give you a speaking part.'

He handed me a page about one quarter filled with typescript. I glanced at it. There was certainly nothing much here to tax me as my lines consisted of, 'Very good, Sir, I will request milady to attend you,' give a curtsey and back out. Then later I had to come in and say, 'Milady is confined to bed with a bad attack of the vapours, she sends her regrets' and withdraw. Even these few words would break the monotony of standing around all day.

Sol strode on to the middle of the set, leaning heavily on his stick. 'First positions, folks and make sure you get the eyeline right.' He turned to Perry, 'Lights and camera.'

A sudden explosion of light illuminated the set as Harry ran forward, swinging the boom with the microphone at the end over the spot where Franklin and Quentin were standing. Harry's job was a more important one than he was given credit for - a clumsy boom operator could ruin a shot and Tracy, who'd been standing nearby, instinctively ducked.

'And action!' Sol grabbed Matt by the elbow and they went over to the far corner where there were two monitors, the black and white one side by side with the newly restored colour one, and positioned themselves to keep track of every movement.

The boy ran forward with the clapperboard and we were off into the scene with the brothers arguing over the best way for James to proceed.

'I am your brother. I only want what is best for you. You can't stay here while that woman spends all your money on her profligate friends in the den of iniquity that is Edinburgh.'

229

'She is my wife. That is a burden of responsibility I have to bear. I shall summon her down.'

This was my big moment, the one I'd been both looking forward to and dreading, but to my great relief I managed my dialogue on the first take.

Then I noticed a very curious thing. Franklin and Quentin weren't keeping to their allotted places on the black tape that criss-crossed the floor and several times Quentin placed himself between Franklin and the camera so that on at least two occasions, Sol had to leap up from his seat behind the monitors and shout, 'Cut. What the hell do you think you're up to, Quentin?'

'Trying to keep in shot, of course,' said Quentin smoothly as though he considered Sol was making a fuss about nothing.

'He's bloody well trying to upstage me, that's what he's doing. I knew it was a mistake to hire him. He's always been like this.'

Quentin whirled round, his face contorted with anger. 'What exactly are you suggesting, Franklin? It isn't possible to upstage you, because you don't do anything. You think because you've had a part in some two bit soap opera that everyone should cow tow, should allow you to take centre stage all the time. Well, I for one am not impressed.'

'Stop it, stop it, you guys. Calm down.' Now it was Sol's turn to be angry as he placed himself between them. Meanwhile the rest of the cast and the crew looked on with amusement, relishing this welcome diversion.

'Are you professionals or not? I'm the director and what I say goes. It's not up to you. All you gotta do is deliver the dialogue, though even that seems to be beyond you at times. Now let's take that from the top and this time keep to the script and to the positions.'

He stomped back to join Matt at the monitors, swearing under his breath.

Tracy pulled her mobile out as it vibrated and stared at the screen, then gestured to Sol that she was going out to take a call.

Fortunately this time the scene went off without a hitch. Whether Franklin and Quentin had been shamed into sticking to the script and the movements as they'd been told I wasn't sure, but once Sol sprang forward shouting, 'Cut, brilliant take,' they turned away from each other without a word, unkind or otherwise.

Tracy came running on to the set as the technicians were wrapping up, breathless and tearful and made straight for Sol. ' It's the police,' she said, 'they want to speak to you at once.'

Sol shook his head. 'Must be some news about Derek's death, I guess,' he said.

'No, no,' said Tracy, gulping, 'it's not about Derek. They've found Juliet.'

'Why would the police be c …c…coming along to tell us that?' Matt sounded scornful.

'Because,' sobbed Tracy, 'because…she's dead.'

'What happened to her? Has she had an accident?'

'No, no,' hiccupped Tracy, 'her body was found early this morning by a dog walker, hidden in the Skeogh woods. He heard her phone ringing and went to investigate.'

'What on earth was she doing there?' Matt grabbed Tracy by the elbow. 'S...s...she was supposed to be going up to Glasgow.'

Tracy turned her tearstained face towards him. 'I've no idea, but it looks as if her death wasn't an accident.'

32

It was no surprise when we heard the news. Not only had Franklin no alibi for the time of Juliet's death but word was she'd been strangled with his missing cravat.

When she heard this, Tracy broke down and confessed she'd lied about him being with her the night Derek was killed. There was almost a collective sigh of relief when he was arrested, led away, loudly protesting his innocence.

'I didn't do it, I'd nothing to do with either death,' he said over and over again. Trouble was, no one believed him.

'I knew all along the police suspected him,' Linda said. 'Only they didn't have any conclusive proof. Though why Tracy agreed to give him an alibi for the time of Derek's death I can't fathom.'

'It was only because she believed what he told her - that he was innocent.'

'That ...and the fact she was besotted with him. As if Franklin would have any time for someone like Tracy.'

Strange how everyone was now eager to say how they'd suspected all along he was guilty, not only of Juliet's death, but also of Derek's.

'As for that story about being with Tracy... I never believed it - it was preposterous.' Quentin was almost gleeful as he spoke till he saw the look of anger on Linda's face. 'I mean,' he blustered, 'it's all too awful, no matter what the truth.'

This feeling of relief didn't last long. With Franklin under arrest and Tracy taken in for questioning, Sol was left with an even bigger difficulty and in the hotel bar the rest of the cast and the crew huddled round the tables, talking in subdued tones.

'How will you manage with the leading man gone?' I said timidly, sitting down beside Sol. After all, I did have a stake in this.

'Yes,' said Matt who was passing our table carefully balancing a tray with several drinks. 'Your leading man and your leading lady both out of action. How will you finish the film now?' He sounded more assertive than I'd ever heard him. Was this because there might have to be a major re-write and Sol would have to rely on him?

Quentin had heard this exchange, judging by his grin as he came sauntering over to join us.

'I guess it'll be down to me to pick up the pieces now. Some of the scenes will have to be re-written to give me more to do.'

Sol glared at him, ignoring me and Matt. 'Don't talk crap. We're at the editing stage, only a few more scenes to shoot. All the scenes with James Hamilton and his wife are over.' A pause. 'Or we can end without seeing James Hamilton again.'

He stood up and shouted over to Linda. 'Let's get cracking with the last few scenes. We only need Quentin and,' whirling round, 'you, Alison. Come on guys, we have to get it together, there's work to do. We can get this film wrapped up, then we can all get on with our lives.'

Possibly there was a way of pulling all those disjointed scenes together and the secret was in the editing. So although a thousand questions rattled around in my head, I kept silent.

There was a buzz of noise as Sol stopped speaking. One or two of the crew remained seated, finishing up their drinks, but most of the cast stood and hurried out of the bar.

'Hey, w…w…wait a minute, what about all these drinks,' called Matt to the rapidly disappearing backs.

'Help yourself.' Linda turned round just long enough to comment to Matt, before she too made a rapid exit.

He plonked the tray down on the nearest table, none too carefully and the drinks sloshed and spilled off on to the table as he ran to catch her up.

Over in the make-up caravan there was a curious flatness about proceedings, none of the usual banter and high spirits. It was more a determination to see it all through, finish as best we could and resume our lives, no matter what the outcome for Franklin.

Outside the caravans the minibus which took us from venue to venue was sitting waiting, its engine running, and Quentin and I, now costumed and made up, scurried to find seats.

Mick the driver gazed at us as we boarded. 'Heard the terrible news. I guess the film will have to be abandoned? Your main actor's been arrested?'

'Of course not. We're well ahead,' said Quentin, making it clear he had no intention of indulging in further discussion, much to Mick's disappointment. 'Let's get a move on.'

'Right oh!' Mick sighed, realising there was no chance of gossip.

The drive to the set took no more than a couple of minutes and I gazed out of the window as we drove along the shore past the tenements and the rows of holiday cottages.

Already the Port was slipping back to its sleepy state - the public toilets stripped of their false frontage as a backlot, the Submarine Memorial garden back on view, the notice boards of the Petanque court again facing the front, the park with its swings, slide and play tractor once more resounding with the laughter of children.

Sol had arrived before us, earnestly talking in to his mobile. As reception on this part of the island can be difficult he kept moving backwards and forwards, lifting the phone in the air, swinging round to try to catch the signal and when he turned to face us it was clear he was very unhappy.

'Another problem?' Quentin arched his eyebrows, almost as though he was hoping the answer would be 'yes'.

Perry sidled up, whispering, 'The producer has been on again. Sol has tried to explain our difficulties, but the sponsor wants us to enter the film for the *Silver Hart* awards.'

'Isn't that a good thing?' Visions of being able to tread the red carpet in Hollywood came flashing into my mind, though as a lowly assistant scriptwriter I might not merit an invite.

Perry chewed his bottom lip before explaining, 'It's an award night in Glasgow where producers and directors get to showcase a specially made excerpt from the answer print, the first print of their latest film.'

Visions of rubbing shoulders with a galaxy of Hollywood stars, of smiling and waving on the steps at the garlanded entrance left me, to be replaced by a vision of heavy rain, and a very soggy red carpet, somewhere in Glasgow on a windy November evening.

Quentin's face took on a look of exhilaration.

'Brilliant. A proper showcase for the film. The *Silver Hart* Award is one of the most prestigious there is. You should be pleased about that, Sol.'

Sol turned to glare at him. 'It's all a lotta work for very little. This isn't the kinda film that wins awards. Anyway, there's still editing to do. I've no idea if we'll manage to finish it in time to enter. Places, everyone.' He strode off into the main room where the final scenes were to be shot.

'Surely even Sol can manage to come up with twenty minutes of edited film,' muttered Quentin, as he strode on to the set. 'This is a major opportunity for some of us.'

In the end Matt had made some adjustments to the script and in the new version Daniel had arrived at Kames Castle to make a final effort to encourage his brother to come back to Edinburgh, only to find Harriet had gone off to the continent and James had died.

As the maid I had to impart the immortal words, 'Forsooth, sire, you are too late. Milady Harriet has gone and my master was interred yesterday.'

This seemed a ridiculously sudden ending to the film with Daniel, apparently not the least put out by the sudden demise of his brother, saying, 'I must pay my respects at his grave,' before heading off to Cnoc-an-Rath. Perhaps the longer this production ran, the more he was becoming accustomed to sudden deaths, so a fictitious one made little impact.

'The final scene will pan away from you, Quentin,' said Sol, gesturing with his stick, 'and then out over Kames Bay before the credits.'

The crew headed up towards the little copse where James was buried, lugging the camera and a glow light, together with a collection of ditty bags, while Quentin came up behind them, practising a suitably moody look for the final scenes.

About to say this version was completely inaccurate, I decided not to interfere. The film had to be ended in some fashion and with neither Juliet nor Franklin now available, it was as good a way as any.

Here was yet another puzzle, one even more important than these problems with the script. It was difficult to understand why Sol was making this film, investing all this time and money, if he thought it would be a flop.

33

It was with some reluctance I faced the final couple of days with the cast and crew of *A Man Alone*. In spite of all the difficulties, an uneasy camaraderie had grown up among us, a friendship cemented by the terrible occurrences of the past weeks. All credit to Sol and to the rest of the team that they had gone ahead, completed the filming.

Now any success was all down to the final edit and the compilation of a 'short' for the gala performance in Glasgow. No one had any expectation of winning the *Silver Hart* award but the occasion would provide an opportunity to dress up, and for those more intent on a film career than I was to network, to hope the next offer would be the big opportunity, the career changing role.

Besides, there remained the problem of Robert. He had returned to the island and was hanging around for much of the time, sitting with us in the Coronet, taking every opportunity to engage people in conversation. I'd not yet found a suitable opportunity to ask him about his meeting on the mainland with Juliet, though from the information circulating on set, she'd never made it off the island.

'Anyone would think he was w...w...writing a book about the film,' said Matt on another occasion when he'd appeared in the bar, hailing all and sundry as if he was a long established member of the team. Matt's short spell of bravado had disappeared and he was as nervous as ever.

'Stop it, Matt.' Linda put on her frostiest look. 'He's a friend of Alison - a good friend, isn't that so?' Her raised eyebrows gave an indication of what she meant by "a good friend" and I replied, 'Just someone from the past I caught up with recently,' mindful of the speed with which rumours spread.

Simon hadn't been able to make his planned trip to the island. 'There seem to be many more loose ends to tie up than I imagined,' he'd said gloomily in our last phone call. 'I will most certainly have to settle for returning to Glasgow instead of joining you on Bute.'

'Plenty of golf courses there,' I'd responded. 'Besides, I'll have a lot more time now this film is finished.' No matter what the inducements, there was no way on earth I'd be persuaded to be an assistant scriptwriter or any other kind of scriptwriter ever again, not even if Hollywood did come calling.

Knowing my time with Pelias Productions would soon be over, I gritted my teeth, joined in the final events and counted the days till my house in Glasgow was free again. I vowed my next trip to Bute it would be for a holiday, nothing more.

'Fancy a last meal out at the Kingarth?' Robert came up behind me so stealthily he made me jump.

'Fine. Good idea.' This might be the chance I was looking for to ask him about Juliet and what he was really doing on the island.

Linda arrived as Robert headed out, waving to everyone. She stared after him. 'Why does he want to know so much about the film? He's forever nosing round here asking questions.'

'I suppose he's curious.' I shrugged. 'He's on his own on the island and perhaps he's not used to the solitude, likes company, or perhaps he has a professional interest.' It was clear no one knew about his connection with Juliet.

Linda sniffed, but she didn't appear convinced by this explanation.

'Well, if that's the case, he's learned enough about making this film to make a sequel.'

I laughed at the expression on her face.

'He's been involved in this kind of thing for most of his academic life. He was a lecturer in accountancy, specialising in media, for many years.'

'Mmm. That's as maybe.' She wandered off, leaving me gazing after her, thinking about what she'd said. Was Robert's interest purely because he was bored, had found island life too relaxing? But why arrange to meet Juliet on the mainland, unless, unless... could there have been the beginnings of a romance there?

The question of the awards ceremony now loomed large. Important as it was to so many of the cast and the crew, it was the only topic of conversation and the set buzzed with questions. Who'd be invited? Was there any chance of winning? Given the level of excitement, Sol had decided to make the best of it.

'It's the sponsors' decision,' said Quentin, trying to disguise the fact he was as eager as any of us. 'They want to have something for their money and this will be an opportunity to show what the film is about. There are so many films jostling for a place these days and sponsors increasingly want the credit for backing a production, I'm not the least bit surprised Zach wants to make a bid for the award.' He laughed harshly. 'Not that we stand the slightest chance of winning. Not with this production. It will go straight to DVD - you mark my words.'

This was what I suspected, but it was bad news to have it so carelessly confirmed and I couldn't help but experience a feeling of disappointment. The only consolation was I'd be able to purchase the DVD as soon as it was released and, if it really was terrible, be forewarned.

The only remaining problem was my meal with Robert. I wanted to ask about his links with Juliet, why he'd asked her to meet him in Glasgow but couldn't think of a way to broach the subject. I hoped he'd be willing to tell me... and have a good explanation.

'I'm off for the evening,' I said to Sol with no intention of waiting for a reply and left before anyone could ask where I was going.

As I drove over to Kingarth, I tried to sort out the questions that were troubling me. One loomed larger than the rest. If Juliet had planned to go off the island to meet Robert, why had the police not pulled him in?

'Are you staying on here for a while?' I asked Robert as we sat in the restaurant waiting for our order, knowing full well what the answer would be, but trying to find a way in to what I really wanted to ask.

'Yes, I've another week or so at the cottage and then I'll head back over to the mainland for the rest of the summer.'

'I'll be going in a couple of days,' I said.

'I'll miss you, Alison,' he said, hastily adding, 'I'll miss everyone. It's been interesting to meet the people involved in making the film.'

'Yes, it's certainly been an experience,' I admitted.

Robert had been a good friend during my time on the island.

'It's very strange about poor Juliet,' I ventured. 'No one has any idea why she had to go over to the mainland so suddenly...and why she was murdered before she could leave the island.'

Robert gazed at me, not betraying by a flicker that he was the writer of the note Juliet had dropped.

I tried again. 'It must have been something really important to make her ask for time off when filming had reached such a crucial stage. It all seems very strange.'

He shrugged. 'I daresay the police will find out eventually.' He drained the last of his coffee. 'Do you need any help packing tomorrow?'

It was evident he'd no intention of revealing his hand and unable to ask him outright about the note, perhaps because I was afraid of what he might say, I declined his offer. 'I'm sure I'll be fine - I have the car.'

'Another coffee?' He gestured over to the waitress.

While pretending to search for something in my handbag, I watched him furtively. Robert knew more than he was saying, a lot more, but it was obvious he had absolutely no intention of telling me, no matter how many questions I asked.

34

On the last evening before we all went our separate ways, a dinner had been arranged in the Coronet for everyone who'd worked on the production, but in the end there were so many people, when you added in all the extras, it was agreed the hotel would do the catering for a buffet in the Port Bannatyne hall.

One thing led to another and before we knew it the local Ceilidh band had been hired and a drinks licence arranged with the council.

The invitation was extended to anyone in the Port who wanted to come along "to make up for all the inconvenience they've had to put up with over the past few weeks" as Sol put it. There were a few mutterings about this being unfeeling in the circumstances, but in the end the event went ahead as planned.

Tracy had been released by the police, but warned she'd be called in again and as most of those attending were locals unaware of the details of the events of the past few weeks, there was much merriment, fuelled by a generous supply of alcohol and excellent food.

It was as if, now all the traumas and problems of the production were over, everyone wanted to forget it all and enjoy the moment.

We left at midnight with much hugging and kissing and promises to keep in touch, promises which were unlikely to be kept.

Tracy was tearful, the black mascara she favoured making little rivers down her cheeks as she hiccupped, 'I'll soooo miss you all. You've been wonderful.' She started to sob, until Perry came up and took her by the elbow. 'For goodness sake, Tracy, get a grip.'

'But I sooo… don't want it all to be over,' she wailed, trying to disengage herself and not succeeding.

'You shouldn't have had so much to drink.' Perry showed no sign of sympathy for her plight. 'You'll regret this in the morning.'

With a final tug, she pulled away.

'What do you know? I know all about you, you and Derek.'

Perry went pale and backed off. 'What are you talking about, you stupid girl.' He turned to the rest of us, now transfixed by this real life drama. 'It's all nonsense. She's had far too much to drink,' he said. 'Can you get her up to bed, Linda?'

Linda moved forward.

'Come on, Tracy. Let's go.'

Tracy shouted, 'Get away from me. That's what you wanted to do with Derek, wasn't it Perry? Get him into bed, but he turned you down? I saw you with him the night before he died - you wouldn't let him out of your sight.'

Even those residents of the Port who had been heading home, trying to avoid involvement in this drama, stopped to look and listen, fascinated by this disclosure.

Perry whirled round to face the rest of us, but he was laughing rather than angry.

'She's talking nonsense. Why would I have anything to do with Derek? It's all lies. The police interviewed me, they had no problems with my alibi.'

Whatever the truth of his story, he was saved from any further questions as Tracy gave a great wail and slid to the ground.

'For goodness sake, someone give me a hand here. She's passed out,' said Linda. 'There's no way I can manage her on my own.'

Matt and Quentin rushed forward, one on each side and attempted to haul Tracy to her feet but her size and her inebriated state made their efforts futile.

'We'll have to t…t…try to waken her, rouse her from this stupor,' said Matt, wiping his brow from the effort of trying to move Tracy. 'Else we'll be here all night.'

'Someone fetch some water,' said Sol who had come out of the hall in time to witness the spectacle.

'You're not going to throw water over her?'

'Of course not. All we have to do is get her to her feet and then we can manage her up to her room and into bed.'

'There's n…n…no way I'm putting her to bed,' said Matt in horror.

'I'll get her into bed, if you can help move her back and upstairs to her room instead of all standing around talking,' Linda said, glaring at him.

Just then, Quentin came out of the hall carrying some cold water in an ice bucket, with a tea towel draped over his arm.

'Will this do?'

'Give it here.'

Sol soaked the towel and began to wipe Tracy's face. Whether it was the cold water or Sol's vigorous scrubbing, after a few minutes of this treatment Tracy moaned and moved.

Determined not to waste the opportunity, Matt and Quentin grabbed an arm each and with Linda lending a hand at the rear, heaved and hauled Tracy the short distance down the street towards the Coronet.

'Perhaps I should go and help?' I said, but Robert put a restraining arm on my shoulder.

'Leave them be. She'll be fine.'

The others began to drift away in little groups, whispering. Plenty of fuel for local gossip with this event.

Robert and I were left at the door as the caretaker locked up for the night, no doubt relieved the drama was over and he could go home. We stood together under the glow of the streetlamp, an awkward silence between us.

'I suppose I should head back,' I said.

'Yes, I daresay Tracy will have a thumping headache in the morning.'

I couldn't leave like this.

'What do you think she meant about Perry and Derek? Do you think there's any truth in what she was saying? I can't believe the police haven't picked this up, if it's true.' Then I said, 'Sorry, Robert, why would you have the answer.'

He looked thoughtful.

'Mmm. I'm not sure what's been going on, Alison. If this was the case surely the police would have had him as a suspect for Derek's death. They interviewed everyone several times, so it's more than likely Tracy is muddled…and very drunk.'

'My thoughts exactly.'

'So,' he went on as if I hadn't spoken, 'he must have had a good alibi.'

Then he appeared to dismiss the problem and said, 'Let me walk you up to your house for the last time.'

'But how will you get home?

He gestured towards the seafront.

'My bike is chained to the railings down by the slipway. It's a lovely night to cycle back.'

'In that case,' I said firmly, 'off you go.' I held out my hand. 'It's been good seeing you again, Robert. Perhaps we'll meet up again in Glasgow at some point.'

He ignored my outstretched hand and leaned forward to kiss me on the cheek.

'If only things had been different, Alison.'

This wasn't what I wanted to hear and lingering in the moonlight was not a good idea. I grabbed his hand and shook it vigorously. 'Keep in touch,' I said and turned and almost ran along Castle Street and didn't pause till I reached the flat, aware he was standing looking after me. I closed the front door and leaned back against it with a sigh, trying to catch my breath.

Damn! With the way the evening had ended there'd been no chance to ask Robert about his contact with Juliet, not to mention his knowing both Sol and Derek. He was involved in some way with the events of the past few weeks, but I'd no idea how.

All in all, it had been quite some night, especially with Tracy's sudden outburst at the end. There was probably no truth in what she'd said. These people were so given to high emotion, and the amount she'd had to drink hadn't helped.

Perry was a dark horse, someone who was close to Sol, but you didn't see him around much, he didn't make much effort to socialise with the others and I couldn't see him as Derek's lover somehow.

Enough thinking. Time for bed with the pleasant notion that tomorrow night I'd be back in Glasgow in the comfort of my own house. As I stood at the mirror in the bathroom, brushing my teeth, realising the first thing I should do when back on the mainland was make an appointment with my hairdresser, I suddenly wondered, how come Tracy knew so much?

35

Next morning I was packed and ready to leave bright and early, having spent most of the night going over and over everything that had happened since I'd first joined Pelias Productions: the death of Derek, the 'accident' with Quentin and the discovery of Juliet's body in the Skeogh woods... and where Robert fitted in to it all.

There was something at the heart of this, someone had a good reason for wanting the production to be disrupted, but for the life of me I couldn't think who or what it might be. All they had in common was that they were working on the same film and with so many careers riding on its success, no one would want the film to be a flop.

Then again, none of this was any longer my concern. I'd soon be back in Glasgow, ready for the next project. I'd put aside the story of St Blane for the moment and had decided to concentrate on something nearer home - the story of the tobacco merchants of Glasgow. It seemed a lot safer than anything I might write about Bute at the moment.

Out on the little terrace I lingered over coffee, watching the few clouds whisper across the blue sky. It promised to be another fine day, but I had to make tracks for home.

With a sudden realisation time was slipping away and I had to hurry, I rinsed out my cup, locked up the house and with some difficulty stowed the rest of my luggage in the passenger seat of the car. All that remained was to drop the keys off at the estate agents and head for the ferry terminal.

I drove slowly down Castle Street to pause at the parking bay on the seafront. The two large caravans belonging to the production company had gone and the bus shelter was no longer cordoned off, once again restored to its proper use.

Even the seagulls seemed happy, the young with their brown speckled plumage strutting about on the foreshore, reclaiming their territory now they were no longer being harassed by one or other of the crew.

The Coronet Hotel was also strangely quiet. Most of the large contingent from Pelias Productions had departed, leaving only a few visitors, but I was certain it would soon be busy again.

With a sigh, I put the car into gear and prepared to drive off. This would be my last glimpse of Bute for some time. No doubt I'd be back, though not immediatcly. But as I prepared to leave, Tracy came lumbering out of the Coronet Hotel and rushed over, waving frantically and knocking loudly on the car window as soon as she reached me. I slid the window down. What on earth had happened now, I thought, cross I hadn't driven straight to the ferry terminal instead of lingering in the Port.

'I'm in a hurry, Tracy,' I said. 'Whatever your problem, there's nothing I can do to help. I want to catch the next ferry.'

She pulled back in astonishment and then leaned in again, her face wreathed in smiles. 'What makes you think that there's a problem, Alison? I wanted to catch you before you went off the island to give you the good news.' She showed no signs of the distress of the previous evening.

'And?' There was no longer anything about this production that might concern me, good news or not, unless Sol had decided my contribution was worth some extra money.

'Well!' A deep breath, making her ample chest heave, 'We've had word from the organisers of the *Silver Hart* Award. *A Man Alone* has been shortlisted as one of the entries for this year's award.'

All I could think of saying was, 'That's brilliant. I'm sure you'll all be pleased.' She was right, of course, it was pleasant to be leaving the island in the wake of good news.

She laughed. 'No, no, you don't understand how important this is, Alison. This is one of the most important awards for independent film makers. To win this sets the seal on your career. Sol has been working hard for so many years with not even a nomination. If we win this, or even because we've been nominated, it's bound to propel him to greater work. And if he wins...wow! The film world's his oyster, as they say.'

I hate to admit it, but my first thought wasn't how great for Sol or the rest of them, but how awful for me if my performance as Harriet's maid was to be seen by a wider audience than anticipated. Realising how selfish this was, I forced a smile.

Tracy was so excited, it would be unkind to cut her off. Besides she was firmly stuck half way in through the car window and until she withdrew I wasn't going anywhere at all.

'So what exactly happens?'

'Well.' She took a deep breath. 'The award ceremony takes place in a few months in the Endymion Hotel in Glasgow. It's quite a night, very glamorous. You'll have to buy yourself something really smart, Alison.'

'Me?' Now it was my turn to be astonished. 'Why would I have to buy something?'

She tutted.

'Because you've been invited of course. We're all invited. Although the award will go to the director of whichever film wins, it's an award for the whole team.'

'I'm not sure I'll be able to manage,' I said. 'I've other commitments.'

'Nonsense. You have to be there. It's important we show solidarity, support Sol. Especially after what happened to the stars of the film.' She hesitated. 'I hate to say this...'

But you're going to anyway, I thought.

'I hate to say this,' she repeated, 'but because of what happened to Derek and to Juliet, we may find some of the judges are, how to put it, more kindly disposed towards us.'

She withdrew from the window and straightened up, rubbing her back.

'Ouch. So you see, Alison, you have to clear the decks when your invite comes through.'

'Fine, I'll look out for it. Now I really must go, Tracy.'

She wagged her finger at me.

'Remember we're still a team and you must be there.'

Released from her grasp, so to speak, I accelerated away along the road beside the shore, still thinking about the implications of what she'd said. A bad choice as it turned out. The High Road at the fork beside the War Memorial would have been a better option, as I found myself stuck behind a slow moving tractor.

Past Ardbeg, the road widened and the driver motioned me to overtake him, but precious minutes had slipped away and I had to slow down again as I reached the outskirts of Rothesay, conscious of the speed limit.

After handing in the keys, I drove past the Pavilion, the Discovery Centre and turned left at the traffic lights to arrive at the ferry terminal, but as I drove into the lane the ferry slid away from the pier and out into the open waters of the Firth of Clyde.

I switched off the engine and sat back. The ticket collector came over. 'Bad luck,' he said, 'you missed that one by a whisker. Never mind, there's another one in forty five minutes.'

There was no point in wasting the best of the day sitting in the car and, after locking up, I headed into the town, busy with day trippers, many of them walkers judging by the backpacks they sported. At Guildford Square the tourist bus was ready to depart, packed with excited travellers eager for a tour of the island.

I headed for the Electric Bakery to buy a sandwich then came back down to the front to lean on the railings, watching the boats come and go in the Marina as I thought about the *Silver Hart* Award. It would be churlish to refuse the invitation and if it was the gala event Tracy had suggested, it might be fun.

In spite of her enthusiasm, I didn't see how *A Man Alone* would win. Then I felt a pang of guilt at my disloyalty. No matter what my feelings were about them, about what had happened, about my disappointments at the way everything had worked out, I would go to the award ceremony and support them.

In the meantime there were more pressing matters: I had to go back to Glasgow and meet up with Simon.

36

The weather was exceptionally fine for November, one of those West of Scotland evenings when a day of rain has unexpectedly cleared and the skies are washed a deep blue, peppered with stars. The Endymion Hotel in the centre of Glasgow, the location for the *Silver Hart* Award ceremony, wasn't one of the largest hotels in the city, but its boutique intimacy was ideal for the occasion.

I hadn't seen or been in touch with any of the members of Pelias Production since we'd left Bute and had to admit to being curious about meeting up with them again.

Simon muttered on about what had happened during my time on Bute. 'Is it not possible for you to take on a job without becoming involved in mayhem?' he said.

'If I could answer that, I'd be able to avoid any problems, 'I replied, a little too tartly.

He wasn't so much upset as worried.

'It's only that I fret about you, about what might happen. Let's be honest, you've had some pretty narrow escapes.'

'Nothing that happened was my fault,' I said. I understand his anxiety. Many years ago, when we were both young and living in London, we were involved in a very bad car accident. Simon escaped unhurt, but for some time I suffered memory loss and occasionally he has a concern there might have been a more permanent legacy of the accident. 'All those difficulties are behind me,' I smiled. 'I'm absolutely fine now.'

There had been no more news about Franklin since his arrest, but there must have been enough evidence for a strong case against him.

Those days of filming began to take on the feeling of a bad dream, something that had happened to another person, so it was almost a surprise when the stylish silver and black invitation plopped through the letterbox one morning in late September, inviting me to the *Silver Hart* Award ceremony in November.

'Of course you should go,' said Simon, when I expressed doubts about accepting.

Since Simon's return from America our marriage had resumed a more tranquil state: if not the soul mates we had once been, we were able to live together more or less harmoniously. I'd tried to forget about Sol and the rest of them, hadn't been in contact with Robert, my only desire to resume a normal life.

I hesitated. 'I don't have anything to wear,' I said. 'Least not anything suitable for an occasion as grand as this one.'

'Alison, treat yourself to a new outfit. I'll pay for it.'

It was a difficult offer to refuse. He was right, it would be the final chapter in the saga of *A Man Alone*, would enable me to draw a line under this disastrous venture into the film world. 'All right,

I'll accept the invitation. It will be good to say a proper goodbye to them all.'

'Who knows,' he said with a wicked grin on his face, 'You might even be there when they win the award.'

This was a step too far. 'There's absolutely no chance of that,' I said. 'The only reason Sol agreed to present the extract at this ceremony was under pressure from the sponsors.'

'Didn't you tell me the others were keen because there had been so little money invested in the film?'

'Yes, that's what I heard. There are incentives to make a film of this kind in a place like Bute where there are employment and other opportunities for the locals. I think that was one of the reasons Sol chose this script - and Bute - in the first place.'

The night of the award ceremony saw me decked out in a gown of shimmering pale blue satin, not at all the kind of thing I'd usually wear and certainly not a dress I'd have any other occasion to wear. Deborah had insisted on coming with me to choose it, something I regretted as I gazed at myself in the mirror. What's more it had cost a lot of money and I noticed Simon bite back a comment when presented with the bill. Deborah pointed out, 'This is a once in a lifetime experience, mum, so you shouldn't stint on cost.' Words I repeated to Simon. Wasn't this kind of event all about going over the top?

What's more the invite was only for me, Simon wouldn't be there to hold my hand and give me a bit of courage, so it was even more important to have the right outfit, one that would give me confidence.

But when I drew up at the entrance to the cinema in the black limousine Pelias Productions had kindly provided I realised that far from being over-dressed my gown was the most understated there. There was indeed a red carpet and Linda, leaning heavily on Quentin, had arrived before me. At least I think she was looking to him for support but when I noticed the position of the cameras I wondered if all she was doing was trying to upstage him. Nothing had changed.

A small crowd had gathered outside, but it was apparent they weren't for the most part diehard movie goers but passers-by who had noticed the hustle and bustle and had stopped to investigate.

'Come oan,' I heard a tall heavily tattooed man say to his bright blonde-haired companion, 'never heard of ony o' them.'

'No hang on.' She chewed heavily on a wad of gum as she spoke. 'There jist might be someone famous turn up.'

But after a few minutes he succeeded in luring her away.

'No idea who any of these are.'

Perhaps if Franklin had been there it would have been different. Soap stars are almost universally known, but the rest of us fell into the category of 'unknowns' as far as the onlookers were concerned.

The only photographer was sullenly snapping away, no doubt displeased at this assignment ruining his evening when he could have been in the pub, or settled with a beer in front of the television.

'Have you heard anything about Franklin?' I whispered to Matt as he suddenly appeared beside me, while I blinked to recover from the bright flashlight.

He shook his head.

'Only that he's still in custody. T...t...terrible thing to happen. I can scarcely believe it and of course he's been suspended from *Heart and Home* with immediate effect.'

This was bad news. Personally I didn't understand how Franklin could be responsible, but there was the evidence of Franklin's cravat, the missing dagger and the false alibi provided by Tracy.

By all accounts Derek hadn't been popular and he'd fallen out with several members of the cast, but what motive could Franklin have for killing Juliet? The loss of the leading lady would jeopardise the whole production.

We crowded together for more photos and then the burly young man at the door, attired in a plush maroon velvet suit, ushered us in to the foyer.

The organisers had certainly made a splash. There were several films in contention for the *Silver Hart* award and each had a separate display made up by the PR team. It took me a few minutes to find the stand for *A Man Alone*. Whereas the other films had lavish hoardings, with the main stars and the titles prominently displayed, our film placard was a tiny affair, in black and white.

What's more, it was the only historical film among the contenders. The others were two thrillers, two romances, and something which looked like a Sci-Fi film, judging by the costumes the cut-outs of the stars on the hoarding were wearing. Our chances of the award looked slimmer than ever.

'Looks good, eh?' said Matt. 'T...t...that black and white on our display makes it stand out from the others.'

Yes, indeed it did, but for all the wrong reasons.

'Quite a lot of competition,' hissed Tracy who had come in behind me. I turned round and stopped in my tracks, trying to conceal my astonishment at her outfit.

A long, low-cut dress in glittering stripes of red, gold and black was accompanied by a long feather boa, also in red and she was wearing the highest heels I'd ever seen. Given she was so tall to start with, this ensemble added at least another three or four inches to her height. Her elfin crop had grown a little over the summer and she sported a series of colourful hair slides in an array of matching colours.

She smiled. 'Do you like my outfit? I had it made especially. I wanted something that would get me noticed.' She did a twirl, almost toppling over as she did so and only saved herself by clutching on to the handrail on the stairs. 'Oops, guess I need a bit of practice in these shoes.' She regained her composure. 'Well, what do you think?'

For a moment I struggled to find something appropriate to say. Her outfit most certainly made her stand out: it was impossible to ignore her in this array of colours and fabrics. 'It's absolutely stunning,' I said tactfully.

This seemed to please her. 'Yes, I'm delighted with it,' she said without a trace of humour.

My own outfit, which I'd thought was rather over-the-top, now seemed dull in comparison and I followed her as she mounted the stairs, like a beautiful galleon in full sail.

The main room was a blaze of light and as we went in I was momentarily dazzled by the welcoming glow of the array of crystal chandeliers. From the vantage point of the doorway the room appeared to be an endless vista of round tables, covered by bleached white cloths set with fine china and an array of glasses glittering in the light of the candles in silver candelabra.

At the far end of the room a stage had been constructed. The film screen took up most of the back wall, but the curtains on either side twinkled with a pattern of silver stars and in the centre of the table sat the silver award, beautifully fashioned as a hart raised on its hind legs as though to flee, mounted on a silver plinth.

There was a faint aroma of mingled perfumes in the air, pleasant enough not to be overwhelming in the cool air wafting from the fans set into the walls around the room.

We spied Sol standing near the stage, deep in conversation with Zach. Waiters were already approaching the tables, champagne bottles at the ready. Ah, well, we might not win anything but at least there was the prospect of an enjoyable night ahead.

Sol came sauntering over with Zach and sat down. He didn't seem to mind our table was at the back of the room, far away from the main action. He was the most relaxed I'd ever seen him.

'What's the format?' I hissed to Matt, seated on my right.

'We have a few opening speeches, which with a bit of luck will be mercifully short, and then we see the extracts from the competing films before the judges announce the winner.'

I took a quick sip of my champagne, coughing as the bubbles went up my nose.

'Steady on,' said Matt, but it was a good-humoured remark rather than a reproach. Tonight Matt was even more carefully groomed than ever, but he had given in to the inevitable and his hair was cropped short, close to his skull, the comb over no longer evident. What's more, he seemed calm and composed, all traces of his nervousness gone.

There was a flurry of excitement on the stage and the lights dimmed before a series of spotlights illuminated the man in an over-tight black tuxedo standing by the podium next to the award.

'This might be our big moment,' Zach whispered to Sol who shook his head replying, 'Don't get your hopes up. The competition's pretty fierce.'

'Good evening, ladies and gentlemen,' the announcer said. 'And welcome to the fifth *Silver Hart* Award ceremony. We've had a great number of entries this year but we've managed to whittle them down to those you'll see extracts from tonight. Without further ado, I'll pass you over to Bertie Russell, our compere for the evening.'

Out on to the stage to rapturous applause strode Bertie Russell, someone I did recognise from his many television and film appearances, accompanied by the inevitable blonde in a tight pink sliver of a dress glittering with a wealth of sequins.

As he began his introduction, I thought about Franklin and Juliet. They should have been with us, part of the celebrations. Instead Quentin and Tracy were sitting in the places of honour, flanking Sol and Zach. Quentin looked relaxed, smug, occasionally turning round to acknowledge a greeting.

As though by some strange insight, I thought again about Quentin's part in what had happened. Franklin's arrest meant he was the man in the limelight, would be first choice for any publicity events. But why kill Juliet? Even though it had all been hushed up, why risk that sham accident unless it was to further discredit Franklin? None of it made sense, not from what I knew about Quentin.

With a start, I came back to the present as Bertie said, 'And now for the extracts from the films, to give you a flavour of our difficulty in selecting the winner. As you know, each company was asked to submit a half hour extract, a synopsis of the film and information on the stars. We won't be showing the entire submissions - we haven't ordered enough wine for that.' He paused for the obligatory laugh. 'But we will show a short excerpt of each.'

The curtains swung back to reveal the full size screen and the voiceover announced the first film as Perry leaned over to whisper to Sol. The director looked startled for a moment, then shook his head and put his finger to his lips.

This part was interesting, though the quality of the films was incredibly varied. One of the thrillers, if the excerpt was anything to go by, was noisy and violent and one of the romances could only be described as cringe making.

A Man Alone was fifth on the list and while I looked forward to seeing which extract Sol had selected, my hope was it would be one that didn't feature me.

As the film rolled it became clear the chosen scene featured Franklin and Juliet inside the great hall in Kames Castle as Quentin as Daniel tried to persuade his brother to return to Edinburgh and his post as a lawyer. And horror of horrors, there I was in the background as the lady's maid.

It was one thing to see yourself in the rushes on a small screen but here on the full size screen in colour the effect was quite different. Supposed to look demure and servile, instead the expression on my face could only be described as sullen and I'd obviously forgotten at one point to obey Linda's injunction to stay as still as possible and always face the front. As Quentin, in the role of Daniel, left the room, I turned to watch him and you could see my costume straining at the seams. I put my wine glass down, immediately resolving to go on a diet.

The rest of the evening passed in a blur. All I could think about was my screen performance, if you could call it that, wondering why I'd ever allowed myself to be persuaded to take on the role of Harriet's maid.

As the final credits on the last entry rolled and the curtains closed, there was a burst of applause and an excited buzz in the room as Bertie stepped forward to announce the winner.

Thank goodness we'd soon be out of here. Our film was very unlikely to secure distribution, but in some ways going straight to DVD would be worse, because all my family and friends would want a copy. My cheeks burned at the thought of it.

The room had suddenly gone quiet. The speeches were over, now all that remained was for the winner to be chosen, to say a few gracious words of acceptance and then we could have dinner and go home. I might even make an excuse and leave early.

Zach nudged Sol, but he was ignored and Sol resolutely faced the front.

Bertie racked up the excitement. 'Soon one of you will be the proud owner of this beautiful *Silver Hart.*' He held up the trophy, to allow us to appreciate fully this spectacular piece of solid silver.

He moved over to the dais and lifted the envelope, silver of course, and with an elaborate show slowly opened it before smiling at the expectant audience and saying in a loud voice,

'And the winner of this year's *Silver Hart* award for the best production is...' a long pause... 'Pelias Productions for *A Man Alone*.'

There was a stunned silence in the room. Tracy screamed, Quentin stood up and applauded, closely followed by Zach, Matt said, 'I don't believe it,' while Perry looked shell-shocked.

While everyone else was looking at the stage, waiting for the winner to claim the award, I glanced over at Sol. The expression on his face wasn't one of delight, or even shock. It was a look of fury.

37

With some urging from the rest of us, Sol eventually got to his feet, ignored his stick and made his way a little unsteadily towards the podium. There were a few murmurs at his unsteady gait, but I knew it was nothing to do with the champagne. He'd hardly touched a drop. There was something familiar about the way he was walking, but I couldn't think what it was.

For a moment, as he reached the rostrum, it looked as if he was about to faint, but he grabbed the edge of the lectern and steadied himself as he accepted the award from Bertie.

'Well done, Pelias Productions,' said Bertie, grinning broadly as he handed it over. 'It's a beautiful award, made of solid silver, so if times get hard in this economic climate you can sell it.'

A titter went round the room, but this failed to amuse Sol and he remained stony-faced as he clutched the award to his chest.

'I'm completely taken by surprise,' he said. 'I'm sure there are more worthy winners than our little film. But I thank you guys for making this award to Pelias Productions.'

With that he hurriedly left the podium and wove his way through the crowd back to our table, steadfastly ignoring the cries of 'Well done,' and 'What a great result,' from the other tables.

He slumped down beside Quentin who leaned across and grabbed the trophy. 'I don't think that was at all gracious, Sol, as an acceptance speech. If you don't want it, this award would look very good on my mantelpiece.'

This speech seemed to rouse Sol from his lethargy and he grabbed it back. 'It belongs to Pelias Productions.'

'Only joking, only joking,' said Quentin, raising his hands in mock self-defence.

There was something strange about Sol's attitude. He should have been delighted at this coup. After all, no one had expected *A Man Alone* to be placed anywhere in the list, let alone win.

The rest of the evening passed, not in a spirit of exhilaration but one of sombre reflection. It was as though Sol's mood infected us all and everyone toyed with, rather than ate, the meal that followed the presentation, delicious as it was. There was an air of unreality, of expectation something would happen, but quite what I couldn't imagine.

I kept looking over at Sol, trying to remember what it was that was so bugging me, but no answer came to mind. Perhaps it was all my imagination.

There was no opportunity to talk to any of the others about my concerns as the table was besieged by well-wishers, by those who wanted to be seen and photographed with the winner.

'We'll be on all the front pages tomorrow,' said Tracy in delight. 'I'm so pleased I bought this outfit. It cost a bomb, seemed a bit extravagant at the time, but it's going to be worth every penny.'

'I doubt YOU'LL be on the front page, Tracy,' sniffed Quentin. 'Your part in the production was very much backstage. The Press don't usually make a fuss of helpers.'

Tracy glared at him, no doubt about to make an angry reply, but at that moment another reporter edged over to the table and she quickly switched from a frown to a generous smile. 'Can we help you?' she said sweetly and stood up to block the others from the accompanying photographer's view. 'I'm the PR person and I can assist you with any publicity you might want. This is very much a team effort, that's why it's been so successful.'

Her ploy failed to work. Zach for one wasn't going to let his role be high-jacked and as he, Quentin and Matt jostled for position to talk to the reporter, I stood up and said, 'Off to powder my nose,' and slipped away.

Of course no one acknowledged my leaving: they were all far too busy vying for prime position.

Instead of heading for the Ladies, I went out into the cool of the foyer. The burly minder in the maroon velvet suit was still there, pacing backwards and forwards. I went over and stood at the open door, taking in deep gulps of fresh air.

'Leaving already?'

'No. I'm trying to have a moment or two of quiet away from the noise and bustle of the room.'

'I know what you mean. It all gets a bit too much, all that stuff, especially when well lubricated with wine.'

I was seriously tempted to leave, call a taxi and go home, but a sense of reluctant loyalty to the group made me hesitate. This would be the last time I'd see them. Wild horses wouldn't persuade me to become involved ever again in a film production, not as a scriptwriter and certainly not as a member of the cast.

'I'd better go back in,' I said, shivering a little in the chill air. 'They'll be wondering where I am.'

'At least you've something to do. I'm stuck out here for the duration.'

'Do you do this all the time then?' As a way to earn a living it must be incredibly boring.

He laughed. 'Only when I can't get a film or TV role. I'm an actor, specialising in 'heavy' roles, but those parts seem few and far between at the moment. Hence my role as a doorman for this event. At least I get to be a bit close to the action and who knows,' jerking his head towards the room, 'someone might spot me, offer me a part.'

As a way of gaining employment, even in the film world, this seemed a dodgy proposition but all I said was, 'We won tonight,' and then corrected myself. 'Pelias Productions won with *A Man Alone*.'

'Ah, that would be Sol Makepeace's film? I've worked with him before.'

This conversation was becoming interesting.

'He doesn't seem too happy to have received the award. Everyone else is delighted, but from the expression on his face when he was called up to the stage, you would think he'd been placed last.'

'That doesn't surprise me. Now he might actually have to finish a film, get it out there.'

'What on earth do you mean? This film is finished. He submitted a short because that's how this competition is organised, to allow the maximum number of entries. Some of them will still have to be edited, but from what I know Sol has completed the entire film. All that he needs now is a distributor and that will be easily done, now he's won the award. I guess distributors will be knocking on his door, vying to take *A Man Alone* on board.'

He tutted and wagged his finger at me.

'I can see you're not a real movie person. You've no idea. If Sol finishes this film, it will be the first, the only one.'

Before I could question him about this strange statement, Tracy came rushing out. 'Oh, there you are, Alison. We wondered what had happened to you. We need everyone back in the main room for a photo. Do hurry, the champagne will be finished if we're not through soon.'

I allowed her to tug me gently by the arm out of the foyer and into the stifling heat and excitement of the main room.

What had the doorman meant by saying Sol hadn't completed a film? If it was true, what might his reason be?

38

The next day, in spite of all my protestations about not having any interest in the film world, or even the *Silver Hart* Award, I couldn't resist purchasing several newspapers.

'Anxious to see yourself in the news after all?' Simon was in an exceptionally good humour. He seemed pleased and relieved to be home again.

Any questions about his time in America were met with a vague reply or, 'I'll tell you about it later,' kind of response, making me suspect all hadn't gone according to plan and there was no mention of a return visit.

Whatever the reason, the experience had made him more appreciative of home. 'Ah, a decent cup of tea at last,' he said regularly.

How long it would be before he again got itchy feet I'd no idea, but meantime each day saw an improvement in our relationship, we were more at ease with each other. I'd even managed to slide a bit about Robert into the conversation, quite casually, without giving too much away.

'It was strange meeting someone from so long ago and entirely by chance.'

'He was also on Bute?'

'Mmm...yes, he was on holiday there and we met up a couple of times.'

Simon didn't seem interested, nor the least bit concerned about Robert and I quietly let the subject drop.

That still didn't solve my difficulty about how to get in touch with Robert again, to persuade him to tell me what he knew, but the problem was resolved easily in the end, because Robert phoned me later that afternoon while Simon was out playing golf.

'Fame at last, Alison? I saw the story about the *Silver Hart* Award in today's newspaper.'

'Hardly fame for me,' I laughed, 'though I daresay Sol and the others will benefit from it.'

'Still, you must be pleased you were involved. Any idea when the film will be released?'

'No, actually no one has said anything about it to me.' Now that Robert had reminded me, I wondered why there had been this silence. 'In fact, there seems to be some doubt if it'll be released at all.'

'There's nothing in the newspapers and I thought that a bit strange, that Sol would want to cash in on the publicity.'

There was nothing more I could tell him, but as he was about to ring off, I said, 'I wouldn't mind a catch up sometime.' I hoped that sounded vague enough to throw him off the scent, to disguise why I really wanted to see him.

To my disappointment, he didn't suggest anything definite and instead replied in a casual way, 'Good idea. I'll give you a call.'

I put the phone down, cross I hadn't been more assertive and suggested a time and a place to meet, but if he didn't call me back soon, I'd get in touch with him.

Back in the lounge I went through the newspaper articles again, more carefully this time and almost an hour and a pile of newspapers later, I sat back in disbelief. Robert was right. There was absolutely no mention of a release date for the film. Most of the articles centred on interviews with Quentin and there was much made of the 'unlucky' episode of the two murders.

The only answer I could come up with was that Sol had decided in the circumstances not to put the film forward for distribution, but then again, surely it would be better to put it out and acknowledge the contributions of Juliet and of Derek. And the sponsor would want to recoup some of the money he'd invested, more likely now with the success at the *Silver Hart* awards.

With only a moment's hesitation, I lifted the phone to call Tracy hoping she might have some news. Easier said than done, because I couldn't remember where I'd put her number, but eventually, after a bit of searching, I found it.

No point in beating about the bush, better to go straight to the point.

'Tracy, I've looked through all the newspaper articles and I can't see anything about a release date for the film. Have you any info?'

There was a silence at the other end and then she said, 'I think there's been a small problem about that, Alison.'

'What kind of a problem? What do you mean, Tracy?'

Another silence.

'Tracy, are you still there? Surely all this publicity has been good for the film?'

'Well…it's not as simple as that.'

Her evasive replies were beginning to annoy me. 'For goodness sake, Tracy, tell me what's going on. I can't bear the suspense. I was part of this production as well and I've every right to know what's happening,' I said, trying hard to keep calm.

'It's nothing to do with your part in the film, Alison, nor even the rest of us. The trouble is…' there was a gulp as if she was trying to hold back tears, '…the trouble is, there is no film.'

39

At first I thought she was making a mistake or being over-dramatic.

'What do you mean there is no film? We saw it on screen at the award ceremony. It even won the *Silver Hart*. How can there be no film?'

Then light dawned.

'You mean it's not all been properly edited yet? There's still work to do before it can be distributed?'

Trust Sol not to have completed the editing. This explained why he'd looked so unhappy at winning. He'd known that he wasn't yet ready to go ahead with it, that his laziness meant all the publicity attached to winning would be wasted. By the time the film was completed, the opportunities to cash in on the *Silver Hart* award would have well and truly dissipated.

'So when will it be ready? Surely there's some indication now of a completion date?'

'No, you don't understand. THERE IS NO FILM. All that we have is not much more than the extract you saw at the ceremony.'

'So what happened to all those scenes we shot, all the days of working in Port Bannatyne?' This couldn't be true.

On the other end of the phone Tracy was snivelling and I held it away from my ear for a moment before saying, 'Will you please explain?'

'There's nothing to explain. I knew there was something odd going on - all those changes of script, all the behind the scenes conversations. I was supposed to be the PR person, but Sol told me nothing.'

As she spoke, her tone of voice became more and more anxious. It was hard to believe what she was saying, that all the time and effort, not to mention the money invested in the film, was for nothing. There had to be some rational explanation.

'So what happens now?'

'I guess the sponsors will be keen to see something for their money - though how, I've no idea.'

'Why don't you ask Sol straight out? He does owe you that much, given how much work you did.'

'If I could find him. There's no answer to his mobile and his landline is dead.'

She sounded so desperate, so upset, the words were out of my mouth before I thought about the consequences.

'Have you tried going round to his flat? I don't mind going with you, if that would help.'

Then I thought, for goodness sake, Alison, why are you getting involved in this? It's nothing now to do with you. But some sympathy for Tracy, plus a natural curiosity, drove me to continue.

'That would be a good idea.' This suggestion of a plan of action seemed to calm her. 'When do you suggest we do this?'

'There's no time like the present. The sooner we go to see him, the sooner we'll have some answers.' And before I have second thoughts about this whole mad idea, I muttered.

We agreed to meet later that afternoon in front of the Kelvingrove Art Gallery and Museum in the west end of Glasgow. Sol, according to Tracy, lived up in Park Circus, a fine semicircle of large Victorian houses that had been converted to offices, but in recent years had been converted back again to houses in a spectacular fashion. Because of the size, many were subdivided into flats and it was in one of these Sol lived, on the top floor in a flat that would have magnificent views over the park and the city beyond.

We walked together through Kelvingrove Park, crowded at this time of year with families with young children enjoying the unexpected bonus of some late sunshine, the children whooping as they ran about kicking up the last of the autumn leaves. On the bowling green it looked as if the final match of the season was being played, judging by the concentration on the faces of the players and the tennis courts were full, a little queue of young people lounging on the benches, waiting their turn to play. It was as though everyone was aware this spell of fine weather wouldn't last, that winter was on its way.

Tracy wasn't her usual communicative self. Too much hinged on this meeting with Sol and we made our way through the park in silence, each of us lost in our own thoughts.

At the far end we climbed the steep flight of steps leading up to Park Circus and stopped at the top while Tracy and I, if I'm being honest, caught our breath.

'What number is it?' I asked, gazing round at the semi-circle of tall houses in front of us.

Tracy swung off the backpack she was wearing and dumped it on the ground before beginning to scrabble through the front pocket. 'Yes, here it is,' she said eventually, pulling out a crumpled piece of paper and smoothing it out. 'Flat Three Left, number Twelve.'

'A few doors down,' I said beginning to walk in that direction. 'Come on, we're almost there.'

She trotted after me, cramming the paper with Sol's address on it back into her bag.

We stopped outside number Twelve and stood for a moment before going up the steps to search for the buzzer for Sol's flat.

'This must be it,' said Tracy as she leaned on it heavily, 'though there's no name beside the number.'

We could hear the sound echoing down the communal hallway, but there was no response.

'Try again,' I urged her.

'You try,' she replied a little crossly. 'He may not be at home.'

That was something which, rather foolishly, we hadn't considered. I pressed the buzzer again. Still nothing and I walked back down the steps.

'Where are you going?' said Tracy in some alarm.

'I'm trying to spot which are the windows of Sol's flat,' I said, crossing to the pavement opposite and craning my neck to count the floors. 'It must be one of those two at the very top of the building.'

Tracy came over to join me and we stood for a moment looking up at the windows on the top floor in silence.

There was little we could say, because it was very unlikely Sol lived here. All the windows at that level were completely filled by posters with TO LET in large letters on them.

'How can that be?' Tracy was puzzled. 'I'm sure this was the number we were given.' To confirm it, she pulled out the paper with the address on it. 'Yes, this is certainly the right place and the right flat.'

'Perhaps we should buzz someone else in the block? They might be able to give us some information. He might have moved recently.'

'Good idea.' We crossed back to the block of flats and before I could stop her, she pressed the buzzer for the first flat on the right on the ground floor.

We had more success here, because within a few seconds a quavering voice replied, 'Yes, who is it?'

Tracy leaned close to the entry phone. 'Sorry to trouble you, but we're looking for Sol Makepeace. He has a flat on the top floor.'

'Who did you say?'

'Sol Makepeace,' shouted Tracy so loudly I had to back away.

'Just a moment,' said the disembodied voice. 'I don't hear too well through this thing. I'll come out.'

A few moments later there was the sound of the door being unlocked and a little white-haired lady peeped round, suspicion written all over her face. She was hanging on tightly to the door, no doubt so she could slam it quickly if we turned out to be dubious characters. Behind her I caught a glimpse of the elaborate ornate plasterwork and original terrazzo tiling from the time when this was a family house.

'Where did you say your friend lived?'

'The flat on the top floor.'

'I don't think so. You must have the wrong address.'

She made to close the door, but quick as a flash, Tracy wedged her foot in the doorway.

'Are you certain? He's been living here for some time as far as I know.'

'Nonsense. That flat was rented by the McKinlay family for years and the only one left is Mrs McKinlay. She went in to one of those care homes six months ago and the flat has been vacant ever since. There's no lift here so it's awful hard to let, all those stairs, you know. It was the servants' quarters once, when this was a fine family house.' Now that she had decided we weren't burglars or worse, the old lady had become chatty.

But interesting as the history of the house was, it wasn't the reason we were here.

'Thank you, anyway,' I said, pulling Tracy away and the old lady stood looking after us as we went back down the steps.

'Why did you do that?' said Tracy crossly. 'I was about to ask her if we could have a look round, just in case.'

'In case what, Tracy? You heard what she said. Sol doesn't live here, never did live here.'

'So what's going on? Why would he tell us he lived here when he didn't?'

A question to which I had no answer.

40

We stood looking at each other, equally perplexed about what to do next.

'It can't be, it can't be,' said Tracy over and over again as if this mantra might make everything come right.

'There's no point in waiting around here,' I said, taking her by the arm. 'That little old lady was suspicious enough of our motives.'

A twitch of the net curtains at the ground floor flat window convinced me it would be better not to linger here. Wherever Sol lived, it wasn't in Park Circus.

'Is there anyone else in the cast or the crew who might know more about him?' This was the time for a practical approach to the problem.

'No idea.' She looked dazed, as if she couldn't quite believe what was happening.

'Tracy,' I repeated patiently, 'Is there anyone else who would have this kind of information?'

'But I'm the person who deals with all of that.'

'No matter. Think of one of the others who know Sol well.'

'I suppose we could call Matt. He worked closely with him, being the scriptwriter.'

This wasn't the time to be reminding Tracy Matt hadn't been the only scriptwriter on the production.

'Well, let's give him a call.'

She struck her forehead.

'Oh, wait a minute. Matt's gone off to another job, scripting a corporate video being filmed in Portugal.'

I racked my brains.

'There must be someone who knows what's been going on? What about Perry? He and Sol seemed to be pretty close from what I could see.'

Tracy nodded.

'Yes, they go back a long way. They've worked on a number of projects together.'

'Let's try Perry then.'

'Okay.' She pulled her phone from the pocket of her jacket.

'No, not here. Let's walk down to the café at Kelvingrove. We can get a decent cup of coffee there and you can phone Perry in comfort.' Instead of hanging about here in the street under the suspicious gaze of the little old lady I thought, as I saw the curtain twitch again.

We made our way down back through the park, each of us mulling over this latest episode in the strange world of Pelias Productions. Perhaps Tracy had the wrong address for Sol and the answer was as simple as that. Most of the people who'd been involved with the film hadn't inspired me by their efficiency. Anyway, it would be a simple matter to look up Pelias Productions in the Register at Companies House, find out more about them.

'How did you get that address for Sol?'

'He gave it to me,' muttered Tracy. 'I had to have a contact address off the island for all of the cast and the crew, but I'd no reason to check them. We were pulled together for the production and that was it.'

We went in through the back door to the Art Gallery and Museum and along to the tearoom. It wasn't far off closing time and as soon as we entered the waitress came bustling over to take our order.

'Right. Phone Perry while we're waiting,' I said.

She opened her phone. 'Damn,' she said, 'the battery's dead.' She shook it, as though that would help.

'Here, borrow mine,' I said, pulling my mobile from my handbag.

She dialled the number, then frowned. 'No reply. There must be someone else we can contact.' Her eyes lit up. 'I know, let's try Linda.'

It took her a few attempts to remember the correct number but at last she succeeded and explained our problem. It's always difficult when you only hear one side of a conversation, but I'd a good idea of what was going on. At least I thought I did, until Tracy almost screamed, her voice echoing round the café.

'He's what? I can't believe it. Surely it's all a mistake?'

Another silence at her end as Linda continued with whatever story was so upsetting her until finally she rang off and sat staring at the phone.

287

'What's wrong? Did she not know Sol's address?'

'It's nothing to do with that. Sol's been arrested.'

'Arrested? Surely he didn't have anything to do with the deaths on the film set? That's ridiculous.'

'What! No, no. All Linda knows is that he's been taken to the police station.'

I should have been surprised, but then I thought about what the doorman had said that night of the award ceremony, about Sol's strange behaviour on receiving the award. Whatever the answer, this was something beyond my area of experience.

I'd no idea how to find out the truth. But I knew someone who did. Time to contact Robert... and at last I'd a good reason for asking all the questions I'd stored up.

41

As so often happened of late, my action was pre-empted. Robert phoned me.

'Everything going well, Alison?'

'Yes, I'm fine thanks. And you?'

We exchanged desultory chit chat for a few moments and then he said, 'Do you have time to meet up?'

Of course I had to see him, find out what he knew about the film. With his background he was sure to have heard something, or have an idea why Sol had been taken in for questioning and besides I was still intrigued about his relationship with Juliet and what he really knew about Pelias Productions. I said, 'Coffee would be good. I've a lot on at the moment - a new commission.'

'A new commission? What's this one about?' He sounded interested.

'Not really, it's not quite at that stage. I've a few ideas I'm hoping to pitch to publishers and I'm working hard on them.'

'Ah, it's not another film script you're trying?'

'No way! I've had enough of film scripts to last me a lifetime,' I said.

My strength of feeling must have come over because he chuckled.

'That I can well understand. But that's in part why I'm phoning you. There are a few things have come up about the film of *A Man Alone* and I think you may be able to help.'

Better and better. Now I could question him while he thought he was grilling me. Even so, I had to dampen his expectations. 'I don't see how I can be of much help,' I said. 'Others knew more about the production than me.'

'No, no, Alison. It's not about the production itself - it's more to do with the various problems and before I could reply, he hurried on, 'I'm speaking to a few people and I'd very much appreciate your input.'

'If you think I know anything that'll be useful…' I said cautiously. This sounded more hopeful by the minute. Let him think he was pumping me for information, but I'd every intention of quizzing him.

'Fine. How about we meet somewhere in Glasgow tomorrow, if that's not too soon?'

We arranged to meet in one of the cafés in the Merchant City for coffee after I'd refused his offer of lunch. 'Coffee will be fine,' I said, when he tried to persuade me to join him for a meal.

As I put the phone down, Simon came wandering in. 'Have you seen my car keys?' he said, moving around the random bits and pieces that had accumulated on the hall table.

I shook my head.

'Where did you last have them?'

He frowned.

'I thought they were here. No, wait a minute, I must have left them in my jacket pocket when I came in last night.'

As he turned to go upstairs to retrieve his jacket he paused and said, 'Who was that on the phone? You didn't sound happy.'

I was about to tell him about my plan to meet Robert, but something made me hesitate.

'Oh, someone from Pelias Productions. Apparently they're trying to tie up all the loose ends and are arranging to have a chat to each of us individually.'

This answer seemed to satisfy him and he continued on upstairs with no more than, 'I see. I only hope they won't go upsetting you again. I thought you'd finished with all that.'

'Oh, this will be the end,' I said - and I meant it. Once I'd prised the information I wanted out of Robert, I planned to sever all connections with the cast and crew.

There'd be no harm in having a quick coffee with Robert and while I'd be happy to answer his questions if I could, I'd plenty of my own to ask.

42

Anxious about the meeting with Robert, I arrived at the café in the Candleriggs at the far end of Argyle Street way too early. I peeped in briefly, but the only customers at this time in the morning were a couple of elderly women, enjoying a gossip as much as the coffee and cake in front of them.

Coffee was an enticing prospect - I'd been too jittery to have anything before leaving home, but didn't want to go in and sit on my own waiting for him, appear too eager. He had asked me, not the other way round, which suited my purposes very well.

I started to walk down to Argyle Street, but here, near the Trongate, there were few shops of interest and I contented myself with a slow stroll twice round the block until I judged it near the appointed time.

Sure enough, when I returned to the café, Robert was sitting at the table in the far corner, one that had a good view of the door and he jumped to his feet as soon as he saw me appear.

'Over here, Alison,' he waved, though it would have been impossible not to spot him in such a small and sparsely patronised place.

'Hi, there.' I sat down on the seat opposite as he beckoned the waitress over to take out order.

'I thought I'd wait for you,' he said. 'What will you have?'

It was on the tip of my tongue to say, 'Coffee will be fine,' but the cakes in the display looked tempting and now seriously feeling the lack of a proper breakfast, I added a slice of carrot cake to my order.

'Same for me,' said Robert as the waitress came over.

The initial conversation was stilted as we chatted about the weather as if it was the most important event in our lives until somewhat exasperated I finally said, 'Well, now that we've discussed every possible aspect of the climate, perhaps we could get to the reason you invited me to meet you.'

There was a hesitation that didn't bode well as he fiddled with the crumbs on his plate and then licked his fingers, a way of stalling.

'Well?' I pulled up my sleeve and looked at my watch. 'I've other things to do today, so I can't wait much longer.'

He laughed then changed it into a sigh.

'Okay, Alison. I've been trying to think how to say this to you, but there is no easy way.'

I felt my heart begin to pound and bent down to scrabble in my bag to hide my confusion. As I lifted my head again, it was to see him looking at me earnestly.

He leaned across the table.

'Alison, I haven't been entirely honest with you.'

Oh, no, I thought, here we go. He was going to tell me something awful about his involvement with Pelias Productions. 'I'm not sure you should be talking to me, Robert, it's the authorities...' I tailed off as I saw the look of puzzlement on his face.

'When I said I hadn't been entirely honest, I meant about my time on Bute, how I was involved with the making of the film.'

Now it was my turn to look surprised. 'How were you involved with the film? You weren't one of the backers were you?' Perhaps he'd invested his pension pot in the production. If so, heaven help him.

He shook his head.

'Nothing like that. You'll remember my previous post was in the department of Accountancy at the University of West Maple in British Columbia. And that I retired early.'

I frowned. 'Yes, yes, I do remember that. That's how you came to know Alastair. But not the reason you left early.' I wasn't going to repeat what Alastair had told me - all that gossip.

'I'd had enough of the changing academic world and then one of my students accused me of stealing some of his research work, claiming it as my own.'

Ah, this was the correct version of what Alastair had found out. But why should Robert want to tell me? His past life was no concern of mine.

He went on, 'It was all nonsense of course and I was cleared of any wrongdoing, but it left me feeling things had changed too much for me to continue. I had to go through the whole process of an investigation, ward off all the suspicions, try to maintain my academic credentials. So I took the option to retire early.'

This was all well and good, but nothing to do with me, far less Pelias Productions.

'So where does the film come into this?'

It was as if, having come to the nub of the matter, he was reluctant to finish, but he said, 'Not long after I retired I was approached by a company specialising in fraud and asked to look into what was going on with Pelias Productions. They needed an accountant with experience in the media. That's the reason why I was on Bute, why I was so interested in the film.'

'Surely you're not talking about Sol?'

'Afraid so. There have been suspicions about him for some time, I'd met him before and this was the biggest suspected fraud yet.'

It was all becoming clear. The sponsors had put up the funding and Sol had failed to complete the film, had siphoned off the money. Zach must have realised what was going on, had complained to the police and Sol had been found out.

'So I've been involved in a fraud of some kind?' Visions of court appearances and perhaps even prison, loomed before me.

He laughed.

'Don't worry - there is no way you'll be accused. The authorities are only interested in the big fish. We're trying to gather the evidence together to put him away for a long time.'

'So why are you telling me this?' I took a sip of my coffee and made a face as I realised it was cold.

'Another one?' Robert pointed to my cup.

'No thanks.' I didn't want to interrupt the flow of this tale. 'So how do I come into this?'

'The evidence would include statements from everyone involved in the production. You wrote the original story, wrote the script. Is that correct?'

'I certainly wrote the original story, and helped with the script.' I thought of Matt Trickle and his dismissal of my efforts.

Then something else struck me.

'So it's true Sol's been arrested?'

Robert smiled.

'I'm pleased to say yes, that's what has happened.'

'Well, it's certainly been some production, 'I shivered. 'I won't be getting involved again with anyone in the film world ever.'

'A wise decision. Now if we could agree a time and a date for you to come along to my office and make a statement? I wanted to explain to you first though, since we are old friends.'

I stood up and then sat down again as I remembered what it was I wanted to ask him.

'So why were you involved with Juliet? Was it something to do with this?'

He grimaced. 'Yes, you've guessed correctly.' He tapped the spoon against the side of his cup. 'I had to have someone who knew about film production and especially what was going on with this one. I thought you might be able to help,

Alison, but then I realised your knowledge was very limited,' he went on, completely oblivious of my seething resentment.

I'd thought he was a friend, someone from the past whose company I'd enjoyed - perhaps a little too much - and now he was telling me the reason for his friendship was to find a way in to Pelias Productions.

I bent my head to cover my embarrassment at this turn of events as he said hastily, 'Not that it wasn't good to meet you again, have your company on the island.' He resumed the story. 'It was Derek who first went to the authorities, they recruited me and luckily Juliet also had her suspicions and was more than willing to help.'

'And...'

'And as you know, Juliet never left the island. Someone didn't want her to tell me what she'd found out. Now I have to ask everyone who was involved for a statement, so that I can put the evidence together, help make a solid case. So I hope you will be willing to help and then all the information will go to the police.'

'Just text me. Any time next week will be fine. Thanks for the coffee,' I said. And with that I fled.

Out in the street I stopped for a moment before heading back to the train station. Was what Robert had suggested true? Had Sol really been involved in some kind of scam? And did that mean he'd something to do with the deaths of Derek and of Juliet?

None of this made sense. In spite of Robert's explanation, there was something perplexing about this business. Any one of the cast or crew could be the murderer, but I could come up with no good reason for any one of them to do it. Surely each and every one of them was more interested in finishing the film, making a success of it.

And could I trust Robert to be telling me the truth, in spite of his alleged role as the lawman in this affair? Why would he have been recruited for a case like this? Surely it was all a matter for the police? He was an academic, not a detective.

I was so busy trying to think through these issues, make sense of the events of the past few months, it was only while sitting on the train on the way home I realised I'd forgotten to ask if he'd heard any more about Franklin.

43

When I thought about it later, much later, I had to admit I should have told Simon everything. Hadn't I had more than one experience of keeping a secret to myself, only to regret it later? But I didn't and that was what caused more trouble.

The next week, as requested, I went along to Robert's office, a tiny eyrie of a place in one of the converted Victorian blocks on the edge of town. At one time these had been houses, but unlike the flats at Park Circus, they were still offices. I suspected Robert's office had originally belonged to the lowliest of the servants as I climbed the several flights of stairs which twisted and turned, becoming narrower and narrower as you reached the top.

Robert was brisk, businesslike and this time there was no offer of coffee though I did spy a kettle and the makings of a brew on a little table in the corner of this sparsely furnished room. The seat he offered me was hard, the lighting dim: not a place you'd want to linger. Perhaps that was the idea.

Half an hour later and we were shaking hands goodbye.

'Thanks for your help,' he said.

'I don't know that I've been of much help,' I replied. 'There's not been much I can tell you.'

'Every piece of information adds to the case,' he said.

Interestingly, he made no suggestion of meeting up again, though at my prompting he did promise to let me know the outcome, saying,' Though you may read about it in the papers, if the case is successful.'

'Am I the last person to be interviewed?'

He shook his head. 'There is one person still to interview, someone who has more involvement in this than we realised.'

'Oh, who's that?'

He hesitated then said, 'Best you don't know, Alison. These are ruthless people.'

I said a hurried goodbye, wondering who this "one person" could be. Whoever it was, Robert was going to gather the evidence and I could withdraw, let him do the job he'd been recruited for.

So why was there a niggle of doubt which I couldn't explain to myself as I left the office. Why had I accepted his word for everything without question? I hadn't seen Robert for years until our chance encounter, yct here I was accepting his version of events without a shred of proof. For all I knew he might be involved in the scam, might be the prime mover, intent on covering his traces.

There had to be some way of checking out his story without giving too much away. Who'd be able to help? Tracy was as much in the dark as I was, Quentin too self-absorbed to care.

Then I remembered Perry. As director of photography he would know exactly what was going on with Sol, if it was true he'd been arrested and why. He and Sol had appeared to be close, to know each other well from working together on previous films. I should be able to track him down without too much difficulty.

How could I get his phone number? Of course, Tracy had borrowed my phone because her battery was dead. His number would still be logged.

I scrolled through until I found it. He answered on the second ring and said he'd be happy to see me. 'Problem is, I'm tied up till mid evening,' he said.

'That's not a difficulty, 'I said, all the while wondering what excuse I could give to Simon for yet another excursion.

After some discussion, Perry and I arranged to meet by the Clyde Walkway. 'An odd choice of venue,' I said when he suggested it.

He laughed. 'Not really. If you meet me where the statue of La Pasionaria stands down by Custom Quay at the riverside, we can go along to a pub I know in King Street. It's a cosy place, good to have a chat uninterrupted.'

'Okay,' I replied, quashing my doubts. Why am I so trusting?

44

It was dark in this corner of town, the streetlamps sparse along the water's edge, making little impact on the blackness of a December night. Further up I could hear the city alive with noise, but down here on the walkway beside the river all was silent and there was no one else about. The statue of La Pasionaria stood, her arms outstretched, beside what had once been a busy jetty, but now there was an air of neglect, weeds growing through the flagstones, the railings broken.

In the quiet I stood looking over the silver grey of the River Clyde, shivering as I pulled my jacket tightly round me, watching the reflections of the streetlights glinting and shimmering in the water as it flowed out to join the Firth of Clyde.

Years ago this had been a bustling port, down here by the Broomielaw, where boats were crammed together so tightly you could walk from one to another without any danger of falling into the water. Many of these had been destined for Rothesay and other popular holiday resorts down the Clyde, but now the place was deserted, a silent shadow of its former glory.

I heard a soft footfall behind me and whirled round to see Perry standing grinning at me.

'Hello, Alison. Glad you could make it.'

'Gosh, it's cold standing here. A drink would be most welcome.' A gentle reminder he'd invited me to join him in the pub.

'In a minute, in a minute.' He waved his hand impatiently. He moved closer and I instinctively backed away, grabbing at what was left of the railings. He grinned again, but this time there was more than a little threat of menace in his smile. 'I should have guessed you were the kind of person who wouldn't let things lie.'

'What do you mean?' What did he think I'd been doing? 'I wanted to see you because you might know the truth about what Pelias Productions was up to, what has happened to Sol.'

He showed no inclination to move, to take me to the "cosy pub" he'd mentioned and I was growing colder and colder standing here by the edge of the river. At least I think that was the reason I was shivering.

'You and Sol were really close. Is it true he's been arrested?'

'Mmm, I heard as much.'

He moved a little closer, his profile sharpened in the hazy lamplight and I instinctively drew further back, putting out my hand to steady myself and feeling only empty space.

With a sudden flash of insight, I said, 'You and Sol are related.'

'How do you know that?' he growled.

I tried to recover my balance. If he came any closer I'd be in the river. 'There's no point in denying it. I can see the resemblance,' I blurted out, too late realising the effect this might have on him.

He laughed, but it was a mirthless sound. 'Yes, you're right. We're cousins, so I guess there is a family resemblance.'

'But...' I put my hand to my mouth, stopping myself just in time. Put a white wig on Perry, give him a walking stick and in a dim light he could pass for Sol. Of course, as the sudden thought struck me, it was Perry who'd been spying on Juliet when she'd met me down by the quay at Port Bannatyne. He must have heard everything. And if that was the case... I didn't dare follow this line of reasoning through, but my face must have betrayed me.

'Ah, so you've worked it out,' he said, edging closer to me, moving me nearer and nearer the unrailed part of the walkway. The heel of my shoe felt suspended, had lost contact with the ground.

'Now what about that drink,' I said briskly in an attempt to move us away from here, out of danger, but my voice was quavery, trembling.

He grabbed me by the arm. 'Why didn't you keep your nose out of this,' he said.

Exactly the question I was at this very moment asking myself. The chance of a drink in a nice warm pub, crowded with people and safety looked like a very remote possibility.

Well, if I was in trouble, I might as well find out the truth. I took a bold leap of imagination, probing for his reaction.

'So you murdered Derek and tried to blame it on Franklin?'

He wrinkled his nose as though he smelled something rotten. 'What else could I do? Sol and I had it all worked out. How many films do you think we've made, how much acclaim have we had. Zilch. We set up this scheme - at least it would make us money and then Derek comes in with his suspicions - little goody two shoes, worried about his reputation, and then he brings in that friend of yours.' He paused. 'Though we didn't realise that until much later, of course, when he roped in Juliet.'

'You killed Juliet?'

He shrugged. 'We were too far along the line then, had to get the film finished somehow, bring in the money.'

Too astonished now to feel fear, I said, 'And what about Quentin?'

'Oh, the accident with the gun?' A dismissive wave of the hand. 'That was nothing to do with us.' He laughed. 'When he saw Franklin was being blamed for Derek's murder, Quentin was delighted, saw it as no more than Franklin deserved for stealing his role.'

'Quentin tried to arrange his own killing?'

He shook his head. 'No, no. Of course not. It was all a ploy.'

I remembered Linda's explanation, but before I could say anything, Perry went on, 'In a way I can understand his frustration. When Franklin was released because that stupid girl, Tracy, provided him with an alibi, he had to try something else. He set the whole thing up himself. He was never in any danger. It was an incredibly stupid thing to do, because he was sussed pretty quickly, but he obviously thought it was worthwhile to upset Franklin, even for a short time.'

'But everyone saw the blood.'

Perry looked highly amused at this suggestion. 'The blood was fake -Vichner no 11- but Franklin had no idea. He's not even a real actor, just some jumped up participant in a soap opera.'

This explained a lot, confirmed what Linda had said, but I wanted to get to the truth of it all, no matter what the consequences.

'And Sol was arrested because he misspent the sponsor's money?'

Perry threw his head back and roared with laughter, but he didn't loosen the grip on my arm. 'No - who'd be interested in that?'

He narrowed his eyes. 'It was the Taxman we were up against. Set up a film, claim all the tax benefits, including matched funding, then only shoot enough to keep everyone happy, make them think you've finished the film, then quietly drop it. You're quids in.'

There was a terrible tightness in my chest and, aware of the danger of my position so close to the edge, I tried to move forward on to the pavement, but Perry was barring my way.

What could I say? 'Excuse me, that was very interesting, but I have to go now,' hardly seemed appropriate. Perhaps I could catch him off guard and make a run for it?

Even as I thought about this line of action, he grabbed my arm more tightly.

'As well we met here, Alison. You'll have a nasty accident. Don't worry, the riverman will find your body and your family will be able to give you a decent burial.'

Of course, he'd have no idea I'd already given Robert a statement. Would it help my situation if I told him? The gleam in his eyes indicated that might make matters worse.

Was it all over? I was certainly no match for his brute strength as he now grasped me with both hands and propelled me backwards towards the edge.

One last attempt to rescue the situation. 'But Sol's been arrested,' I said, 'so it's all over. Why add more crimes to the tally.'

'Not quite. I've made my own plans.' He let go of me with one hand and patted his jacket pocket. 'Once you 'slip' into the river, all I have to do is walk up to the corner, find a taxi to take me to Glasgow airport and I'm off. You don't think I'd have trusted everything to Sol, do you, even if he is a relative? Everything about him is false, including that accent.'

Why, oh why, had I been so stupid? It had been nothing to do with the actors and their rivalries; it was all about making money by cheating the system, setting up a scam, a fake film in order to defraud the Inland Revenue. Now Franklin would be convicted of crimes he didn't commit and Perry would escape scot free.

If only my brain would work, if I could think of a way out of this, but no great idea came to me and I felt paralysed, incapable of speech.

Perry had now grabbed me again with both hands and moved me backwards, inch by inch as I put all my remaining strength into resisting. I tried to dig my heels in, but with nothing to stop my fall, I'd be in the river in no time.

Suddenly there was the sound of heavy footsteps and loud shouts of laughter as a crowd of young men in brightly coloured rugby shirts came running round the corner, whooping along the walkway, pushing and pulling one other in mock fight.

Startled by this sudden upset to his plans, Perry pulled me close to him. These might be the only people along here for some time and I'd only a split second to act. These youngsters might think we were lovers having a cuddle down by the walkway, though why a woman of my age would be doing this on a cold December evening might strike them as strange, if they bothered to think about it at all.

As they passed beside us, one of them nudged another and he bumped into Perry. Startled, Perry let go his grip of my arm as the young man raised his hand and said, 'Sorry, sorry, mate,' and given this opportunity, almost as a reflex action, I grabbed the young man at the end of the line.

'Okay, missus?' he said, stopping for a moment to grin at me.

'Where are you going?' I said, trying hard to make my voice sound as normal as possible, aware Perry still had a tight grip of my other arm.

He smiled good-naturedly at this odd question. 'We're heading for the *Canny Man* pub up in the Saltmarket,' he said.

'Then I'm coming with you,' I said and he was too amazed to refuse me as I shook myself free from an astonished Perry and grabbed the young man's arm even more tightly to hurry off with him and the rest of his crowd towards the busy Saltmarket.

As I was swept along in their merriment, I glanced back quickly. Perry was standing staring after me, as still as the statue of La Pasionaria, incandescent with rage.

EPILOGUE

The lights in the cinema dimmed and there was an expectant intake of breath from the audience. We were few in number in this small cinema, but at last the film *A Man Alone* was ready.

After all the hard work, all the problems and the disappointments, it was good to know something had been salvaged from the wreckage. Not that this film was going to make the big screen, but thanks to Matt and his contacts there was at least a film of sorts.

Simon squeezed my hand. 'Feeling okay, Alison? Not too upset by this?'

'I'm fine,' I whispered. 'Just glad it's all come together at last.'

The credits rolled and the film began. It was so strange seeing everyone again in their costumes as the story unfolded.

One of Matt's friends had had the bright idea of filling in the missing parts of the story with a voiceover and had made great use of the spectacular vistas of Bute and the area round Kames Castle to fill in any missing scenes. So when Franklin and Juliet in their roles as James and Harriet Hamilton came to the end of a take, the next phase of the story was taken forward by the

310

voiceover as the camera panned across one of the sites associated with their lives.

I was particularly curious to see how the ending would be managed, with Juliet dead and Sol and Perry now under arrest: Sol for tax fraud and Perry for the murders of Derek and Juliet.

Robert had worked hard and the evidence he'd gathered was enough to put both of them away for a very long time. I shivered when I thought of my narrow escape. When I'd reached the Saltmarket with the crowd of young men I'd latched on to, I said, 'Thanks. Your help was much appreciated.'

They didn't take this amiss but replied, 'No bother,' showing no curiosity about my strange behaviour as they made their way to the pub and I whipped out my phone to call the police. Perry was arrested before he could make it to the airport.

The film was very tastefully done, with the final chapter of the story told as the camera panned away from Kames Bay towards the site of James Hamilton's grave, now restored to its Victorian splendour.

As the lights came up, there was a long silence and then a loud burst of applause. Matt left his seat and went up on to the stage.

'Thanks, everyone. We wanted to complete this as a mark of respect to those who so sadly suffered for their art. And a special word for Franklin, wrongly accused of murder. Those responsible have been caught and you can be sure they'll get what they deserve.'

Matt was assured and confident, a different man from the one I'd known during filming. Only now did I realise how much working with Sol had terrified him.

Franklin acknowledged this comment on his innocence with a gracious nod of his head, while in the corner, Quentin glowered. I turned my attention back to Matt.

'It's not the film we thought it would be,' he was saying, 'but it is finished and I'm pleased to announce it's been bought by the History Channel, so all is not lost.'

This announcement was greeted with a resounding cheer. Something had been saved and the story of James Hamilton and Harriet would have the audience it deserved. I felt genuinely pleased for the cast and the crew who had so unwittingly been caught up in these terrible events.

Matt was still speaking.

'The History Channel is so pleased with the final product they've indicated a willingness to commission another film, this time about the Stuarts of Bute. It may be a great opportunity.'

Simon leaned over and whispered, 'There you are, Alison. You could write the script for that.'

'No way! There's not the slightest chance. I've had enough of films to last me a lifetime. From now on I'll be content with being a member of the audience.'

And I meant it.

Acknowledgements

Many thanks to:

Joan Fleming, Bill Daly and Judith Duffy for assistance with editing, Sergeant Wilkinson of the Rothesay Police for help with technical questions relating to police procedures (any errors are entirely my own), Joan Weeple for proof reading, Paul Duffy for technical assistance, Mandy Sinclair for the cover design and, as always, to Peter for checking the nautical descriptions and for his support.

Further Information

In 2011 a community archaeological dig took place at Cnoc-an-Rath, where James Hamilton is buried. Much of the detail of his story was researched as part of this project by local expert John MacCallum. Further details can be obtained via Brandanii Archaeology and Heritage at www.discoverbutearchaeology.co.uk